Rebel Winter

CAPTAIN SEBASTEV of the Vostroyan Firstborn has risen through the ranks, much to the chagrin of some of his fellow officers. His mettle is truly put to the test during a posting on the ice-encrusted battlefields of Danik's World, fighting against a fierce rebellion. Caught between rebels and hordes of orks, Sebastev's company is tasked with holding the line, while the rest of the Vostroyan army makes a tactical retreat. But the withdrawal goes horribly wrong, and Sebastev and his men are cut off and stranded behind enemy lines. Worse still, when new orders come in, the captain must not only try to ensure the survival of his company but escort a traitor back to Vostroyan high command or all efforts in the war thus far will have been for nothing!

D0311224

More Imperial Guard action from the Black Library

FIFTEEN HOURS
Mitchel Scanlon

DEATH WORLD
Steve Lyons

A WARHAMMER 40,000 NOVEL

Rebel Winter

Steve Parker

To Mum and Dad, with love and gratitude.
Additional thanks to Kev for his faith,
and to Kana for her kindness.

A BLACK LIBRARY PUBLICATION

First published in Great Britain in 2007 by
BL Publishing,
Games Workshop Ltd.,
Willow Road, Nottingham,
NG7 2WS, UK.

10 9 8 7 6 5 4 3 2 1

Cover illustration by Alex Boyd.

© Games Workshop Limited 2007. All rights reserved.

Black Library, the Black Library logo, Black Flame, BL Publishing,
Games Workshop, the Games Workshop logo and all associated marks,
names, characters, illustrations and images from the Warhammer
40,000 universe are either ®, TM and/or © Games Workshop Ltd 2000-
2007, variably registered in the UK and other countries around the
world. All rights reserved.

A CIP record for this book is available from the British Library.

ISBN 13: 978 1 84416 483 7
ISBN 10: 1 84416 483 7

Distributed in the US by Simon & Schuster
1230 Avenue of the Americas, New York, NY 10020, US.

No part of this publication may be reproduced, stored in a retrieval
system, or transmitted in any form or by any means, electronic,
mechanical, photocopying, recording or otherwise, without the prior
permission of the publishers.

This is a work of fiction. All the characters and events portrayed in this
book are fictional, and any resemblance to real people or incidents is
purely coincidental.

See the Black Library on the Internet at
www.blacklibrary.com

Find out more about Games Workshop
and the world of Warhammer 40,000 at
www.games-workshop.com

IT IS THE 41st millennium. For more than a hundred centuries the Emperor has sat immobile on the Golden Throne of Earth. He is the Master of Mankind by the will of the gods, and master of a million worlds by the might of his inexhaustible armies. He is a rotting carcass writhing invisibly with power from the Dark Age of Technology. He is the Carrion Lord of the Imperium for whom a thousand souls are sacrificed every day, so that he may never truly die.

AMONGST THE EMPEROR'S many servants, waging His eternal war are the Imperial Guard. Harnessed from countless worlds across the galaxy, their numbers are legion. From the ice-wreathed factory world of Vostroya come the Firstborn. They are a noble race, a warrior brotherhood ruled over by the Techtriarchs and worship both the Immortal Emperor and the Machine God of Mars. In maintaining the fighting strength of their regiments with continuous replacements, they honour the ancient pact they swore with the Emperor long ago.

The Vostroyans are master artificers, who supply the many armies of humanity with munitions, their own regiments bearing handcrafted weapons of exceptional quality. Stoic, resolute, experts in fighting in the most adverse of conditions, the Vostroyan Firstborn regard themselves as more dedicated than any other Imperial Guard regiment and as such are fierce foes, but even fiercer allies in what is a war-torn galaxy.

FORGET THE POWER of technology and science, for so much has been forgotten, never to be re-learned. Forget the promise of progress and understanding, for in the grim dark future there is only war. There is no peace amongst the stars, only an eternity of carnage and slaughter, and the laughter of thirsting gods.

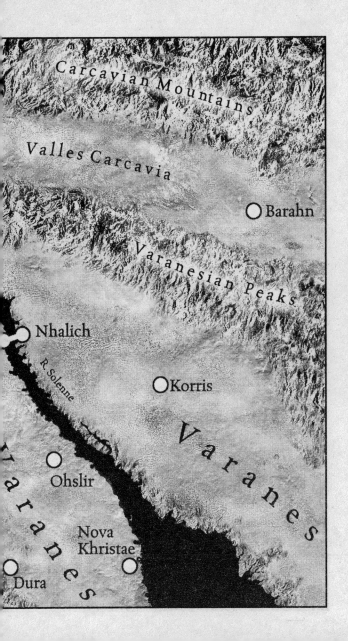

'Secession - let a single rebel world go unpunished and countless more will rise up, all clamouring for those religious and economic freedoms better known to loyal citizens of the Imperium as heresy and ingratitude.

'On Danik's World, the seeds of rebellion were planted in the deep snows of an ice age that ravaged the planet for two thousand years. It began when volcanic eruptions on the southern continent filled the atmosphere with debris and plunged the land into darkness. The sudden climatic change wiped out over half the human population and reduced planetary productivity to almost nothing. On countless occasions in the years that followed, one loyalist governor after another begged the Administratum for aid. Eventually, the Administratum approved the deferment of Imperial tributes, but more direct aid in the form of food and technologies was repeatedly denied. Imperial coffers, the Danikkin were told, were being drained by anti-xenos campaigns throughout the segmentum.

'When Danikkin scientists finally announced the beginning of a slow return to warmer temperatures, the population had climbed to two-thirds of its pre-catastrophe figure. An estimated ninety-three per cent of that population supported open revolt against the Imperium. The central figure behind this movement *was Lord General Graush Vanandrasse, High Commander of the Danikkin Planetary Defense Force.*

'Vanadrasse had spent his life rising through the ranks of the PDF, finally attaining absolute command at the age of sixty-one. Mere months after his accession, he led his forces in a bloody coup against troops loyal to the Planetary Governor. He celebrated victory by renaming his force the Danikkin Independence Army. To ensure absolute loyalty to his vision of planetary independence, he established a brutal organization of elite officers called the Special Patriotic Service.

'Agents of this so-called Special Patriotic Service publicly executed the legitimate Planetary Governor and his family, and sent a formal notice of secession to the Administratum.

'Two years later, in 766.M41, Lord Marshal Graf Harazahn of the Vostroyan Firstborn - then charged with overseeing all ground operations in the Second Kholdas War - relented before pressure from the Administratum and agreed to send a small punitive force to Danik's World. Twelfth Army was formed for this purpose and deployed under the leadership of General Vogor Vlastan - a man for whom Harazahn allegedly bore little genuine respect.

'Twelfth Army's orders were to crush the Danikkin rebels, restore order, and return to action in the Second Kholdas War with all due haste. As the old adage goes, however, few plans survive first contact with the enemy.

'The climate and the rebels were bad enough, and Twelfth Army underestimated both. But there was another force present on Danik's World for which General Vlastan and his Guardsmen were unprepared - a force that would claim all too many of Vostroya's firstborn sons.

'The old foe, you see, had got there first.'

Extract: *Hammer and Shield: Collected Essays on the History of the Second Kholdas War,* eds. Commissar-Colonel (Ret.) Keisse von Holh (716.M41-805.M41) & Major (Ret.) Wyllum Imrilov (722.M41-793.M41)

A TRIAL BEGINS

THE EXEDRA UDICIARUM Seddisvarr was a grand place indeed, as grand and dark as an Imperial mausoleum. The ancient court had stood for millennia, echoing with the sounds of innumerable trials, both military and civil. Stylised images of the God-Emperor and His saints stared with unblinking eyes from great stained-glass windows, weighing the souls of the innocent and the guilty.

Tapestries hung from the dark marble walls, their fading colours struggling to contrast the aura of the room: here, an image of Tech-Magos Benandanti, who'd rediscovered the Kholdas Cluster in M37 and restored it to its rightful place in the Imperial fold; there, Saint Hestor, who'd led loyalist forces against the dread armies of the Idols Dark, which had spilled from the warpstorm at the cluster's centre in M39. Around these worthy historical figures, pre-Winter Danikkin iconography spoke of better days, days before the people had turned from their God-Emperor's light.

Had the faith of these people remained unbroken, the Vostroyan Firstborn might never have set foot on Danik's World. Dead men might yet live. Then again, thought Captain Grigorius Sebastev, as well to die on this world as on some other, so long as one dies well.

As commanding officer of the Firstborn Sixty-Eighth Infantry Regiment's Fifth Company, Sebastev went where his Emperor needed him. It was as simple as that. For now, he stood patiently in the dock, awaiting the beginning of his trial, uncomfortable and self-conscious in his ill-fitting dress uniform.

He was a stocky man, short for a Vostroyan, but thick-set and powerful. In the days since his return to Command HQ in Seddisvarr, with solid meals and little to do in his cell but practise the forms of the *ossbokh-vyar*, he'd quickly regained the size and strength he'd lost since being posted to the Eastern Front. His bright red jacket, piped with shining gold brocade, strained to contain the thick muscles of his chest and back.

He'd have given anything for the familiar comfort of battle fatigues and a greatcoat. Strutting and posturing like the highborn officers had never interested him. Sebastev was a fighter, a brawler. His men called him the Pit-Dog, though rarely to his face since it tended to ignite his temper.

A dozen servo-skulls drifted overhead, carrying braziers filled with hot coals, but the air would hardly be warmer by the time the judges took their seats. That would set them in foul spirits from the outset. No matter. His future was in the Emperor's hands, as it had always been.

Sebastev shifted his gaze to the most central of the hall's windows and looked up at the glowing image of the Emperor. 'Light of all Mankind,' he said, uncaring that the bailiffs behind him would hear, 'I've lived my life on the battlefield, serving your will. Let me die doing so.'

Someone coughed off to Sebastev's right, and echoes chased each other up the stone walls to the shadowy reaches of the high ceiling. Sebastev turned.

'Really, captain,' said a man sitting alone on the observers' benches, 'must you be so gloomy this early in the morning?'

It was the commissar. He looked well rested, healthy. A few days away from the fighting had taken the sunken look from his cheeks. His oiled black hair shone as it had when they'd first met. The ubiquitous cap, the symbol of the man's rank, sat neatly on the bench by his side.

'Commissar,' said Sebastev with a nod. He was surprised to note a feeling of comfort at the man's presence. No matter what transpired during this hearing, the commissar had been right there in the thick of things. He'd played his part and knew the truth. But how would he testify? For all they'd been through together, the man was still something of an unknown quantity to Sebastev. He was brave enough, yes, and had demonstrated his dedication and loyalty to the Emperor, but he was also *chevek*, an outsider, a non-Vostroyan. The minds of such men were frustratingly difficult to comprehend.

A flicker of movement on the balcony above the benches caught Sebastev's eye. He lifted his gaze from the commissar and saw a curious duo sitting in the balcony's front row. Two figures diametrically opposed in bearing stared back at him, a man and a woman, though the term 'man' seemed hardly adequate to describe the former.

The woman sat hunched, almost drowning in the black folds of her robe. Her back was bent, her body twisted with age. She appeared no larger than a child of ten, but from the shadows of her cowl, her eyes shone with wisdom and a sharp intellect.

Was she Danikkin? An off-worlder? The sight of her made Sebastev uncomfortable, but he couldn't fathom why.

Next to the crone, dwarfing her utterly, sat a man who seemed nothing less than a statue cut from living marble. His skin was the white of daylit snow, and his spotless robes did little to mask the gargantuan body beneath. He was absolutely hairless, reinforcing the illusion of stone construction, but that illusion was shattered when Sebastev met the man's gaze. His eyes were blood-red, even where they should have been white.

Sebastev had never seen such a figure, so ghostly and yet so overwhelmingly solid, in all his travels across the Imperium of Man. Who were these people? And what in the blasted warp were they doing at this trial?

He might have asked them had the silence not been shattered at that moment. Doors banged as they were thrown open, and the air filled with the tumult of booted feet on marble flooring. A mixed crowd of Munitorum staff and Vostroyan military personnel poured into the room, chattering loudly as they took their seats.

Sebastev scanned the crowd for familiar faces, but could find no sign of his men. He wasn't surprised. In all likelihood, *Old Hungry*, or General Vogor Vlastan, as the bastard was more properly known, had forbidden their presence among the spectators. Sebastev turned his eyes from the crowd and faced forward, just in time to see the door of the judges' chambers crack open. A wash of warmth and orange light spilled into the hall. The general's military judiciary entered slowly and in single file.

Sebastev couldn't keep a scowl from his face as his eyes tracked the bloated figure of the general. He was a ruin of a man, confined to a multi-legged mechanical chair wired directly to his nerves via data-plugs at the base of his skull. The chair carried him to his place at the judges' bench with smooth, spider-like movements.

Sebastev raised his right hand to his brow in a sharp but grudging salute.

'In the name of the Emperor,' called the court secretary, 'all rise!'

The people on the spectators' benches clattered to their feet, and the trial of Captain Grigorius Sebastev began.

CHAPTER ONE

Day 681
Korris Trenchworks – 08:59hrs, -25°C

MORNING AT THE Eastern Front began, as it most often did, with the dark sky shifting from midnight blue to slate-grey. Down on the ground, everything turned a brilliant white. Only regular clearance work prevented the heavy snow from filling the Vostroyan trenches. Out here, eight kilometres east of the town proper, the only true shelter to be found was in the dugouts that the engineering teams had cut into the frozen earth. If Sebastev lived through this campaign – and the odds were against it, given the wretched state of things – he was sure he'd remember it, not for the fury of the warp-damned orks or the desperation of the filthy rebels, but for the relentless assault of the Danikkin deep winter.

Icy winds gusted down the firing trench, catching the snow as it fell, and hurling it against his men with a fury that was almost human. Fur hats and cloaks became coated on their windward side. But the Vostroyan First-born had weathered worse in their time. It would take more than the Danikkin ice-age to shake their commitment to the fight. Vostroyan pride was at stake here.

Sebastev moved up to the firing step, raised his head over the lip of the trench and peered out between coils of rusting razorwire and sandbags frozen hard as rock. The deep winter had pulled powdery blankets over yesterday's dead, and there was little evidence of the violence that had shaken the earth. Only irregular mounds of snow on the otherwise level battlefield hinted at the multitude of dead xenos that lay beneath.

Given the uniform white that lay before him, it was hard to believe a battle had been fought here at all: no scorched ground, no smoking craters. Yet, barely twenty hours ago, Sebastev had led his men in a bloody defence of these very trenches.

Here he was again, called back from the warmth of his bunk after First Company scouts had alerted the regiment to a massing of enemy forces beyond the tree line to the east. Tired as they were, those off-duty had quickly reassembled to face the inevitable attack.

The orks, damn them all, seemed impervious to the deep winter.

On either side of Sebastev, the trenches snaked off north and south into the snow veiled distance, filled with men in greatcoats of deep red, cinched under plates of polished golden armour. These were his men, the men of the Sixty-Eighth Infantry Regiment's Fifth Company. They stamped their feet on the frozen planking of the trench floor, and rubbed gloved hands over their weapons to keep the mechanisms from freezing. Their pockets bulged with lasgun power packs waiting to be loaded at the last minute so that the cold of the open air wouldn't leech their valuable charge.

There were three hundred and thirty-eight men at the last count, spread across five platoons. He'd started with four hundred. Twenty-two had been lost since the last reinforcements had come in. Those same reinforcements accounted for most, but not all, of the recently deceased. That was the way of things in the Guard, of course. Those with the right stuff lived to fight on. As far as most officers were concerned, the rest were just cannon fodder.

Sebastev pulled his scarf down for a moment, so he could scratch his face where the coarse hair of his moustache was itching. The bitter air nipped at his exposed skin. Every face around him was covered against the cold, some with warm scarves, others with rebreather masks that offered better protection against the elements, but reduced peripheral vision. Sebastev had always allowed his men a certain amount of freedom in the way they configured their gear. Each man knew himself best, after all. Even so, he'd have welcomed the chance to read their expressions as they readied themselves for the inevitable ork assault.

Stand strong, he thought. You're tired, cold and hungry, I know, but in three more days, we've a duty rotation. Hold fast until then.

He knew there would be mistakes brought on by exhaustion, and decided to order extra checks on cold climate discipline. Pneumonia and frostbite were constant threats on this world. The deep winter stalked every man, waiting for simple mistakes, for chances to claim the lives of the careless.

Early in the conflict, the youngest and greenest Guardsmen in the Twelfth Army had suffered in depressingly high numbers. Frostbite: for some it was lips or noses, for others it was fingers or toes. The flesh became numb, then shrivelled and turned black. If the dead flesh didn't fall away first, the medics would cut it off. Many of the afflicted didn't need scarves and goggles now. They wore permanent masks, expressionless machine faces screwed into the bone of their skulls by the regiment's techpriests and the chirurgeons of the Imperial Medicae.

Twelfth Army Command had since made instances of frostbite a capital offence, but flogging men for losing a finger or two didn't sit well with Sebastev. He preferred to omit the mention of it from his reports. Since Fifth Company had yet to be assigned a replacement commissar, Sebastev dealt with most infractions in his own way. For frostbite, it meant the confiscation of alcohol or tabac. For other offences, it meant a stint as his sparring partner.

Sebastev tried to gauge the mood of the men around him. Despite their being covered from head to toe against the razor winds, it wasn't all that hard to sense their agitation. Their bodies were in continuous motion, keeping their joints loose and their blood pumping in readiness for combat. It kept them warm. Many were veterans who, like Sebastev, had opted to serve beyond their ten years of compulsory service. Such men would have sensed the coming storm of battle just as he had.

He raised his magnoculars and squinted into the lenses, picking out the tree line just over a kilometre east of his position. The heavy curtains of falling snow hampered his view, but the shadows beneath the trees stood out as a dark border in all that white, marking the far edge of the killing fields. As he adjusted the magnification, bringing the wall of pine into sharper focus, he thought he glimpsed motion between the black trunks.

Lieutenant Tarkarov was right, he thought. We should have cut the trees farther back. We've no idea just how many are massing there.

After watching for another minute with no further sign of movement, Sebastev returned his magnoculars to the case on his belt.

The foothills of the Varanesian Peaks lay beyond the great pine forest, hidden today, as on most days. On those rare occasions when the cloud cover broke and the sky shone bright and blue, the mountains were visible, rendered in sharp detail, the land displaying a rare beauty. It was everything Sebastev's home world might have been were it not covered from sea to poisoned sea in gas belching, city-sized manufactories.

We may not have the same grand vistas, Sebastev thought to himself, but at least Vostroya is no traitor world.

He turned at a muttered curse from behind him. His comms officer and adjutant, Lieutenant Kuritsin, was crouching by the rear wall of the trench, adjusting the frequency dials on his vox-caster back and forth in tiny increments. His motions betrayed a mild frustration.

Still, thought Sebastev, you've a lot more patience than I have, Rits. I'd have blasted the damned thing to pieces by now.

Long-range comms had been unreliable since they'd landed on the planet. Some two thousand years after massive volcanic eruptions in the far south had kick-started this Danikkin ice age, tiny particles of volcanic debris in the high atmosphere still played hell with signals over distance.

Short-range vox, at least, was somewhat less affected.

'Captain,' said Kuritsin as he joined Sebastev on the firing step, 'that was a message from the colonel's office.'

'A full message?' asked Sebastev doubtfully.

'I'm afraid not, sir. The last half was mostly static.'

'Sometimes I feel guilty for making you carry that bloody thing, Rits. Just give me what you've got.'

'Yes, sir. Lieutenant Maro just wanted to let us know, sir. A Chimera left Korris HQ a few minutes ago, heading for our current position. It shouldn't take long to arrive.'

Not an inspection, thought Sebastev. The colonel knows better than to trouble us at a time like this, and Maro wouldn't have warned us if it was good news.

Sebastev frowned under his scarf and said, 'I don't suppose you know who's riding it?'

'I'm afraid we didn't get that far, captain. Would you like me to keep trying?'

Sebastev was about to answer when the vox-bead in his ear crackled. It was Lieutenant Vassilo, commander of Third Platoon. 'Vassilo to company leader. Movement among the trees. Lots of movement.'

'No, Rits,' said Sebastev to his adjutant, 'it'll have to wait. It sounds like we're about to have our hands full.'

Sebastev keyed the company command channel on his vox-bead, cleared his throat and said, 'Captain Sebastev to platoon leaders. I want all squads on full alert. Wake up, gentlemen. Expect a charge from the tree line any minute. I can bloody well smell them coming.'

Sebastev's officers broke through the static with brief confirmations.

'Rits, get a message off to First and Fourth Companies. Tell them we've got activity at Korris East, grid-sector H-5. Make sure they get the message, and keep Korris HQ updated on our status.'

'Yes, sir,' said Lieutenant Kuritsin.

As Sebastev raised his magnoculars again, Kuritsin transmitted his message to the company commanders in the neighbouring sections of the trench. Each Guardsman wore a vox-bead. The devices didn't have much range, maybe five kilometres on a good day, just one or two as standard on Danik's World, but they were absolutely vital for coordinating operations. Anything over that range required a heavy vox-caster set like the one Kuritsin carried around, strapped to his back. Every company and platoon leader in the Sixty-Eighth had a comms officer beside him.

Sebastev didn't have the faintest idea how vox worked, but that was the Imperium for you, he supposed. If the Priests of Mars understood it, they guarded the knowledge jealously. No matter. So long as everything worked as it was supposed to, that was enough. Sebastev's own regular obeisance to the machine-spirits seemed to keep his equipment in working order.

He flexed his fingers. That feeling had descended on him again, the tightness in his muscles, in his gut, as if he needed to piss. He knew it was partly the cold, but it was more than just that. He pulled the folds of his thick, white cloak tighter around his body, glad of its protection from the worst of the winds, and for the tall fur hat that warmed his head.

Slow adrenal increase. He always felt it before they came. Another tide of violence was building, about to spill over, to shatter the relative silence of the deep winter. The feeling was so strong it left little room for doubt.

How many will I lose this time, he wondered? Twenty? Thirty? By Terra, let it be less.

If he worked smart, and if the Emperor was with him, maybe he could keep the numbers down. It was what he excelled at, so Colonel Kabanov had told him. Sebastev hoped the old man wasn't just blowing smoke up his backside. Good men still died under his command, and bad ones, too.

He keyed his vox to the company's open channel and addressed his troops. 'Ready yourselves, Firstborn. Check your kit. Follow your platoon leaders.'

Up and down the line, he could sense the men preparing themselves, switching mental gears at the sound of his voice. These were the times he missed his old friend and mentor, Major Dubrin, the most. The man had always been ready with an inspirational phrase or quote to bolster the troops. Conscious of this, Sebastev struggled for something to say. 'Ask for the blessings of the Emperor. Do your duty without hesitation, free of all doubt, and when those ugly green bastards come charging over the snow, drop them with a lasbolt to the brain, and buy us all another day of righteous service in the Imperial Guard!'

That'll have to do, thought Sebastev. I've never been much of a speechmaker. You should be standing here, Dubrin, girding these men for battle. An old grunt like me has no business in officer's clothes. Any blue-blooded bastard in Twelfth Army Command can tell you that much. If it weren't for my damned promise…

Lieutenant Kuritsin spoke from behind him. 'Captain, First and Fourth Companies report movement all along the line, sir. Looks like a big one.'

As if on cue, an all too familiar sound erupted from the distant trees: the rage-filled battle cry of an ork leader. If the sub-zero temperatures of the Danikkin day weren't enough to chill a man's blood, an alien roar like that would do it. More sub-human roaring sounded on the air, racing over the white drifts to the ears of the anxious Guardsmen, signalling the start of the battle.

Sebastev tapped a finger on his adjutant's vox-caster and said, 'Monitor the regimental command channels for me, Rits. Keep me updated on the status of the First and Fourth. I'll need to know what's going on in their sectors. We don't want any surprises.'

'Understood, sir,' replied Kuritsin, 'but transmissions are really starting to break up between here and Korris HQ. I think the weather is worsening.'

Sebastev looked up at the sky. The snowfall was getting heavier, but the gusting winds had eased a little. He spoke again on the company's command channel. 'Ready yourselves, Firstborn.'

Lasgun charge packs were drawn from pockets all along the trench, and clicked into place under long, polished barrels.

'Maintain fire discipline. Power settings at maximum. Choose your targets. I want redundancy minimised. Remember, all of you, that temperature, visibility and the nature of our opponent have reduced lethal range to approximately one half. Any trooper wasting bolts on long shots will immediately forfeit his *rahzvod* allocation. You don't fire until I bloody well say so.'

Despite the usual groans from nearby soldiers at the thought of losing their alcohol, Sebastev knew he hardly needed to warn them. He was proud of them, his Fifth Company. Their discipline was rock solid. Most of his men were as dedicated and faithful as a commander could have wished for, committed to a life of fighting for the honour of Vostroya and the glory of the Imperium of Man.

Faith is the armour of the soul, thought Sebastev. That's what Commissar Ixxius used to say.

Commissar Ixxius was another friend and mentor who'd been lost to the campaign. The man had been a pillar of strength to Sebastev's company after Dubrin's death. He'd been a fine speaker, too.

In scholas and academies across the Imperium, officers and commissars were taught how to tap that faith. There were entire study programs dedicated to battlefield oration, but that didn't help Sebastev, because his was a field-commission. Everything he knew about leadership had been learnt the hard way, through blood, sweat and tears shed on battlefields from here to the Eye of Terror.

For better or for worse, litanies and the like were firmly the province of Father Olov, Fifth Company's aging and slightly insane priest. Sebastev hoped that the men at least drew some strength from his insistence on fighting alongside them, shoulder-to-shoulder, in these freezing trenches or anywhere else the enemies of the Imperium dared to show themselves.

As if summoned by the thought, they showed themselves now, bellowing their challenge as they broke cover. They crashed from between the trees, a thunderous green tide of muscle-bound bodies, kicking up great sprays of snow as they raced over no-man's land towards the Vostroyan lines.

Orks.

'Mark your targets,' ordered Sebastev. 'First volley on my order. Not one shot till we see their breath misting the air. Let them extend themselves. Grenades and mortars on dense knots only, please. I *will* be watching you. Your platoon leaders *will* be taking names.'

From the bead in his right ear, he heard his officers acknowledge.

'Sir,' said Kuritsin. 'First and Fourth Companies both report enemy charges in their sectors.'

Sebastev raised his right hand to his chest and the holy icon that lay beneath his clothes. An image, rendered in Vostroyan silver, hung from a cord around his neck. It felt cold against his skin. It was a medallion given to him by his mother some thirty years ago on the day he'd left to begin his term in the Guard: the Insignum Sanctus Nadalya, the holy icon of the Grey Lady, Vostroya's patron saint.

He mumbled a quick prayer for the Lady's favour and drew his gleaming, handcrafted bolt pistol from its holster. 'Let's see what they're made of, eh Rits?' he said.

Lieutenant Kuritsin slammed a power pack into position on his lasgun. 'Aye, sir. On your order.'

Sebastev felt his adrenaline surge as he watched the enemy speed towards him, signalling his body's readiness for the fight. The cold lost some of its bite. His fatigue faded and all his long years of training and experience rose to the fore.

Along the trench in both directions, men made ready to fire at the tide of charging orks. 'On my mark,' Sebastev voxed to them. He raised his pistol high above his head. Out on the snowfield, the green horde swept closer.

That's it, you snot-coloured xenos scum. Keep coming. We're not going anywhere.

Bestial roars filled the air, pouring from mouths filled with jutting yellow tusks. The wall of monstrous green bodies closed with frightening speed. All too quickly, with their oversized feet eating up the distance to the Vostroyan trenches, the orks came into lethal range.

Sebastev fired a single bolt into the air and voxed the words his men were waiting for. 'Open fire!'

A searing volley of las-bolts blazed from the trenches, each shot slicing through the air with a distinctive *hiss-crack*. Scores of charging greenskins howled in agony and fell clutching their faces. Massive pistols and cleavers were flung aside as grotesque bodies tumbled to a lifeless heap. But for all those that fell, there were hundreds more that hadn't been blinded or crippled. They kept charging, their hideous faces grinning with bloodlust.

The Vostroyan heavy bolters opened fire, filling Sebastev's ears with deep machine chatter. Pillboxes and gun-platforms up and down the line laced the rough ork formations with enfilading fire, sending fountains of dirt, snow and blood high into the air.

'Fifth Company, fire at will,' voxed Sebastev. 'They do not get to the trenches. Do you hear? Fire at will!'

Enemy slugs, solid rounds as big as a man's fist, bit great chunks of frozen dirt from the sandbags on the trench lip. But the greenskins, despite their obsession with battle, were notoriously bad shots. They represented a far greater threat in close combat. Sebastev had to make sure the charging mass didn't breach the Vostroyan defences, at least not until their numbers were manageable.

'Take those bastards down, Firstborn. The Emperor demands it!'

A knot of massive orks charged straight towards Sebastev's section of the trench. Perhaps they'd marked him out by his white cloak, or by the gold Imperialis insignia on his hat, but it was just as likely that the monsters sought their kills at random.

Troopers to left and right opened up on the orks as they sped nearer, carving black wounds into the wall of green flesh. Lieutenant Kuritsin scored a masterful headshot that put one of the monsters straight down. But, while all this las-fire would have obliterated an army of men, the ork charge barely slowed. Las-bolts could cut and char, but they lacked the raw kinetic punch of solid rounds. The orks shrugged off anything that wasn't crippling. The battle-lust burned bright in their red eyes.

Sebastev brought his bolt pistol to bear on a massive ork charging straight towards him. He slowed his breath, took aim, and squeezed the trigger.

The gun kicked hard, and hot blood misted the air where the monster's head had been. The heavy body ran on, legs still pumping, muscles executing the last orders from an absent brain. Sebastev watched the headless body snag on a tangle of razorwire, ripping open with a red spray before it tumbled down into the trench.

Both Sebastev and Kuritsin stepped neatly aside. Steaming fluids poured from the corpse, freezing quickly on the trench floor. Even through his scarf, Sebastev could smell the pungent fungal stink of the ork's insides. But this was no time to stand gaping. More greenskins boiled towards the Vostroyan defences. Sebastev turned his bolt pistol on them.

Solid firing discipline and Vostroyan accuracy were taking their toll on the orks. Out on the open drifts, the first charge broke. Stragglers turned and sped back towards the trees to join up with the second wave.

The angry rattle of the heavy bolters ceased.

'Good work, Firstborn,' voxed Sebastev, 'but there's no time for smiles and back-slaps.'

Another green tide had already broken from the trees.

'Second wave,' he called. 'Ammo counters and charge packs, all of you.' He pulled a fresh bolt magazine from his greatcoat pocket and slammed it home.

If the first wave of orks had looked large and fierce, they were mere youths compared to the dark-skinned brutes that now swarmed over the snows. Their overlong arms bulged with muscles swollen to unnatural proportions. Some wore crude suits of armour strapped or bolted together from plates of scrap metal and leather. Barring a direct headshot, a lasgun wouldn't do much damage to them, short of making those plates scalding hot. But orks didn't care about superficial burns when the battle-lust was on them. It just made them mad. They'd come straight through, soaking up lasfire until they were right on top of Fifth Company.

Emperor above, prayed Sebastev, give us strength.

'I want heavy bolters to concentrate fire on those armoured bastards. Leave the rest to mortars and lasguns. Is that clear? Flamers, wait for your range. No wasted shots. Mortars, I want focused fire at mid-range, centred on dense knots, as before.'

Heavy weapons teams readied themselves up and down the line.

Sebastev turned to Kuritsin. 'Where's Father Olov?'

'Just north of us, sir, fighting alongside Second Platoon today.'

Somewhat reluctantly, Sebastev voxed, 'Father Olov, a reading if you please. Draw the Emperor's attention to us. I think He might enjoy this.'

And for Throne's sake, he thought, make it uplifting for once.

The priest's gravelly voice came back over the vox a moment later. 'Something to strengthen our souls, captain. Volume II of *The Septology of Hestor*, I think. Ruminations on the Divine Ecstasy of Holy Service at Magna Garrovol is a particularly invigorating piece.'

'A fine choice, I'm sure, father,' replied Sebastev dubiously. He could hear Kuritsin groaning under his scarf. 'Begin at your convenience,' he told the priest.

The second ork wave was closing fast, shooting wildly in the general direction of Sebastev's men.

Lucky for us, thought Sebastev, they couldn't hit the hull of a battleship at point-blank range.

Even as he thought this, a trooper a few metres down on his right was thrown against the rear wall of the trench with bone-splintering force. He slumped dead to the wooden planks of the trench floor. Fully half of his head was gone, as if something had taken a great bite out of him.

Within seconds of each other, two more Guardsmen fell further along the trench, fatal head wounds spraying the rear wall red. The blood froze before it could even run down the wall.

'Gretchin snipers!' voxed Sebastev. 'Keep your heads down.'

They must've moved up under cover of the first assault, he thought. But where the khek are they?

Father Olov's voice sounded in Sebastev's ear as the priest began his reading. 'Saint Hestor dedicated victory at Magna Garravol to the Emperor, as always. Blood was spilled on both sides that day, and many lamented the passing of good men. But he rejoiced in their sacrifice, since paradise belongs only to the righteous.'

'I need spotters,' voxed Sebastev, breaking through the priest's oration. 'I want those snipers taken out, now. Fifth Company, pick your targets. Prepare to fire.'

Someone to the north of Sebastev's position fired off an early shot, hitting a massive ork in the throat. At closer range, the shot might have been fatal, but this far out, the monster just stumbled, regained its footing and continued to charge. A crude banner snapped in the freezing wind above its head: a poorly painted serpent with three heads, its yellow body coiled on a field of black, the mark of the Venomhead clan.

'Damn it, who was that?' roared Sebastev. 'Maintain fire discipline. That's an order.'

Olov continued his reading unperturbed. 'A messenger appeared before Saint Hestor in a dream, and said, "This is your path. There can be no turning from it. False hope fathers forgiveness. Forgiveness lays open the naked heart. There can be no forgiveness for the enemies of our great Imperium. Destroy the forces of the Idols Dark and you will live forever by the Emperor's side"'

Sebastev held his pistol in the air again. 'Steady, Firstborn. Steady. On my mark…'

The musty stink of unwashed ork bodies pushed ahead of the charging mass. An ork round whistled past Sebastev's head, punching into the frozen dirt of the trench wall behind him. Then the second wave came into lethal range.

'Now!' he voxed.

All along the trench, the sharp report of the Vostroyan lasguns drowned out the alien battle cries. From foxholes and pillboxes up and down the line, heavy bolters resumed fire, beating a deep tattoo that resonated in Sebastev's lungs. Mortars sent a deadly explosive hail at any cluster of orks that held together for even a moment. The explosions hurled massive bodies into the air, spinning them end over end, and breaking them open.

Gouts of blood splashed to the snow, the only rain these frozen lands had known for two millennia. But the death of their fellows did nothing to stop the horde. The orks trampled the bodies of their dead and kept coming.

As much as Sebastev detested them, he couldn't deny a grudging respect.

'Hestor led his people across the plains,' droned Father Olov over the vox, 'thirsty and tired, but hungry no more for the knowledge he had sought. The fate of the cluster was clear to him. His hands, stained with blood, carried chalice and censer. Behind him marched the faithful, dedicated to glory, and to a worthy death in the final battle.'

A deep voice broke through the priest's reading. 'Second Platoon to Company Command. We've located two grot sniper teams lying low in the drifts.' It was Sergeant Basch.

'Good work, sergeant,' replied Sebastev. 'Lieutenant Vassilo, did you hear that? Second Platoon has co-ordinates for you. I want Third Platoon mortars on those grot sniper positions now. Sergeant Basch will advise.'

'Understood, sir,' Vassilo voxed back.

Sebastev turned his attention back to the killing field. He fired bolt after bolt into the disordered ranks of the orks as they neared, felling a few with carefully placed headshots. But there were just too many. It was clear to him that the second wave was about to breach the trenches.

When that happens, thought Sebastev, we're–

His bolt pistol gave a loud click. The magazine was spent. The orks came on, waving their massive chipped blades. No point reloading, things were about to get very close and very bloody.

Sebastev knew he had to give the call his men dreaded. 'Fix bayonets!' he yelled over the vox. There was no escaping it. This battle would be won or lost at close quarters.

He holstered his pistol and grasped the hilt of the power sabre at his left hip, but when he moved to draw it, he found the sword frozen in its scabbard. Cursing loudly, he tried to tug the blade free.

He could hear his officers calling for courage as the orks leapt over the banks of razorwire and sandbags. Some of the orks became snagged. Others simply trampled over them, using their backs as bridges over the vicious barbs.

'Everyone back to the cover trench,' yelled Sebastev. 'The firing trench is lost.'

As the first of the orks leapt down into the trenches, the Vostroyans turned and raced off down the communications trenches that led to their fallback positions.

'I want flamers at the trench mouths,' voxed Sebastev. 'We can burn them as they follow us in.'

Sebastev, Kuritsin and the others from his section sprinted along the passage that led back to their secondary defensive positions. He didn't need to turn round to know just how close the orks were. He could hear their heavy boots thundering on the frozen planks as they gave chase.

Trench walls flashed past him as he ran a few metres behind his adjutant. Then, suddenly, the walls on either side ended, and Sebastev found himself in the cover trench, surrounded by his troopers. He spun around and yelled, 'Get me a khekking flamer, now!'

Trooper Kovo of Fourth Platoon stepped across Sebastev's field of vision just as the pursuing orks rounded the last bend. Sebastev's eyes went wide as he saw the enemy. They were monstrous, even for orks, towering hulks of savage muscle far bigger than even the largest of Sebastev's men. He only saw them for an instant before Kovo opened fire. A jet of blazing promethium blasted down the passage, searing away the flesh of the enemy. A moment later, the only evidence that the orks had ever existed was the molten metal that had been their armour, boots and weapons.

'More coming down on us,' yelled Trooper Kovo over his shoulder. 'I'm down to a quarter tank. Get ready.'

He loosed another jet of flame. Sebastev could hear ork screams over the flamer's roar, but they were cut off as the burning promethium consumed all.

Then, with more orks pouring down the passage, Kovo's fuel ran out. 'Incoming,' he shouted as he darted out of the way. Lasgunners moved in to take his place.

'Listen up, fighters,' barked Sebastev over the vox. 'We've got them in bottlenecks. The trenches are too narrow for them to fight properly. I want lasguns on them until they get within bayonet range. You know what to do after that. Hold the line, and remember the Emperor protects.'

Shouts filled the air all along the trench. 'The Emperor protects!'

The greenskins were charging straight down the communications trench. With a last hard tug, Sebastev's power sabre came free of its scabbard. He thumbed the rune that activated its deadly energy field just as a trio of massive orks barrelled forwards, howling in rage as Vostroyan lasfire strafed their bodies. Agony didn't slow them. They slammed troopers aside with ease as they broke into the cover trench.

One of the beasts lunged straight at Sebastev, laughing madly as it raised a huge cleaver above its head. The trench didn't offer any room to avoid the engagement, but that suited Sebastev fine.

As the crude blade came whistling down towards his head, propelled by green arms as thick as his torso, Sebastev darted forward into the blow, throwing his left arm up at the last moment. The ork's wrists clashed with the golden bracer that shielded his arm. The impact was bone-jarring, but Sebastev weathered it. Thanks to the bracer, his arm didn't break. The instant he caught the blow, he rammed his power sabre up into the ork's unprotected sternum.

The effect was immediate, but less than Sebastev had hoped for. The monster's expression shifted from delinquent glee to abject hate and rage, but it didn't die. Instead, it dropped the huge cleaver and wrapped its arms around Sebastev, pulling him into a crushing bear hug. It was a bad move on the ork's part, the motion forcing Sebastev's blade deeper inside its body. Howling in pain, it craned its head forward and tried to snap at him.

Sebastev gagged on the beast's stinking, rotten-meat breath, and reared his head back just in time. Massive yellow tusks slammed together scant centimetres from his face. Making use of the distance he'd created to gain momentum, Sebastev rammed his head forward with all his strength, smashing the metal insignia on his hat straight into the ork's nose.

As the monster reeled backwards, it loosened its grip. Sebastev yanked the hilt of his power sabre hard to left and right, causing massive internal injuries to his foe. Reeking gore poured out over his greatcoat. When the ork's misshapen face finally went slack, Sebastev pushed free and kicked the big body from the end of his blade.

There was no time to revel in the victory. He heard screams and calls for aid from nearby. Close combat raged all around him. Sebastev spun, looking for his adjutant, suddenly aware that they'd been separated.

There! There was Kuritsin, ten paces further up the trench, thrusting his gleaming bayonet at the face of an ork that had just cut down a trooper from First Platoon.

Sebastev ran to join him, and began hacking at the ork's wide back. The broad wounds he carved in the dark green muscle steamed in the freezing air.

Assaulted on two sides, the ork was swiftly overcome, and went down with a final bestial scream. 'Thank you, sir,' said Kuritsin, 'but there's no time for a breather.' He pointed over Sebastev's shoulder. More orks were pushing their way into the cover trench, hacking at Sebastev's men as they came, stomping the bodies of those that fell. Sebastev and Kuritsin both rushed forward to engage, calling others nearby to assist.

'You're not going to horde all the glory for yourself, are you, captain?' someone shouted.

Sebastev looked in the direction of the voice and saw a black figure standing on the lip of the trench, looking down into the mayhem below.

'For the Emperor and Holy Terra!' yelled the stranger. He launched himself into the trench, crashing into Sebastev and barrelling him from his feet. There was a flash of gold at collar and sleeve as the figure spun to face the orks. Sebastev heard the greedy purring of a chainsword before it buried itself in green meat, stressing the motor, changing its pitch.

Sebastev leapt back to his feet with a growl.

'Your wait has ended, captain,' yelled the stranger as he hacked the orks apart with deadly efficiency. 'Your new commissar is here at last. Now, secure the area behind me, for Throne's sake.'

Sebastev's first instinct was to cuff the man, once for knocking him down, twice for his verbal audacity. But there was no time for that. The trench was choked with orks and men fighting on every side. Kuritsin was helping First Platoon troopers to push back the orks attacking from the northern end. The southern end was likewise choked. There was nothing else for it, Sebastev would have to go up and over if he wanted to help his men. Sheathing his blade for a moment, he hauled himself out of the trench. The instant he scrambled to his feet, however, he found himself in trouble. To his right, a large slobbering ork with a black eye-patch had been looking for a place to jump down into the fray. On seeing Sebastev, it changed its mind, bellowed a challenge and stomped straight towards him, hefting a massive axe.

Sebastev drew his blade and hunkered down into his fighting stance, knees bent, sword ready in his lead hand.

The ork's opening move was a sweeping lateral backhander aimed at Sebastev's head. Sebastev ducked under the whistling blade with practiced ease, but the edge of the axe lopped a chunk from the top of his hat. Freezing air rushed into the hole, chilling his scalp. He didn't wait for the second attack. His power sabre flicked out and sliced through the tendons of the ork's thick wrist. Its fingers went limp and the axe spun to the snow. The ork gaped for the briefest moment, surprised and confused by the sudden uselessness of its hand. Sebastev took the opening without hesitation.

He stepped in with a powerful diagonal cut. The humming, crackling power sabre bit into the ork's right trapezius muscle with such force that it passed straight through, exiting the beast's torso below the left armpit.

The ork rolled quietly to the snow in two, lifeless pieces. Steam boiled up from a spreading pool of blood.

'Son of a grox!' cursed Sebastev to himself. *Maro should have warned me there was a new commissar. That's the last bloody thing I need.*

He heard Lieutenant Vassilo's voice over the vox, issuing orders to the men of his platoon. 'The orks are packed in tight. Get up on the trench lip. Fire down into the bottlenecks.'

Behind Sebastev, dozens of men pulled themselves up onto the snowfield and raced along the trench lip, stopping to pour fire down onto the trapped greenskins.

With their numbers cut by the charge over open ground, and their close combat abilities hampered by the narrow trenches, the orks had fared badly once again. Sebastev thanked the Emperor that they didn't learn quickly from their mistakes. But how long could it last? Sooner or later, the greenskins would surprise them.

Sebastev thumbed his power sabre off, giving thanks to the machine-spirit of the weapon before returning it to its scabbard.

Well done, my fighters, he thought. Let's hope it's the last attack before the rotation. But how many did we lose? Will I still call this a victory when the headcounts come in?

It seemed unlikely that the orks would launch a third wave. It wasn't their habit to hold forces in reserve, and they'd waited too long to take advantage of any confusion or cover that the second wave might have offered. Still, it was hard to fathom the workings of the alien mind. From an official standpoint, it was heretical to even try. In all Sebastev's experience with them, ork behaviour was rarely as simple and predictable as Imperial propaganda made it out to be.

Returning to the cover trench, Sebastev sought out his adjutant. He found him standing over the dismembered corpse of a fallen Firstborn.

'Bekislav,' said Kuritsin simply. 'He got himself blind-sided.'

Sebastev bowed his head. Bekislav had been a good man. He'd served with Fifth Company for almost eight years.

Lieutenant Kuritsin bore only a few shallow cuts and scrapes, nothing serious. The vox-caster on his back, however, looked a little worse for wear. It bore a number of fresh dents.

Sebastev tapped it with a finger and said, 'This thing still working?'

'About as well as before,' replied Kuritsin, 'so far as I can tell. It's temperamental, but it's tough. A little bit like–'

'Fine,' said Sebastev, cutting him off. 'Check in with the other companies. Tell them our sector is secure, and make sure the ork bodies are burned quickly. You know the drill.'

Left unattended, the ork corpses would shed their spores. They'd probably begun to do so already. It was best to burn them all as quickly as possible.

As Kuritsin voxed the order over to the platoon leaders, Sebastev walked on, surveying the results of the carnage. It was a grim picture. The red fabric of Vostroyan great-coats peeked out from beneath the heaped bodies of the foe.

Sebastev looked down at himself. His own coat was drenched with splashes of ork blood. He'd have to get inside soon. He was losing too much heat through the hole in his hat. Maybe he could stuff it with something in the meantime.

Warp damn this place, he thought. We can't last like this. If Old Hungry doesn't mobilise us soon, we'll die out here for nothing. We can't afford to play a numbers game with the orks, not with so few men.

Sebastev heard booted footsteps behind him and turned, expecting Kuritsin. But the man who faced him wasn't his adjutant. He wasn't even Vostroyan.

'You, captain,' said a tall, dark figure with a very distinctive cap, 'are an absolute bloody mess.'

CHAPTER TWO

Day 681
Korris Trenchworks – 13:24hrs, -22°C

WITH THE ORKS repulsed, the men of Fifth Company set
about tending to their wounded, salvaging equipment
from the dead, and repairing their defences. The snows
abated for a while, and the air was filled with the black
smoke of burning xenos corpses. Commissar Daridh
Ahl Karif followed Captain Sebastev through the wind-
ing maze of communications trenches to the man's
dugout.

The captain's sour mood was all too apparent to the
commissar, and he resisted any attempts at conversation
while they walked. Despite reminding himself not to
judge the captain too swiftly, Commissar Karif couldn't
help it. First impressions hadn't been good.

Moving south along the supply trench, they arrived at
a flight of steps cut into the frozen earth. Captain
Sebastev descended the steps and tapped a four-digit
code into the rune pad on the doorframe. With a hiss, the
door opened and the captain went inside.

Karif didn't wait for an invitation. It was far too cold to observe such niceties. Instead, he hurried in after the captain, closed the door quickly behind them, and slapped the cold seal activation glyph on the door's inner surface. When he turned, he found himself in a dimly lit room of dirt walls, with shabby furniture and a ceiling of wooden beams so low that they scraped the top of his cap.

The stocky Vostroyan had no such trouble. As the captain removed his damaged fur hat, Karif saw for the first time just how short Captain Sebastev was. The top of his head barely reached Karif's shoulders. At just under two metres, the commissar would have been considered a fairly tall man on most worlds, but he'd met enough Vostroyans to know that Sebastev was below average height for his people. It seemed that this dugout, with its preposterously low ceiling, had been constructed with his exact proportions in mind.

Sebastev's dugout may have been too small by half, but it was infinitely cosier than the freezing trenches outside. A quartet of small thermal coils, one in each corner, hummed as they struggled to take the chill from the air.

Both men removed their cloaks and scarves, and hung them on pegs hammered into the frozen, dirt wall. Karif felt so much lighter without the heavy fur cloak weighing him down, but he'd been glad of its warmth and protection in the open air. Not for the first time since planetfall, Karif cursed this world and the personal disaster that had brought him here.

Damn you, old man, he thought, remembering the gloating look on the face of Lord General Breggius as the man had informed him of his reassignment. *I wasn't to blame for your son's death. You must've pulled some long strings to get me posted out here, but I'm determined to make the best of this. There must be some glory to be had in this campaign.*

Captain Sebastev moved across the room and dropped himself onto the edge of a simple wooden bunk. 'Sit if

you've a mind to, commissar,' he rumbled as he began
unfastening the clasps of his blood-covered boots.

Karif drew a rickety, wooden chair from beside a small,
central table and sat down carefully, half-expecting the
thing to collapse under him. When the chair had
accepted his full weight, he placed his black cap on the
table's grubby surface and pulled a shining silver comb
from his pocket. As was his habit whenever he removed
his cap, he ran the comb through his oiled black hair,
sweeping it back behind his ears.

Captain Sebastev grunted when he saw this.

Karif didn't consider himself a vain man, but he believed
that a position of authority brought with it certain requirements of appearance. It was a matter of self-respect. And if
such an appearance happened to appeal to a particular
class of lady, so much the better.

It was unfortunate that his appearance had also
appealed to the Lord General's son. He'd been a charm-
ing boy with great potential as an officer, but he'd
misinterpreted Karif's friendship as something… deeper.
Karif hadn't expected his rejection to lead to the boy's suicide.

Clearly, Captain Sebastev would never suffer such difficulties. The man was almost beast-like. Then again, Karif
supposed as he watched Sebastev remove his carapace
armour, his breeding hadn't given him much to work
with. Compounding the captain's limited height, he was
so disproportionately thick with muscle that, had he
been painted green and set loose on the snowfield, his
own men could have mistaken him for an ork… albeit a
very short one.

The captain's black moustache was unkempt, clearly in
need of waxing, and his hair was little more than coarse
stubble. His leathery face was split by an ugly diagonal
scar that ran from his forehead, across his left eye, all the
way down to his jaw-line, tugging one side of his mouth
into a permanent snarl. All in all, Karif decided, without

the accoutrements of his position, the commanding officer of Fifth Company would be all but indistinguishable from an underhive thug.

Being a field commissioned officer, rather than an academy man, thought Karif, he may well have come from the underhives. But I'm hardly catching him at his best. He must have some worthy qualities. By all accounts, his fellow officers in the Sixty-Eighth Infantry Regiment rate him very highly. Time will tell.

'Have you anything to drink, captain?' Karif asked hopefully, thinking a little alcohol might take some of the chill off. The room's thermal coils seemed inadequate to the task. 'Amasec, perhaps? I'll even take caffeine if there's any going.'

'Rahzvod,' said Sebastev, indicating a cabinet behind the commissar with a nod of his head. He didn't get up.

Whatever his qualities are, thought Karif, he needs a damned good lesson in manners. A skunkwolf would be a more gracious host.

'Perhaps later,' said Karif, masking his irritation. 'First, let me congratulate you on today's victory. It was most exhilarating to get my hands dirty after such a long trip through the Empyrean. A fine introduction to serving with your company, yes?'

Sebastev growled and shook his head. 'Nineteen dead on my section of the trench, commissar. An unacceptable loss, and one that hardly warrants your congratulations.'

Nineteen men didn't sound like a lot to Karif. In fact, given the ferocity of the fighting he'd seen earlier, it sounded incredibly low. He'd served in conflicts where the daily tolls ran into the thousands. But it was clear from his tone that the captain was genuinely angry about the day's losses. Did he blame himself?

'I'm surprised by your reaction, captain,' said Karif. 'I'd have thought the tally would please you. An ork assault of that size repelled with Guard losses in only double figures? You should be expecting a decoration.'

Sebastev laughed, if the short, sharp bark that issued from his mouth could truly be called a laugh. 'I'll be dead before that ever happens, commissar,' he said, 'and so will you, most likely. It's clear you've no idea how bad things are out here. Weren't you briefed on the way in?'

Karif frowned. 'Perhaps you'd better enlighten me, captain, since you clearly feel the officers at Seddisvarr haven't done an adequate job.'

'Bloody right they haven't,' said Sebastev. 'What does anyone at Twelfth Army Command know about the realities of the Eastern Front? Damned little, that's what. Whichever bigwig you angered knew what they were doing when they posted you out here. You're right in the middle of it, commissar. We're outnumbered, ill-equipped, and so badly supported you'll wonder if the Munitorum isn't just a figment of your imagination. It's only my faith in the Emperor and in the strength of my men that gives me any hope.'

'I haven't angered anyone that I know of,' Karif lied, 'except perhaps you. I was sent here because your company needed a replacement commissar, and it galls me to hear such words from an officer of the Imperial Guard. I've little tolerance for fatalism, captain. In fact, I'm a strong believer in the might of the common man. With good leadership and morale, there's nothing the Guard can't achieve. Be careful not to let me hear you speak thus in front of your men. I'm sure I don't have to remind you of my commissarial remit.'

Sebastev simply stared back at Karif, unflinching, until finally he said, 'Fear won't work for you out here, commissar. I tell you this because you're clearly a man used to being feared. But don't mistake a lack of fear for a lack of respect. I'll admit I wasn't pleased at the thought of a new man coming in. Your predecessor, Commissar Ixxius was a great soldier and friend. We won't see his like again. If he proved anything, it was that the right man can make a great difference. There is a place for you here among the

Firstborn, if you're such a man. It'll take time, perhaps, but once you've earned the respect of my fighters, you'll see what a force they can be. Maybe this conflict could use a fresh pair of eyes to assess it.'

Sebastev stood up, crossed to the cabinet in his bare feet and poured two shots of clear liquid into a pair of dirty glasses. 'Rahzvod,' he said for the second time, placing one glass down on the table next to Karif.

I confess I've never approved of the idea of field commissioned officers, thought Karif, and this one justifies all my prejudices: ill-mannered and contentious, unmindful of his appearance and the protocols of Imperial society, and yet, the man's lack of sophistry is refreshing. He's ugly, brutal and direct, it's true, but if men like me are the surgical scalpels of the Imperial Guard, perhaps men like Sebastev are the sledgehammers. The Emperor has a use for both, I suppose.

He raised his glass to his lips and said, 'For the Emperor.' The liquid ran down his throat, searing the walls of his gullet. He almost spluttered, but caught himself. His cheeks grew hot and he knew they must be flushing.

'For the Emperor and Vostroya,' replied Sebastev, raising his own glass into the air before knocking back the bitter liquid. He sighed happily, as if he'd been waiting all day for that drink.

In the momentary silence, Karif took another look around the little room.

Ill-mannered or not, Sebastev was clearly a pious man: aquilas on every wall, an image of His Divine Majesty set into an alcove there, several holy texts stacked by his bunk, and even a small altar to the female saint they loved so much. That, at least, was gratifying to see.

Sebastev, looking up from his empty glass, followed the commissar's gaze towards the little altar and said, 'Are you familiar with the Grey Lady, commissar?'

Karif nodded and said, 'I read the Treatis Elatii once, the story of her ancient crusades. But that was many years ago.'

'Still,' said Sebastev, 'that's something in your favour. Commissar Ixxius could quote the text from memory. It made a great difference to the men during hard times. I'm afraid Father Olov, much as we revere the man, is a far better fighter than he is a preacher of the Holy Word. If you've any skill in oration at all…'

'Yes, well, I'll keep that in mind, captain, but I didn't come here to replace the regiment's priest. Battlefield oration is–'

Karif was interrupted by a loud knock at the door.

'Come in,' barked Sebastev.

The cold seal hissed and the door cracked open with a sucking sound. Bitterly cold air rushed into the room, causing Karif to pull his coat tighter around him. The promethium lamp on the ceiling swung in the gust, sending the room's shadows into a dance. A Vostroyan with lieutenant's stripes at his collar and cuffs stepped in and quickly sealed the door.

The newcomer had to stoop under the ceiling, and not merely because of his fur hat. The man was almost as tall as Karif. Like many Vostroyans, he was well built. The gravity on Vostroya was slightly higher than on Karif's homeworld.

Throne preserve us, thought Karif as he watched the man stoop, did they fashion these dugouts for children? My own accommodation had better not be like this. I won't spend this campaign bent double like an old ape.

Even as the thought crossed his mind, Karif had a sinking feeling that his fears on the matter would be realised. Cutting trenches into permafrost was hard enough, but Twelfth Army engineers would have taken as many short-cuts as they could while working in the bitter cold.

'Sorry to intrude, gentlemen,' said the lieutenant. He gave a sharp salute before removing his hat and scarf.

Now here's a proper officer, thought Karif. The contrast between the lieutenant and Captain Sebastev was stark. He had a handsome face, a well-groomed moustache, and good, noble bearing. He was an academy man, for certain. How could he stand to serve under this glorified grunt?

Sebastev didn't stand, but he gestured from his bunk and said, 'This is my adjutant and comms-officer, Lieutenant Oleg Kuritsin. Rits, this is Commissar Daridh Ahl Karif from... Sorry, commissar, I didn't catch where you were from.'

'I never said, captain,' replied Karif.

'Tallarn?' guessed Lieutenant Kuritsin with a smile.

Karif wasn't quite fast enough to hide a flash of irritation.

Why does everyone I meet assume that, he thought angrily? Do all men with black hair and a deep tan have to come from that wretched place?

'Delta Radhima actually,' he said, recovering his composure and standing, or rather stooping, to shake the lieutenant's hand, 'but I attended the Schola Excubitos on Terrax.'

Let's see what that does for them, he thought.

He watched the name register with the lieutenant, though Captain Sebastev's grim features didn't change at all. The schola on Terrax was infamous for producing some of the strictest, most militant commissars in the history of the Imperium. Karif didn't care to mention that he'd been considered one of the more liberal graduates.

'Forgive my ignorance, commissar,' said Kuritsin with a short bow. 'I hadn't heard of Delta Rhadima until this moment. In any case, welcome to Fifth Company.'

'Something to tell me, Rits?' interrupted Sebastev.

'An urgent message from Colonel Kabanov's office, sir. The colonel's calling an assembly in the war room. He'll be arriving at nineteen hundred hours.'

'The war room?' asked Sebastev. 'Our war room?'

'Yes, sir,' said Kuritsin, 'at nineteen hundred hours.'

'Is that unusual, captain?' asked Karif.

'Yes,' said Sebastev.

Lieutenant Kuritsin explained. 'Colonel Kabanov usually holds his briefings at the regimental headquarters, commissar. With the scale of today's attack, he may feel he can't pull his company commanders away from the front. In any case, he's chosen our war room, and that means something has happened.'

'Are there any reasons for optimism, gentlemen?' asked Karif. 'Before you arrived, lieutenant, the captain was telling me all sorts of things about poor supplies and the like. The latest reinforcements, at least, must be welcome news.'

'Reinforcements?' asked Sebastev.

'Sorry, sir,' said Kuritsin. 'I forgot to tell you. Some shinies came in with the commissar.'

'Shinies?' asked Karif.

'Aye,' said Sebastev, 'new conscripts, fresh off the assembly line: shinies. How many did we score, Rits?'

'The regiment as a whole, sir? Or Fifth Company?'

'Fifth Company, of course.'

Kuritsin glanced at the floor as he said, 'He's waiting outside, sir.'

Karif suppressed a grin at the look on the captain's face.

'He?' spluttered Sebastev. 'You mean–?'

Kuritsin turned, opened the door, and called out into the icy air.

Answering the lieutenant's call, a Vostroyan of unusually slim build stepped into the dugout, clumps of snow falling to the floor from the top of his hat and armoured shoulders. The lieutenant sealed the door behind the newcomer and ordered him to remove his scarf.

The trooper's face was blue-eyed, red-cheeked and innocent. There was more of the choirboy about him than the battle-ready Guardsman. He looked barely halfway through his adolescence, though he'd have to be at least eighteen years old to be posted to a regiment. His face bore none of the scars from basic training that most new conscripts were so proud of.

Karif recognised the boy immediately. They'd ridden together with a handful of others in the back of a Chimera from the town to the trenches, though he couldn't remember his name.

Captain Sebastev was staring at the youngster with a mixture of disgust and disbelief.

'What the khek is this?' he growled. 'The new company mascot? This one's never old enough for duty. What's your name, trooper? And where's your damned moustache?'

Clearly feeling sorry for the nervous boy, Lieutenant Kuritsin answered on his behalf. 'This is Danil Stavin, sir. His papers say he's eighteen. He came down on the last boat with the commissar and about three hundred others. The Sixty-Eighth was assigned about forty in all. We got this one.'

'Well then,' said Captain Sebastev, 'he must be some kind of Space Marine, by the Throne. Is that right, Stalin? Are you a Space Marine?'

'It's Stavin, sir. With a "v", sir,' said the boy. His voice was little more than a nervous whisper.

The 'boat' Lieutenant Kuritsin had referred to was the Imperial Naval cruiser *Helmund's Honour*. Rather than raise new foundings like most Imperial Guard regiments, the Vostroyan Firstborn was reinforced in the field, a peculiarity that was, according to some, the result of an ancient debt about which no one living seemed to know a great deal. If they did know, they weren't talking.

The newest levies from Vostroya had already settled into the passenger holds when Karif stepped aboard the ship at Port Maw. In the months it took the ship to navigate the warp, Karif had watched the young Vostroyans train, readying themselves for action in the Second Kholdas War. Since Danik's World was considered little more than a backwater with minimal tactical importance to the war effort, those unlucky enough to be earmarked for the Twelfth Army had suffered the taunts of the others. The real glory was on the cluster's spinward side, where those on the Kholdas Line fought to hold back the massive ork armada from the Ghoul Stars.

On the journey out to the Eastern Front, Karif had enjoyed impressing the new conscripts with tales of his battlefield exploits. He told them of his experiences facing the inexplicable eldar. His stories of the terrifying tyranids had drawn gasps of awe from the young men. Karif's ego had been well fed. What did it matter that he'd embellished a little? Karif grinned at the boy as he remembered, and was rewarded with a broad smile in return.

'What are you so happy about, trooper?' growled Sebastev. 'The deep winter'll soon knock that smile off your face.'

Stavin's cheeks glowed and he dropped his eyes to the floor.

'Rits,' said Sebastev, 'who took the most hits today?'

'That would be Fourth Platoon, sir, though not by much.'

'Right. Stavin, I'm assigning you to Fourth Platoon. Your commanding officer is Lieutenant Nicholo. Understood?'

Kuritsin suddenly looked uncomfortable. 'Actually, sir, Lieutenant Nicholo took an ork blade in the shoulder today during the second wave. He's at the field hospital.'

Sebastev loosed a string of curses, the likes of which Karif had never heard. Some of the images they conjured were deeply unpleasant. 'How bad is it?'

'He lost an arm, sir, his left. Full augmentation from the shoulder down, so I'm told.'

The captain was quiet for a moment, visibly disturbed by the news. Then he caught Karif assessing him. His face quickly reverted to its previous snarl. 'Nicholo's a solid man. He's in good hands. Our medics are the very best in the Twelfth Army, commissar.' He turned his eyes to the boy. 'Right then, Stavin, you'll report to Sergeant Breshek in the meantime. He'll get you sorted out.'

It's a fact, thought Karif as he looked at the young trooper, that most new arrivals to the battlefield don't survive their first skirmish. Those that do survive tend to be born fighters, bullies, killers, sociopaths. There are occasionally others, the quick studies. Some of them make it. They learn the hard way. This one doesn't look like a fighter. Is he a quick study, I wonder?

'Excuse me, captain,' said Karif, 'I'd like to present a proposal of sorts regarding Trooper Stavin here.'

'Very well,' said the captain. 'Out with it.'

'You appreciate that newly assigned commissars often experience a regrettable amount of culture clash. It makes things difficult for all concerned. So, in order to help me adjust to Vostroyan ways, I'd like to request an adjutant. Since Trooper Stavin is, in your own words, a shiny–'

'I see where you're going with this, commissar,' said Captain Sebastev. 'I certainly can't assign a more experienced man to spit-polish your boots for you. Very well. Trooper Stavin, you'll serve as the commissar's adjutant. Do as he says except when I tell you otherwise. A commissar's adjutant you may be, but I'm in charge. Make sure you don't forget it.'

Stavin saluted the captain and said, 'Yes, sir. I won't forget.'

'Good.' Sebastev faced his own adjutant and said, 'Rits, take the commissar and his new aide to their dugout. D-fourteen is free, isn't it? Get them settled in. And make sure the relevant people know about the briefing in the war room later. Tell them Colonel Kabanov won't stand for any tardiness, clear?'

'Like good rahzvod, sir,' said the lieutenant with a sharp salute.

The commissar rose from his chair, forced to stoop again, and placed his cap on his head. He lifted his cloak from its peg, fastened it over his shoulders, and joined Kuritsin and Stavin at the door.

'Make sure you're at the briefing, commissar,' said Sebastev. 'You can be sure the colonel has something damned important to say.'

'Naturally, captain,' replied Karif. In truth, his mind was firmly fixed on the weather outside. He was disturbed to find just how much he dreaded re-emerging into the freezing cold. He was somewhat concerned, too, by his impulse to take Stavin under his wing.

Careful, Daridh, he told himself. It was your kindness to Breggius's boy that got you shipped out here in the first place. Where does it come from, this need to look after them? Who looked after me when I was that age? Ah, but perhaps that's it.

Lieutenant Kuritsin hit the cold seal rune, opened the door of the dugout, and ushered the commissar and his new adjutant out into the cold. Karif threw the captain a salute before he stepped out into the howling wind and snow. He drew his cloak tight around him, sinking his chin into the thick fur. Lieutenant Kuritsin stepped out last, closing the door of the dugout behind him. Karif heard the hiss of the cold seal as it re-activated.

So that's Grigorius Sebastev, he thought. That's the man to whom my fate is bound. Emperor above, did you have to make him such a bad-tempered little grox? I'm eager to see how he interacts with other officers at the briefing.

'Follow me, commissar,' shouted Kuritsin over the noise of the wind. 'Let's double-time it so you don't catch your death.'

Karif nodded, and he and Stavin fell into step behind Kuritsin, moving north up the trench with some haste. They bent almost double against the whipping snow, eager to get to shelter as soon as possible.

CHAPTER THREE

Day 681
Korris Trenchworks – 19:09hrs, -29°C

COLD AIR SCYTHED through the war room as the door was flung open. Lieutenant Maro of the colonel's personal staff limped through, and pulled his scarf down to reveal a round face with a clipped brown moustache. His cheeks had been pinched red by the cold. 'Stand to!' he called. The pistons in his augmetic leg hissed as he stepped away from the door.

The assembled men pushed their chairs back from the long, central table and stood, snapping to attention with crisp salutes.

Colonel Kabanov hurried inside, his shape lost in the thick folds of his white fur cloak. He stamped the snow from his boots and shook it from the top of his hat. 'At ease, all of you,' he said after a brief but sincere salute of his own. Then he shuffled forward, moving straight towards the nearest of the room's thermal coils. 'Talk amongst yourselves while I get some heat back into me.'

A stream of officers and command-level personnel entered the room behind him, eager to get out of the punishing winds. Last to enter were the servants of the Machine-God. Tech-priest Gavaril and Enginseer Politnov swept into the room like shrouded ghosts, and sealed the door firmly shut behind them. The machinery that sustained their ancient bodies clicked and hummed as they turned their cowled heads to greet the others.

The newly arrived officers from regimental HQ hung their hats and cloaks on wall pegs and took their seats. Soon, Colonel Kabanov was the only man still wearing both his hat and his cloak.

I suppose I'd better take them off, he thought.

Turning from the heat of the coil, still rubbing his hands together, he said, 'I don't suppose there's a pot of ohx' on, is there? I could use a cup.'

He grudgingly removed his outdoor gear, revealing a pristine formal jacket of bright Vostroyan red trimmed with white and gold. In truth, the jacket was far too ostentatious for the occasion, but it was well made and warm and, for these reasons alone, he'd put his modesty aside, adding another valuable layer of insulation against the deep winter.

Captain Sebastev's adjutant, Lieutenant Kuritsin, stood from his place at the table and moved to a cabinet in the far corner to fix a steaming mug of ohx' for the colonel.

'If there's any going about, lieutenant,' added Kabanov, 'you might put a little shot of rahzvod in it. Do an old man a favour.' The men chuckled. More than a few drew Guard-issue flasks from their pockets and offered them to the lieutenant, but Kuritsin had already unscrewed his own flask. Kabanov saw him pour a generous measure of the strong Vostroyan liquor into the mug.

Good man, he thought. *A dash of that will do the trick.*

The war room filled with low chatter as officers from different sections of the trenches discussed the day's defensive actions. Two men were notably absent:

Lieutenant Nicholo of Fifth Company and Lieutenant Vharz of the Tenth. Nicholo looked set to recover given time, but Vharz had met his end. As the uninformed were told of this, the tone of the conversation changed, and the mood in the room became sombre.

It will get a lot worse before I'm through, thought Kabanov. May the Emperor help you in particular, Sebastev, because you're going to need it.

Lieutenant Kuritsin crossed the room and presented Kabanov with a mug. 'Thank you, lieutenant,' said the colonel with a smile. 'There's nothing like a hot drink on a night like this, eh? So long as there's a drop of the liquid fire in it.'

Kuritsin grinned. 'You're not wrong, sir.'

The ohx' was thick and salty, just as it was meant to be. The drink's proper name was *ohxolosvennoy*, but no one ever called it that. It was a staple on Vostroya, cheap and easy to make. In its dry form, it was simply powdered grox meat with a few added stimulants and preservatives. Workers in every factorum on Vostroya swore by ohx'. It was the only way to get through double shifts. On Danik's World, the Firstborn drank prodigious amounts of the stuff.

Kabanov sighed happily as the hot liquid warmed his belly. Low enough not to be heard over the general hum of conversation, he said, 'Fifth Company did well today, soldier, holding back the greenskin filth. You and your men did the regiment proud. The late major's faith in the captain is vindicated once again. Don't tell the captain I said so. His head will swell and his hat won't fit anymore.' The two men shared a quiet laugh, while Sebastev, busy conversing with other officers around the table, sat oblivious to them.

Kabanov nodded towards the far corner of the room where a small group of commissars conversed around another of the room's thermal coils.

Not one of them had removed his black cap.

The shadowy group reminded Kabanov of nothing so much as a flock of giant crows, the kind he'd seen gather to feast on the dead in the aftermath of so many battles. He immediately felt a twinge of guilt at the comparison. Commissar-captain Uthis Vaughn, the regimental commissar, was a close personal friend. Despite the man's intimidating public persona, Kabanov knew him to have a wonderful sense of humour, a deep appreciation of art in its many forms, and a frustrating talent for the game of regicide. He was the best player Kabanov had met in all sixty-eight years of his life. But it wasn't Vaughn the colonel was concerned with. 'How about the new man, lieutenant?' he asked Kuritsin. 'How are you getting on with Ixxius's replacement?'

Kuritsin shrugged and, with his voice barely more than a whisper, said, 'It's early days yet, sir. The man seems to be a fearless fighter, at least. He literally threw himself onto the orks today. Unfortunately, he threw himself onto the captain first. He's lucky the orks took the brunt of the captain's rage. I'd say they're not off to a very good start.'

'And you expect more trouble between them?' asked Kabanov reading the lieutenant's expression.

'I'd say they have very little in common, sir. The commissar seems a very proud man, a man of fine breeding and aristocratic ancestry. I'm sure that the reputation of the Schola Excubitos on Terrax is well earned, but that'll carry little weight with the captain. You know what he's like with the proud ones, sir.'

Kabanov frowned and stroked his long white moustache. 'Perhaps you could caution the captain, lieutenant. He mustn't underestimate Commissar Karif. Commissar-Captain Vaughn considers his posting to Fifth Company a most perplexing turn of events. The man is an unknown quantity.'

'How so, sir?' asked Kuritsin. 'Didn't the commissar-captain request a replacement after Ixxius was lost?'

'He did, but, at the last possible moment, the postings were changed. Commissar-Captain Vaughn was expecting another man entirely.' Kabanov leaned close and added, 'According to Vaughn, Karif's record is conspicuously impressive. He's been decorated for success in some very high profile campaigns. Foremost among his achievements, so I'm told, is the Armoured Star for a pivotal action on Phenosia.'

If Kabanov remembered rightly, and it was difficult to be sure after a lifetime of trying to stay current on the Imperium's countless wars, Phenosia had been won back at great cost from the forces of the dreaded Traitor Legions.

'If that's true, sir,' said Kuritsin, 'it begs the question: why has the man been shipped out here, of all places? And to a mere company-level commission? It seems most irregular, sir.'

'I'd hazard a guess that our new commissar recently made a powerful enemy, lieutenant.'

'I hope it's just that, sir.'

Kabanov raised a querying eyebrow. 'What do you mean?'

'I wouldn't like to think that it was anything more sinister, sir. Captain Sebastev isn't very popular with Twelfth Army Command.'

I know, thought Kabanov. If General Vlastan didn't owe me his life twice over, he'd have bounced Sebastev back down to sergeant the moment Dubrin breathed his last. The idea that some grunt from the Barony of Muskha, of all places, has been given a company command... Now it seems the general's patience has run out. He's been listening to the wrong people. I can't shield the captain any more. The politics in Seddisvarr are out of hand, but if they think I'll just drop the man like a hot ingot, they don't know the White Boar, by Terra.

Colonel Kabanov realised with a start that he'd drifted off into his own thoughts. The lieutenant was staring at him, waiting patiently. 'Sorry, lieutenant, old men like me have these moments.'

'Not so old, sir,' replied Kuritsin with a grin and a shake of his head, 'and still the best of us by far.'

Kabanov was caught off-guard by the look of admiration in the lieutenant's eyes. Hero worship: he'd never gotten used to it, though he'd had to endure it since winning his first regimental combat tournament. He'd earned his nickname during that contest.

By the Throne, he thought, that was fifty years ago.

At least his time away from the frontlines didn't seem to have impacted on his reputation among his men. Clearing his throat, he put a hand on the young officer's shoulder and said, 'It's time we got this briefing started. Call this lot to order for me, lieutenant.'

'At once, sir,' said Kuritsin. He turned to face the crowded table and called out, 'To order, Firstborn. Colonel Kabanov will begin the briefing.'

The younger man moved off to take his seat, and Colonel Kabanov stood alone, scanning the faces of his patient officers.

No more procrastinating, Maksim, he told himself.

SEBASTEV WAS GLAD he was sitting down when the colonel gave them the news, because he could hardly believe what he was hearing. The words stunned him. It was a bloody disaster. That was the only way to put it. Twelfth Army Command's gross mismanagement of the Danik's World campaign had now cost them an entire regiment of men and a vital beachhead in the north-east. The Vostroyan Firstborn 104th Fusiliers had been decimated. Over two thousand souls had been lost defending the city of Barahn against the concentrated might of the Venomhead clan. Warp blast and damn the orks.

But if the news itself was grim, the implications were even worse.

Someone a few seats to Sebastev's left banged a fist on the table. The hololithic projector studs set into the surface jumped, and bands of static rippled across the ghostly green projection of the Danikkin landscape that floated before them. Sebastev's eyes were fixed on the glowing three-dimensional representation of Barahn. Even now, as the officers of the Sixty-Eighth sat in silence with their jaws and fists clenched, hordes of filthy orks were ransacking the city, stripping it of anything they could use to fabricate their shoddy war-machines, enslaving or murdering anyone they found alive.

Sebastev had seen what ork slavers would do. Though the ork intellect was universally denigrated, he'd worked enough reconnaissance in his past to know better. He'd seen greenskins threaten to devour captive children, forcing their parents to work themselves to death. He'd watched laughing gretchin torture innocent men and women to instil fear and obedience in the enslaved. He remembered, too, the Marauder air strikes he'd guided in to deliver the Emperor's justice. He'd known that, given the choice, the enslaved would gladly give up their lives to ensure the destruction of their captors.

Old memories mixed with fresh anger and made his blood surge. He fought to stay in control.

Most of the officers in that room were looking at the map, giving thanks for the range of high mountains, the northernmost extents of the Varanesian Peaks, which separated the fallen city from the town of Korris by almost three hundred kilometres of difficult terrain.

So far, the Sixty-Eighth had only ever had to contend with roaming bands of ork scavengers or, like today, warbands that spilled over the mountains from the battle in the north-east. Even so, the number of orks in the region and the frequency of attacks had been increasing. Despite the losses they were surely taking, it seemed as if the ork horde was actually gaining in size, strength and ambition. It didn't make sense.

Since taking Barahn in the opening stages of the Twelfth Army's eastern push, the 104th Fusiliers had suffered the brunt of the ork attacks. Twelfth Army Command had believed the city's defences to be far beyond the greenskins' siege capabilities. What fools! Sebastev would have wagered every bottle of rahzvod in Korris that the men assembled tonight felt the same guilt that he did twisting their guts.

'Now that the orks have pushed through our northern line,' said Colonel Kabanov, breaking the silence, 'the entire Valles Carcavia is open to them, from its easternmost mouth all the way to the outskirts of Grazzen in the west.'

The colonel lifted a light quill and inscribed a small circle on the projector's control tablet. A circle of light appeared on the shimmering holomap, circling a riverside city about one hundred and fifty kilometres west of Barahn.

'There's no doubt,' continued the colonel, 'that General Vlastan's tactical staff will be expecting to stop the ork advance at Grazzen. The Thirty-fifth Mechanised Regiment is stationed there. They need only fall back to the west bank and destroy both the city's bridges to prevent the orks from advancing into Theqis. The river Solenne is over two kilometres wide at its narrowest point, and runs so fast and deep that even our Chimeras can't ford it. Without the bridges here and here, the orks will have no way across.'

'Meaning that they'll turn southwards and crash down on us like an apocalypse,' said a gruff voice. Sebastev looked across the table at Major Galipolov, commander of First Company. 'When they hit the banks of the Solenne and find themselves checked, they'll turn and follow it all the way down to Nhalich, isolating us and cutting off our supply lines. Isn't that right, colonel?'

What supply lines, thought Sebastev bitterly? With things the way they are out here, would we even notice?

Colonel Kabanov nodded, his face grim. 'I'd call that a certainty, major. With these changes to the campaign map, Korris sticks out like a grot's nose. But I'm afraid the orks are only half of the problem. It pains me to say it, but I've more bad news. Listen up.'

All eyes rose from the holomap and fixed on the colonel as he said, 'At daybreak this morning, armour columns from the traitor-held towns of Dura and Nova-Kristae laid siege to the town of Ohslir. The 212th Regiment fought back, but their defences were overcome. This is the first direct offensive action taken by the Danikkin Independence Army in over a hundred days, and the timing can't be a coincidence. The possibility that they received real time intelligence from observers at Barahn is something I find both significant and disturbing, especially since our own comms have proven so damned unreliable.'

The colonel suddenly looked over at the attending members of the Cult Mechanicus. He bowed by way of apology and said, 'Of course, I meant no offence.'

'None taken, colonel,' said Tech-priest Gavaril. His voice crackled from a sonic resonator sunk into the pale flesh of his chest. 'We are in agreement.'

'The machine-spirits are discontent,' added Enginseer Politnov. Unlike Tech-priest Gavaril's, the enginseer's mouth moved as he spoke, but the sound was exactly the same, toneless and electronic. 'More obeisance must be made. More obeisance!'

'Indeed,' said Colonel Kabanov. 'We ask much of the Machine-God.'

'Wasn't any support sent out from Helvarr?' asked the Eighth Company commander, Major Tsurkov. 'Surely the 117th were sent east to flank the rebel armour? Didn't Major Imrilov send out a call for emergency support?'

The question had occurred to Sebastev, too. Tank columns from Helvarr could have reached Ohslir in just a few hours, but had they been sent out to help?

'No support was sent,' said Kabanov darkly. 'From what I understand, storms over Theqis prevented Twelfth Army Command communicating with our bases in the south until it was too late. We didn't receive news of the attack until the relay station at Nhalich was finally able to boost the signal to our array. The 212th took heavy losses, but I've been told that a few companies did manage to escape under the leadership of Major Imrilov. As far as I know, they've joined up with the 117th at Helvarr.'

Old Hungry will have a fit, thought Sebastev. I wouldn't want to be Imrilov the next time they meet.

On the hololithic map, Kabanov again drew a small circle of light, this one marking the town of Ohslir. 'With the campaign map altered so dramatically, we are extended well beyond our lines of support. With Ohslir under their control, it's a fair bet the Danikkin Independence Army will strike out for Nhalich next. So, if the orks don't cut Korris off, the rebels will certainly try.'

Major Galipolov leaned forward on his elbows, tugging a waxed end of his grey moustache, and said, 'It's a classic pincer, only each claw belongs to a separate beast. If the dirty xenos were anything but orks or tyranids, I'd suspect some kind of collusion with the rebels. The timing of this DIA push can't be a coincidence, but, given that we're talking about orks here, the notion is preposterous.'

'Speculation won't get us very far,' said Captain Grukov of Third Company. 'We need action.' Refusing to meet Major Galipolov's furious stare, he addressed Colonel Kabanov directly. 'What's to be done, sir?'

'The decision has been made for us, gentlemen,' said Kabanov. 'The Twelfth Army's tactical council have assessed the situation. I received new orders this afternoon.'

Colonel Kabanov's expression told Sebastev he wasn't going to like what he was about to hear. The old man's face betrayed his disgust, as if he'd bitten into a piece of fruit only to find it riddled with Catachan pusworms.

To Sebastev's mind, the smart answer was to move companies from the 117th across from Helvarr to engage the rebels at Ohslir. Then flank the enemy on its north side using companies from the 701st at Nhalich. While the orks were engaged with the Thirty-Fifth at Grazzen, the Sixty-Eighth could move up to flank them from the south. If they were lucky, there might be a chance to take the orks out permanently.

Of course, it would mean abandoning Korris, but, in Sebastev's opinion, Korris's only strategic value was as a launching point for Vostroyan assaults on the rebel-held hive-cities in the south-east. Such an action didn't look likely. The discovery of the Venomhead presence on Danik's World had brought a swift halt to the Twelfth Army's original plans.

The colonel cleared his throat and said, 'The Sixty-Eighth Infantry Regiment has been ordered to pull back to Nhalich. When we arrive, we're to join up with the 701st and assist them in readying their defences against a possible siege from the south. Our redeployment is scheduled to begin at first light, two days from now, preparations to start immediately.'

Redeployment, not retreat: retreat was practically a curse word to many of the Vostroyan Firstborn. Sebastev had never liked it much, but he didn't try to deceive himself now. It *was* a retreat. The Twelfth Army had suffered a devastating double blow. They had to consolidate their forces, and that meant pulling back, at least for now. It wasn't how Sebastev would have fought the war, but at least it made some kind of sense. That was more than he'd expected from Old Hungry and his advisors.

Major Galipolov, on the other hand, was typically direct in voicing his displeasure. 'So we're to just up and leave?' he asked. 'After two years of hard-fought occupa-tion? Does General Vlastan know how many of my men died holding this place? This doesn't sit well with me, colonel. It doesn't sit well at all.'

'Noted, major,' replied Colonel Kabanov.

Captain Grukov added his voice, saying, 'I can't stomach the idea of just letting the damned greenskins roll right in here. The least we can do is leave a few surprises for them, wouldn't you say? What's to stop them following us to Nhalich and attacking at the same time as the Danikkin rebels?'

Colonel Kabanov frowned. 'Now that Barahn has fallen, General Vlastan is betting that the orks will stop crossing the Varanesian Peaks to attack Korris. As a buffer of sorts for our forces at Nhalich, Twelfth Army command has decided that a single company will remain behind in Korris to continue our occupation of the town.' The colonel paused. 'Captain Sebastev's Fifth Company has been selected for this honour.'

'By the Throne!' exclaimed Grukov. 'With respect, sir, you can't be serious. A single company?'

'Honour indeed,' said Major Galipolov, banging the table. 'It's a bloody death sentence!'

Others spoke up, eager to voice their protests. Only the members of the Commissariat and the Cult Mechanicus remained silent, masking their reactions well, if they had any at all.

Sebastev was unsure what to think or feel. A single company, even his outstanding Fifth Company, might hold off a minor assault if they could stomach the heavy losses, but an ork charge like today's...

So, thought Sebastev, the blue bloods have finally made their move. I knew it would come sooner or later.

Not for the first time, Sebastev wished he'd never made his promise to Dubrin, but his friend had been dying. How could he have done any less than swear, on the Treatis Elatii no less, that he would lead Dubrin's company to glory and honour? That he would get them through this wasteful mess of a campaign? And, because some men cared about things like lineage and Vostroyan military politics, and Throne knew what else, Sebastev's whole company had been ordered to hold the line or die.

The other officers were talking over each other. There was such a cacophony that no single voice could be made out.

Colonel Kabanov rose to his feet, toppling his chair to the cold, wooden floor. His fists struck the tabletop so hard they cracked it. 'Silence, all of you!' he bellowed. 'I'm not finished, Throne damn it!'

The protests stopped dead. Sebastev, Galipolov and the rest of the assembled officers gaped at their leader. His eyes blazed from under his thick, white eyebrows, and he seemed to crackle with power. This was Maksim Kabanov, the formidable White Boar and the most decorated man in the Firstborn Sixty-Eighth, former combat champion in the regimental games, and master exponent of the ossbohk-vyar. One ignored or disrespected him at great risk.

Colonel Kabanov stared each man in the face, daring him to open his mouth.

Silence gripped the war room, broken only by the buzzing of the overhead strip lights and the soft humming of the field-cogitator banks by the rear wall.

'Fifth Company will not be holding Korris alone,' said the colonel through gritted teeth. His eyes settled on Sebastev. 'Commissar-Captain Vaughn and Major Galipolov will be taking joint command of our main force during the redeployment.

'I, Colonel Maksim Kabanov, will be staying to lead Fifth Company.'

CHAPTER FOUR

Day 686
Korris – 10:39hrs, -17°C

THE TOWN OF Korris, half-ruined and abandoned but for the presence of Fifth Company, basked in a wash of rare sunshine. Overhead, the yellow globe of Gamma Kholdas crossed the blue sky in a lazy arc, turning the snowfields that surrounded the town into an endless blinding carpet of white light. Sebastev's men patrolled the town's perimeter in pairs, wearing dark goggles to prevent snow-blindness, their booted feet cutting deep channels in the glittering landscape.

Many of the old buildings were little more than angular piles of black rubble, having collapsed under heavy burdens of snow during the last two millennia of the Danikkin deep winter. Metal beams jutted at all angles from the ruins, turned red with rust, flaking away or crumbling to powder in the frequent gales. The corners of those buildings that remained intact were rounded and smooth, as if sandblasted. Particles of ice driven by gusting winds had scoured away all but the most subtle signs of the decorative carvings that had once graced many of the structures.

Here and there, the rough outline of an Imperial eagle could still be seen over some of the doorways. The Danikkin had pulled out of Korris at the start of the deep winter, long before the current rebellion had erupted across the planet. No rebel had defaced the Imperial icons, only time.

Today, the air was still, and visibility was better than it had been for weeks. Fifth Company had moved back from the trenchworks to occupy the town. There were simply too few of them to hold the trenches against any kind of attack. Colonel Kabanov had posted scouts out there to watch the foothills of the Varanesian Peaks for any sign of an ork advance, but so far, Old Hungry's supposition that the orks would stop crossing the mountains seemed to be holding true.

Sebastev was far more comfortable with the prospect of fighting in an urban area. The Vostroyan Firstborn were quite probably the finest city fighters in the Imperial Guard. They were bred for it: trained in close quarters combat from a young age, and taught to fight from cover in the ruins of the old factorum complexes that dotted so much of their home world. Korris suited Sebastev and his men fine. It almost didn't matter than Old Hungry had ordered them to remain out here.

For the last two years, Colonel Kabanov's home had been the abandoned councillor's mansion that stood just north of the town's central market square. The building had served as regimental headquarters since the arrival of the Sixty-Eighth. It was a natural choice, its superior construction having allowed it to weather the very worst of the winter storms with only minor erosion. The regimental engineers had easily restored the mansion's interior to a habitable condition, but despite their best efforts, it was still too cold to be called comfortable.

It was in this building, in Colonel Kabanov's spacious office, that Sabastev now stood, still dressed in his full winter kit, facing his commanding officer.

Colonel Kabanov sat behind a broad desk carved from dark Danikkin pine. The surface of the desk was covered with a disorderly arrangement of rolled maps and message scrolls. On either side of him, placed close to offer maximum warmth, two thermal coils hummed softly, casting a red tinge over the colonel's face that made him look almost healthy.

'Three days,' grumbled the colonel. 'Three days since the regiment departed, and the third day in a row that you've come to me to register a formal protest.' He scowled at Sebastev. 'Am I to suffer this every day, captain? I'm not logging these protests, you know.'

'I'll continue regardless, sir,' said a frowning Sebastev, 'at least, until you see sense and ship out.'

Kabanov shook his head. 'By the Golden Throne, you're stubborn, and insolent too, damn it. That's Dubrin's doing. You get more like the old scoundrel every day, Throne bless him.'

'I thank the colonel for his compliment.'

'It wasn't a compliment, blast you,' said Kabanov, but a grin twitched at his moustache nevertheless. 'Good old Alexos, eh? Arrogant, proud, cocky. Then again, one might suppose the same is true of all Vostroyans, damn our pride. I'm a victim of it myself, I expect.'

'Am I to understand from that statement, sir,' said Sebastev stiffly, 'that pride is the reason for your insistence on staying here with us?'

Colonel Kabanov didn't answer. Instead, he lifted a hand to stall any further questions while he coughed wetly into a handkerchief. Then he folded it, and returned it to his pocket.

When he'd composed himself, he leaned forward on his desk, stared Sebastev in the eye and said, 'I attached myself to Fifth Company because it's what I wanted to do, captain. I've never been in the habit of explaining myself to my subordinates, and I'm not about to start now. I'm your commanding officer, so you'll just bloody well accept it. Now, let this be an end to it.'

There was an uncomfortable pause. When the colonel spoke again, his tone was less contentious. 'In all your time under my command, have I ever done anything to betray the faith my fighters have placed in me? Have I ever put myself above our men? Never, not in all our time serving the Imperium together. Stop these daily protests, captain. If a simple request is not enough, you may take that as a direct order.'

Sebastev bowed his head, resigned.

Colonel Kabanov sat back in his chair and sighed. 'I do hate clashing blades with you, Grigorius. Are we not friends as well as comrades? Thirty years have seen us struggle through some hard times together, after all.'

'You honour me by saying so, sir,' said Sebastev. He meant it, too.

Urgent knocking sounded on the room's broad double doors. Colonel Kabanov sat forward again. 'Enter,' he called out.

Lieutenant Maro walked awkwardly into the room, his metallic foot clattering on the marble floor with every other step. He was gripping a sheet of parchment in his right hand and looked anxious.

'What's wrong, Maro?' asked the colonel. 'You look like you sat on a spinefruit.'

'A communiqué from Nhalich, sir, from Commissar-Captain Vaughn: It just came through this minute.' Maro moved across to Kabanov's desk and handed him the parchment. The colonel quickly unrolled it and scanned it with his eyes.

As Sebastev and Maro waited for Colonel Kabanov to finish reading, Maro threw Sebastev a meaningful look that told him the message wasn't good news.

Colonel Kabanov finished reading, loosed off a few curses, rolled the parchment up, and sat tapping the surface of his desk with his knuckles.

Sebastev's lack of patience finally got the better of him, and he cleared his throat. Colonel Kabanov looked over at him. 'Captain,' he said, 'the message states that the Danikkin Independence Army has moved into position around Nhalich. There's a lot more to it than that, however. Saboteurs have attacked Vostroyan vehicles and supplies there, and the men of the 701st seem to be suffering from some kind of illness. The commissar-captain says he has tried everything to make contact with Twelfth Army Command. Nothing is getting through to Seddisvarr. Damned storms again, it seems.'

'Attacked from within by civilians?' asked Sebastev.

'These people are desperate,' said Kabanov, 'desperate and doomed. Assemble the men. We're the closest assistance on offer. Since Command HQ is still unreachable over the vox, I'll have to take the matter into my own hands. Fifth Company must ride to the aid of our regiment. I want all our transports ready and waiting on the western edge as soon as possible. Since I'm in command, the decision is mine to make. I'll answer to the general later.'

It was suddenly clear to Sebastev that Kabanov had been expecting this all along, possibly even counting on it. He'd known the chance to withdraw from Korris would come all too quickly. He'd probably ordered Galipolov and Vaughn to request aid at the first sign of trouble.

You knew I wouldn't pull the company out, thought Sebastev. No matter how I feel about Old Hungry, orders are orders.

'I'll order the transports assembled at once, colonel.'

Sebastev saluted the colonel and turned to leave, his mind fixed on the task of organising his men. But just as he was crossing towards the door, sound poured into the room, stopping him in mid-stride. The air filled with a terrible ululating wail. It was so penetrating that it made the thick stone walls seem like paper. Sebastev had been dreading that sound. The timing couldn't have been worse.

'Raid sirens on the east towers,' he shouted over the din. 'Orks, sir!'

His vox-bead burst to life with a dozen frantic voices. Reports came flooding in from his scouts. Orks were pouring over the snow from the east. They'd already reached the abandoned trenchworks. The scouts were heading back to the town with all the speed they could manage.

Fifth Company was in trouble.

COLONEL KABANOV HAD established procedures for repelling enemy assaults on Korris back when the Sixty-Eighth Infantry Regiment had first moved in to occupy the town. Of course, those plans had been built around command of an entire regiment, so they were mostly useless now. Instead, his strategy for holding Korris with only Fifth Company under his command relied in no small part on the colonel's many previous experiences with orks. In Kabanov's opinion, the greatest advantage one had in fighting the greenskins was that they were particularly easy to bait. That knowledge was being put to use right now by the squads of men tasked with drawing the oncoming orks into a trap in the market square.

Kabanov stood with Captain Sebastev and Lieutenants Maro and Kuritsin, around a table covered with a large tattered map of the town. Kabanov didn't intend to occupy the place for long, but this building, the remains of a once grand, three-storey hotel overlooking the market square from its eastern edge, was well suited to his current needs. The construction of the old hotel was solid. Thick stone walls offered reassuring cover for the men stationed at shattered windows on each floor.

Vox traffic was still heavy. Snipers were calling in the movements of the orks. The baiting squads were in constant contact as they drew the orks in. Enginseer Politnov and his small staff of Mechanicus servants had assembled Fifth Company's vehicles, a few Chimeras and heavy troop transporters, outside the town on its western edge.

Kabanov tapped the map with a gloved finger and said, 'Squads are waiting at these intersections, ready to converge on the square once the orks are in. We've got heavy bolter nests set up here, here and here to provide enfilading fire. And you've ordered snipers onto rooftops and balconies at these points. Is that right, captain?'

'As ordered, sir,' said Captain Sebastev.

'Good,' said Kabanov. He traced a street to the point where it opened onto the square and said, 'When they reach this point, our men stationed around the square will have visual contact. I want everyone to wait for my order. No firing until the orks have fully committed themselves. It's imperative that the orks aren't distracted from their pursuit of Squads Kashr and Rahkman. Absolutely nothing must draw them away from the trap.'

'Understood, sir,' said Sebastev, 'but, with respect, we can't expect to just herd them like cattle. I think we have to accept that there will be ork elements outside of the trap that could cause us significant problems.'

'That's a given, captain. Our troopers will have to deal with stray groups of orks as they encounter them. Deal with the unexpected as it arises, I say. Our biggest priority is establishing a crossfire. It's the only feasible solution we have at this point for inflicting massive casualties with minimal losses of our own. We need to hold them just long enough for our sappers to achieve their objective.'

From the room's empty window frames, Kabanov heard the sounds of ork pistols and stubbers firing into the air. Over the vox, Sergeant Kashr reported that the greenskins were shooting wildly as they followed his squad. A moment later, Sergeant Rahkman reported the same. Both squads were drawing the ork force closer and closer to Kabanov's trap.

Kabanov took a glance outside. The day was still bright, and snow sparkled on the roofs of the other buildings around the square. The orks weren't in view yet. Everything looked peaceful, frozen and still like a landscape painting or a high resolution pictograph. Kabanov knew this sensation well. It was the quiet before the storm.

Lieutenant Kuritsin suddenly looked up from the map and lifted a hand to the vox-apparatus over his right ear. He was getting a message from beyond vox-bead range. 'Enginseer Politnov, sir,' he said. 'He wishes to inform us that the transports are assembled as ordered. They're ready to move out on your command.'

'Thank you, lieutenant,' said Kabanov. 'Please ask the enginseer to keep the engines running... and keep trying to reach Nhalich, will you? I'll want updates on the battle as soon as they come in.'

'Aye, sir,' said Kuritsin. He relayed the message to Enginseer Politnov, and then resumed his attempts to re-establish contact with Nhalich.

From the vox-bead in his ear, Kabanov heard breathless reports from Squads Kashr and Rahkman. Both squads would be entering the square at any moment. The orks were close behind.

Kabanov moved into the cover of the window frame. He raised a finger to his vox-bead, keyed the command channel, pressed the transmit stud and said, 'Everyone to firing positions, now! Squads Kashr and Rahkman will be crossing the square any second. The orks are right behind them. All squads prepare to fire on my order.'

All five platoon leaders voxed back their affirmations.

Down in the square, on its east side, two squads of Firstborn pounded into view. Sunlight winked at Kabanov from the troopers' golden pauldrons as they sprinted in his direction, pumping their arms for extra speed. Their breath billowed out behind them in clouds. Both squads merged together, sprinting straight towards the ground level entrance of the hotel that the command staff occupied.

Seconds later, roaring and laughing, and firing their weapons into the air, the great green horde spilled into the square. It was impossible to guess their number: hundreds, perhaps even thousands. They were a seething mass. The moment they reached the mid-point of the market square, Kabanov hit his vox-bead and called out, 'Open fire! All squads converge!'

COMMISSAR KARIF KNEW it didn't do to underestimate man's oldest foe. The ork race was a disease of which the Imperium might never truly be cleansed. Munitorum propaganda underplayed the greenskins' strengths, leading many to underestimate them. But anyone who met the greenskins on the battlefield quickly developed a grudging respect for this most violent and relentless of enemies.

Once orks gained a foothold on a world, it was almost impossible to shake them off without the employment of devastating ordnance. The Twelfth Army had been tasked with purging the human rebellion, and they were determined to fulfil their orders, but, according to Captain Sebastev, no one had prepared the Firstborn on Danik's World for a war against the orks. They hadn't been detected here until after the Twelfth Army had deployed.

Karif wasn't prone to negativism, but it was depressing to think the Second Kholdas War was such a desperate drain on Imperial resources that the Munitorum couldn't ship a few more Vostroyan regiments out to help cleanse this planet.

What does that say about the state of play on the Kholdas Line, Karif wondered? The cluster must be in more danger than I'd imagined.

He stood with the men of Squad Grodolkin at an intersection just south of the market square, awaiting the order to converge with the others and catch the orks in the colonel's planned crossfire.

Stavin stood quietly by Karif's side, checking his lasgun in preparation for the firefight. Sergeant Grodolkin, a monstrously ugly man in Karif's opinion, stepped up beside him and said, 'It looks as if the order to advance is about to come through, commissar. Kashr and Rahkman are crossing the square. My men and I wondered if you might like to lead us into battle.'

Karif was taken aback by this. He'd expected to have to push his oration onto these men, perhaps competing with a vox-cast from Father Olov. To be asked like this was a pleasant surprise.

Perhaps my judgement of this sergeant was a little harsh, thought Karif. *He's not even that ugly, now that I look at him. Yes, his disfigured face is more a badge of honour.*

'I accept your request, sergeant. I'd be delighted to lead you and your squad against the foe. When the battle is won, our contribution will be regarded with great envy by all.'

Grodolkin's eyes lit up.

'Open fire!' crackled the vox-bead in Karif's ear. 'All squads converge! This is the White Boar commanding that you do your duty for the Emperor and for Vostroya!'

'Right, you lot,' Sergeant Grodolkin yelled, 'into formation. Power packs locked and loaded.'

'Stavin,' said Karif, 'stick to my left, a few metres behind me. Stay sharp and keep pace. I expect you to cover me at all times. If I move, you move, understood?'

'Understood, sir,' said Stavin plainly. As usual, there was no hint of disrespect or resentment in the young trooper's tone. Karif was almost disappointed. There had to be more to him than the diffident exterior he always presented.

'Sergeant Grodolkin,' said Karif, 'let's move it out.'

'Right behind you, sir,' replied Grodolkin.

Karif drew his chainsword with his right hand. With his left, he drew his laspistol. He faced Grodolkin's squad and thrust the chainsword into the air, shouting, 'With me, Firstborn! To glory and honour!' Then he turned and led the charge towards the square.

SHALKOVA.

The name of Trooper Zavim Sarovic's beloved rifle was Shalkova.

Sarovic had named her after the first and only Vostroyan woman he'd ever bedded. There had been women on other worlds since, but none of them had ever made such an impression on him as Shalkova.

He'd been a teenager at the time, freshly graduated from basic training, and released from duty for the last few days he'd ever spend on his home world. It was extremely rare for the firstborn sons of Vostroya ever to return. Just like the other graduates, Sarovic had been given a roll of notes and told to go out and find himself a willing partner. He was supposed to give the gift of his seed back to the world that had raised him.

It was a Firstborn tradition that Sarovic's drill-sergeant insisted he keep.

Sarovic had always considered himself a fumbler where the opposite sex was concerned. With no real idea of how to secure a willing partner, he'd attached himself to a group of troopers that were going to one of the more notorious entertainment districts not far from the base.

He hadn't had much luck at first. It was getting late. Most of the others had paired off with women who seemed very keen to accept the honour of Firstborn seed. Sarovic's lack of confidence was letting him down. The only thing he was confident about was his skill with a sniper rifle. He'd already been singled out for special training. He'd almost given up on meeting anyone, when a skinny girl staggered drunkenly through the door, tripped on her own feet, and spilled her drink over his good, clean uniform.

He'd been livid, and had chewed her out immediately. But rather than cower before his anger, the girl, unremarkable but for her big brown eyes, had shouted right in his face, telling him to shut up, sit down, and get over himself. Sarovic still didn't know why he'd done exactly that. Maybe basic training had conditioned him to take orders on reflex.

A few moments later, she reappeared from the bar, slamming two drinks down in front of him. Without waiting to be invited, she dropped herself into the chair next to his, and began to ask him about himself. Sarovic couldn't remember even the smallest snippet of the conversation, only that he'd thought over and over again that her perfume smelled nice. Before he knew it, they were back at her scruffy little hab, thrashing around on the bed together as if every second counted.

In the morning, when Sarovic woke up, he'd been confused by his surroundings. Then he'd seen her standing over a blue flame, cooking breakfast. He'd thrown her a smile. She didn't smile back.

Shalkova: cold and silent and deadly. She never missed.

He racked the slide, chambering his next bullet.

He'd never understood why the girl had turned nasty on him. From the moment he got out of her bed, she'd attacked him with a vicious critique of his efforts at lovemaking the previous night. Her taunts were cruel, and her laughter, more so. The breakfast she cooked was hers. He could buy his own or go hungry. She didn't care. She'd chased him from her door, his uniform stained and in disarray, her taunts following him along garbage filled alleyways as the Vostroyan sky brightened overhead.

Did she bear me a son, he wondered? *A daughter? Anything?*

He'd asked himself a dozen times, but he supposed that it didn't really matter. He would never know for sure. She represented a single wonderful, terrible night in his life. Her touch had thrilled him. Her words had been as cold and cruel as bullets, fired to inflict maximum damage. So, he'd named his rifle after her.

He pressed his right eye to the scope and adjusted the zoom to bring his target into clear focus. Range, about six hundred metres. Wind, negligible.

Snipers from other companies tended to favour the long-las. It was a fine weapon, highly accurate, but its bright beam gave the shooter's position away. On the orders of the late Major Dubrin, Fifth Company snipers employed hand-crafted, Vostroyan-made rifles that fired solid ammunition. It was a harder weapon to master than the long-las, but a sniper with good cover could take down target after target without giving himself away.

Shalkova was fitted with flash and noise suppressors. Sarovic enjoyed friendly competition with another sniper from First Platoon called 'Clockwork' Izgorod. Each man had made a wager on who would rack up the most kills throughout this Danikkin Campaign. So far, old Clockwork was in the lead, but his numerous augmetics gave him something of an advantage.

Sarovic centred his sights on the target. It was a massive, dark skinned ork in the front ranks of the charging horde. The monster wore a necklace of severed human hands strung on barbed wire.

Emperor above, thought Sarovic, these beasts are foul.

He breathed out slowly as he squeezed Shalkova's trigger. There was a whisper of rushing air. In the scope, he saw the ork's head jerk backwards. The fiend sank to the ground with a neat black hole punched in its skull. The other orks trampled over the body, hardly noticing it.

Another deadly word from the lips of Shalkova, he thought. You never tire of killing, do you, my love?

Sarovic imagined he could smell perfume. He racked the slide and chambered another bullet.

THE SQUARE WAS full of them now, orks of every shape and size stumbling over each other in their eagerness to engage the Vostroyans. Hundreds, maybe thousands more, were still trying to push their way forward. Retreat for the orks trapped in the square was impossible, such was the crush at their backs. Kabanov watched it all play out as he'd known it would. In the course of his career, he'd seen them make the same mistakes time and time again.

The greenskins just couldn't control their urge to fight. If they'd landed here on Danik's World to find a lifeless rock, they'd have simply fought amongst themselves.

Kabanov leaned from the window and loosed another shot down into the orks. He'd already lost count of his kills and the battle had been raging for mere minutes. He pulled the trigger of his hellpistol again, but nothing happened. The power pack was spent. As he drew a fresh one from a pouch on his belt, he remembered other scenes just like this one. The press of orks out there in the square was almost as dense as it had been on the bridge at Dunan thirty-five years ago. It had been the same in the canyon on… where was it again? There had been so many battles.

He slammed the fresh power pack into the pistol's socket and resumed firing. With the orks bunched so tight down there, every single shot found a mark. Green bodies crumpled to the ground clutching the black pits the pistol burned in their chests and bellies. The hellpistol, a House Kabanov heirloom, still performed with lethal efficiency despite over three centuries of service.

From positions of cover, both high and low, Firstborn troopers fired again and again into the mass of enemies. There was so much lasfire it hurt Kabanov's eyes, but the orks were fighting back. Some began throwing grenades at the windows from which Kabanov's men fired.

Most of the grenades clattered off the walls, falling to the snow below or bouncing back towards the orks at the fringes. They detonated noisily on open ground, causing welcome greenskin casualties, but a percentage of the grenades found their mark, gliding through the openings they'd been aimed at.

Muffled booms echoed over the square, and black smoke billowed from old habs. Tumbling red forms plummeted from some of the smoking windows, to land in unmoving heaps on the snow.

'Men are dying out there!' barked Kabanov. 'Where are my flanking squads?'

On the colonel's right, Captain Sebastev was pouring shots down on the horde from a smashed window, his bolt pistol barking aggressively. There was a feral look on the man's face as his finger squeezed the trigger again and again. 'We need some fire on those black, battle-scarred ones,' said Sebastev. 'They're leading the charge.'

Kabanov scanned the green mob and found the individuals in question, three of them standing in the centre of the horde. These ork leaders bellowed orders to their kin in the inscrutable series of grunts and snorts that constituted the ork language.

'Colonel,' said Captain Sebastev between shots, 'I'd like to send an order to First Platoon's snipers to take them out.'

'Do so at once, captain. The enemy is pressing uncomfortably close to the east edge of the square. I'm still waiting for my bloody flanking squads.'

'They're on their way, sir,' reported Lieutenant Kuritsin, 'but Third Platoon reports contact with orks sneaking through the backstreets. They're engaging them now.'

'Sneaking?' said Captain Sebastev. 'Orks don't sneak, Rits.'

'Lieutenant Vassilo was very specific about it, sir. He reported a squad of orks employing something almost like stealth tactics, sir.'

Captain Sebastev turned to look at Kabanov and said, 'If our flanking squads are engaged before they get to the square, sir, we're in a lot of trouble. The orks are still pouring in. We need those squads here. The crossfire must hold until the sappers are done!'

'We've got to be on our way,' said Kabanov. 'What's the word from our demolition squad?'

Lieutenant Kuritsin voxed an update request to Fifth Company's sappers. The men under the command of Sergeant Barady of Fifth Platoon had been given a special mission of their own. Like most Danikkin towns, Korris had been built around a geothermal energy sink. The massive structures generated tremendous amounts of electrical power. Barady's sapper team was charged with denying the orks this valuable energy source. Enginseer Politnov had advised the sappers how the charges might be set to cause a significant explosion, one that would level most of the town. With Colonel Kabanov personally ordering a full withdrawal, Fifth Company had one final chance to deal devastating damage to the orks that had troubled them for the last two years.

'Our sappers report a problem, sir. They're proceeding to rig the charges, but they're under fire. Sergeant Barady says he'll need twice as much time to complete his mission if his men keep having to defend themselves.'

'Damn it,' barked Kabanov, 'it's all going to hell. There is no more time.'

Just as he spoke, however, the orks began falling back to the centre of the square, desperate to escape a sudden and massive increase in las-fire from the avenues to the north and south.

'Our flanking squads are here, sir,' reported Captain Sebastev. He began firing again from his position at the window.

Kabanov saw the full might of Fifth Company hit the orks. It was a wonderful sight, reminiscent of so many old victories, proud Vostroyan Firstborn marching in ordered rows from the openings on north and south sides, loosing well-ordered volleys into the desperate alien foe.

The square was being covered, metre by metre, under a growing carpet of dead orks. Ork blood had turned the snow into a dark red slush.

'Outstanding,' said Kabanov. He turned to his adjutant, Maro. 'Now that's a wonderful sight, wouldn't you say?'

'Wonderful, sir,' said Maro.

'Sir,' said Kuritsin. 'Squad Barady is again calling for urgent assistance. What is your response?'

Kabanov quickly assessed the situation in the square. The orks were being murdered in great numbers. They returned fire and tried to charge the Vostroyans with cleavers held high, but Vostroyan discipline was unbreakable and, no matter how great the difference in numbers, the enemy rabble was faltering in the face of it.

'Very well, lieutenant,' said Kabanov turning, 'order Squad Breshek to break from the attack on the market square and divert to the power plant. The sooner we get that thing rigged to blow, the sooner we can pull out and leave Korris to the orks and their doom.'

Sebastev spoke from his position at the window. 'Commissar Karif looks to be enjoying himself.'

The commissar was down in the streets, alongside Sergeant Grodolkin and his men. The commissar's gleaming chainsword was raised aloft, and he seemed to be orating to the squad as they fired volley after volley at the massed foe.

I'd like to hear what he's saying, thought Kabanov. I notice Father Olov is conspicuously quiet. I wonder if he's wary of broadcasting a reading with the new commissar around to hear it.

At the thought of Fifth Company's battle hardened priest, Kabanov scanned the square and saw him almost at once. He stood out clearly in his tan robes, brightly chequered at the hem and sleeves, yelling at the top of his voice to the men of Squad Svemir. He swung his massive eviscerator chainsword again and again, hewing apart the luckless orks that came at him.

Half-mad he may be, thought Kabanov, but what a fighter.

One of the squads on the north side, Squad Breshek, broke from the battle in the square and pounded north, racing to the aid of the beleaguered sappers. The other squads tried to cover the gap this created, but the orks noticed the absence of pressure from that quarter and immediately moved to take advantage.

Without waiting for Kabanov's approval, Captain Sebastev ordered Squads Ludkin and Basch to spread out, cutting off any chance of an ork pursuit of Squad Breshek. Sergeant Breshek would have enough to deal with at the power plant without having to worry about orks at his back.

Kabanov felt momentarily irritated by Sebastev's presumption, but the order was exactly the one he would have given, had he been quicker off the mark. Sebastev must have sensed his colonel's irritation, because he stopped firing briefly, turned to his superior officer and bowed. 'My apologies, colonel. It was wrong of me to... usurp your authority.'

'Less talking, more firing, captain,' said Kabanov, realising how foolish it was to damn the man for his quick thinking. If anything, the speed of Sebastev's reflex had prevented the other officers from seeing just how slow Kabanov had become. 'You're used to leading these men in battle, and they are used to you. I'll have no apologies for that. In my own way, I'm the usurper here.'

Sebastev straightened. 'Never that, colonel. This company follows the White Boar.'

Kabanov grinned, and then turned and resumed firing.

Sometimes your behaviour drives me to distraction, captain, he thought, *but at other times, you're an exemplary officer. Let's have more of the latter.*

The greenskins' next action disgusted Kabanov, highlighting the fact that orks lacked even the least comprehension of honour or pride. Pinned down without adequate cover, they began to haul the carcasses of their dead into piles to be used as shields. They pulled the heavy corpses up and over their bodies. It was something the proud Vostroyans would never have stooped to, but it was immediately effective. The shields of dead meat soaked up lasfire and bolter fire alike, giving the orks the protection they needed to rally.

Grenades exploded. Orks armed with cleavers and axes darted forward. More Vostroyans began to fall from their positions in the smartly ordered lines. Kabanov could hear increased vox-traffic, officers and sergeants calling for order and courage among the men.

'Two of the ork leaders are still standing, captain,' said Kabanov. 'Where in the warp are my snipers?'

Even as the colonel barked at Sebastev, the largest and darkest of the orks rocked on its feet, and collapsed, its skull perforated by a masterfully placed shot.

'Trooper Sarovic reports a successful kill, sir,' said Kuritsin.

Out in the square, the monstrous form of the last ork leader crumpled soundlessly, a sniper's bullet cutting a neat hole in its chest, punching an exit wound in its back as large as a man's head.

'Corporal Izgorod also reports a successful kill, sir.'

'My compliments to both men. It's time we started pulling back. What news from our sappers?'

Lieutenant Kuritsin checked in with Sergeant Barady, but it was another member of the sapper squad that answered in his place. Kuritsin reported to the colonel. 'Squad Breshek is at the power plant, sir. They're engaging the orks. I have reports that Sergeant Barady has fallen, sir. As have three others from his squad. The remaining men... what? Please confirm that.'

'What is it, Rits?' asked Captain Sebastev, moving from his position at the window to stand before his adjutant.

'Our sappers confirm that the charges are set, sir. We've got twelve minutes to evacuate the town before the power plant blows. The blast will reach our current position.'

'Then we'd best be away from here,' said Kabanov.
'Lieutenant, broadcast the order. I want our men to fall
back to the transports in a well-organised relay. Pull
squads Breshek and Barady out first, and then the squads
on north and south. I want the heavy bolters to cover the
final retreat.'

'Understood, colonel.'

'Very good,' said Kabanov. He faced Sebastev and said,
'Let's get ourselves down to ground level and ready to
move out, captain. We want to be as far away as possible
when the power plant blows. I expect the blast will make
a proper mess of things here.'

'No doubt about that, sir,' said Sebastev with a wicked
grin. 'The bloody orks won't know what hit them.'

THINGS IMMEDIATELY LOOKED different to Sebastev from
the open street. As he raced from the old hotel's side
entrance with the colonel and the men of First Platoon,
he glanced left towards the market square. From behind
the heaps they'd made of their dead, ork mobs raced
swinging their blades, only to be cut down before they
could engage the Vostroyans at close quarters.

The Vostroyan squads had been ordered to fall back,
but as they did so, they were forced to keep the pressure
on the orks by utilising a staggered retreat formation that
made pulling out far slower than Sebastev would've
liked. Just as he was turning from the scene, ready to race
west to the transports with Kabanov and the others, the
ground began to shake. Great piles of snow slid from the
rooftops around the square, and rubble began to topple
from the tops of half-shattered walls.

'What the Throne is going on?' asked a wide-eyed
Maro. 'An earthquake?'

It was a fair guess given the amount of regular seismic
activity that Danik's World endured, but this was no earthquake. The shuddering of the ground was different
somehow. It was rhythmic and regular, like giant footsteps.

'Get moving, now!' barked Sebastev. But the others stood transfixed as a building on the far side of the square exploded outwards into spinning, tumbling chunks of broken masonry.

The orks turned to look, and were showered by a hail of flying fragments. Some of them were crushed to death, rendered little more than smears on the snow by the passage of the largest tumbling blocks. The others ignored the casualties, and began to hoot and cheer. As the great cloud of dust and debris slowly settled in the still winter air, a monstrous silhouette appeared from within, the massive form of an ork dreadnought.

Thick black fumes boiled up from its twin exhausts as they coughed and chugged. The sound of its engines was a throaty, bass rumble that vibrated the plates of Sebastev's armour.

It was absolutely huge – even taller than a sentinel and far bulkier. A moment ago, the powerful bodies of the orks had looked formidable to Sebastev, packed with dense slabs of muscle that could tear a man apart. Now they looked small by comparison.

As soon as the dreadnought stomped into the middle of the square, the orks swarmed around it, seeking shelter between its gleaming piston legs. Vostroyan las-fire continued to slash across at them from the mouths of alleys and streets, a few beams licking harmlessly across the dreadnought's armour.

For all its size, the killing machine looked as if it had been slapped together in the most haphazard way. Its bucket-like torso was covered with thick plates of metal that looked as if they'd been stripped from security doors or tank hatches, and bolted to it at all angles. Massive twin stubbers sat fixed above its thick piston legs.

From either side, long steel arms extended outwards, covered in snaking cables and powerful hydraulics. The bladed pincers at the end of each arm clashed together restlessly, eager to tear weak, fleshy beings to bloody tatters.

A ragged banner of black cloth with a familiar image painted in bright yellow hung from the top of the machine. It was the three-headed snake of the Venom-head clan.

'By the Throne,' gasped Kabanov, 'we'll need more than heavy-bolters to take that out.'

'The power plant explosion should do the job, sir,' said Sebastev, 'but let's not stick around to find out. We've less than six minutes to get clear of the blast radius.'

Even as he spoke, the dreadnought turned towards the retreating Vostroyan squads on the south side, and Sebastev's stomach lurched. 'Rits,' he shouted, 'tell our lads to move it. Forget the covering fire. Retreat at speed! That thing's going to–'

A deafening staccato beat tore through the air. Fire licked out from the fat barrels of the stubbers, illuminating the whole square in stark, flickering light. A blizzard of large-calibre bullets spewed forth, stitching the front of the south-side buildings, ripping through the walls, and pounding the thick stone construction into so much dust and stone chips. The upper floors of the ancient habs, untouched for two thousand years, tumbled to the ground in billowing clouds of dust.

Sebastev could hear yelling over the vox. His officers were calling their men to cover. 'Throne damn it,' voxed Sebastev to them, 'forget cover. I want a full-speed retreat, now! Get yourselves out of there. Head to the transports at once. That's an order!'

The order came a little too late for some. Firstborn were getting slaughtered under the dreadnought's devastating hail of fire. If the rest lingered even a moment longer, the orks would take their chance to rush forward and engage them at close quarters before they could escape west.

Sebastev saw Colonel Kabanov looking at him. He realised that, for the second time today, he'd bulldozed his superior officer, trampling on the colonel's authority. But there wasn't time to offer another apology. They had

to get moving. Sebastev figured he'd face the conse-
quences later.

'Colonel,' said Sebastev, 'we should run now, sir.'

'First Platoon,' said Colonel Kabanov, 'get us safely to
the transports, please.'

Lieutenant Tarkarov immediately ordered his men into
a defensive formation around the command staff officers.
At another word, they took off down the street at speed.

As Sebastev ran, he noticed that the colonel was struggling to keep up. Kabanov was pushing himself hard to
match the speed of the others, but his age had eroded his
former athleticism. Maro, on the other hand, had mas-
tered a kind of loping run that negated the disadvantage
of his augmetic leg.

In the square behind them, the thunder of the dreadnought's heavy footsteps had been joined by others. More
of the ramshackle, red killing machines lumbered into view
between the ruined habs. The orks roared and cheered as
they raced forward in pursuit of the retreating men.

Sebastev saw that the colonel was gasping hard, but
there was no time to stop. They were almost at the western edge of the town. Then the assembled heavy
transports and Chimeras came into view, waiting
patiently in a snow covered field. Their engines idled
noisily. Their exhausts, like those of the ork dread-
noughts, spouted dark fumes into the air. The men of
Fifth Company who'd already reached the site were hurriedly loading their gear onto the vehicles.

As First Platoon and the command squad emerged
from the avenues of buildings, Sebastev saw more men in
red and gold running up ramps and into the bellies of the
heavy transports. There wasn't time for any kind of accurate assessment, but at a glance it looked to Sebastev as if
Fifth Company hadn't fared too badly.

As the command squad slowed to a trot, and then a
walk, Kabanov scrambled in his pocket for a handkerchief. He raised it to his mouth and gave a series of

hacking coughs that made him hunch over. On the colonel's behalf, Maro faced Lieutenant Tarkarov and said, 'Thank you, lieutenant. You and your men should board your transport now. Prepare to move out at once.'

Tarkarov nodded, though it was clear from his face that he was concerned, and perhaps a little shocked, by the state of Colonel Kabanov. Throwing a quick salute, he spun and led his men away.

Maro ushered Colonel Kabanov up the ramp and into the colonel's command Chimera. Sebastev hesitated for a moment. He and Kuritsin looked at each other unhappily.

'It seems the colonel isn't a well man, sir,' said Kuritsin.

'You're not joking,' said Sebastev.

More Vostroyans raced from the edges of the town, sprinting towards the safety of the waiting vehicles. The orks could be heard from between the buildings, their grunts and roars getting louder as they closed.

'We need to get moving, captain.'

'There must be more to come, Rits.'

'You know there isn't, sir. Anyone who hasn't made it here by now isn't coming.'

'Father Olov? The commissar?'

Kuritsin quickly voxed a call out for the priest and the commissar, and received prompt answers from Second and Third Platoon lieutenants.

'Third Platoon reports that Father Olov is safe with them in transport three. The commissar has apparently decided to travel with the men of Second Company. Our drivers await the colonel's order to move out.'

The first knot of ork pursuers emerged from the edge of the town, firing their pistols in Sebastev's general direction. Sebastev turned and marched up the ramp into the back of the rumbling Chimera, Kuritsin following a pace behind.

Inside the cramped rear compartment, Kuritsin hit the control rune to raise the ramp. Kabanov was already strapped in, covered with a thick blanket, drinking rahzvod from a silver flask. Sebastev had expected the man's face to be red from his exertions, but it was ghostly white.

'May I give the order for all transports to move out, sir?' asked Kuritsin.

'Do so at once, lieutenant. Get us away from this accursed place.' The colonel's voice was scratchy and subdued. He lifted the flask to his lips and took a deep draught.

Kuritsin voxed the order, and the rumbling of engines intensified outside. Lieutenant Maro gave two sharp knocks on the inside of the hull and, with a jolt and a shudder, the command Chimera accelerated away from Korris, leaving the frenzied orks and their monstrous contraptions behind.

Sebastev and Kuritsin strapped themselves into their seats, a quiet look passing between them. No one spoke. A minute later, a flash of bright light poured through the Chimera's firing ports, followed by a distant boom that rocked the vehicle.

Colonel Kabanov managed a small grin, perhaps imagining the utter devastation the explosion had wreaked on the orks. Sebastev took the colonel's reaction as a cue. He leaned forward, stared the old man straight in the eye, and said, 'No more grox-shit, colonel. It's high time you levelled with me.'

CHAPTER FIVE

Day 686
82km West of Korris – 17:48hrs, -22°C

THE SETTING SUN painted the land in hues of reddish gold before it slid from the sky. Cold, dark evening descended. The stars glittered overhead, a billion icy pinpricks of light, and the Danikkin moon, Avarice, rose fat and glowing.

Over the moonlit snows, a column of rumbling vehicles charged west with all available speed. It wasn't much, the unbroken drifts averaged over a metre deep. Fifth Company's Chimeras were forced to run slow, matching the speed of the massive, Danikkin-built troop transporters that moved up front, carving broad channels through the snow with their huge plough blades.

The local machines, called Pathcutters, had been sequestered from captured depots throughout Vostroyan occupied territory on Danik's World. They were ponderous compared to the smaller, better Imperial machines, but they hadn't been built for speed. Instead, their design stressed large capacity and a ruggedness that could handle the very worst of the Danikkin terrain. The troop compartment at the rear could accommodate over thirty personnel and was split into upper and lower decks. The chassis sat high on twinned pairs of powerful treads, well clear of the ground and any obstacles the vehicle might encounter. The height of the troop compartment called for a long ramp that dropped from the vehicle's belly rather than from the rear like most other APCs.

Commissar Karif had opted to travel in one of these relentless giants, committed to his belief that a commissar should provide a role model to the rank and file. So, as the Pathcutter juddered and forced its way through the deep snow, he moved along the rows of seated Vostroyans, using the handgrips that hung from the ceiling to maintain his balance. Everyone else was strapped into their seats.

'What's your name, soldier?' Karif asked, stopping to look down at a thick necked man with a waxed, brown moustache and piercing, grey eyes.

'Akmir,' replied the man. 'Trooper Alukin Akmir. Third Platoon, sir.'

'Good to know you, Akmir,' said Karif with a nod, 'and how many of the foe did you slay back there in Korris?'

'Not enough by half, sir,' said Akmir. There was a quiet anger in his voice. He turned his eyes down to his hands and rubbed at them, feigning preoccupation with some invisible mark. He didn't seem the talkative type.

Karif wasn't finished. 'How long have you served in this regiment, Akmir?'

The trooper paused before he answered, perhaps gauging just how open he should be with this newcomer to the Sixty-Eighth. After a moment's thought, however, he threw the commissar a lop-sided grin and said, 'Long enough to know when things are properly khekked, sir.'

Karif was about to ask for specifics when another trooper spoke from behind him.

'He's not wrong, commissar. We've all served long enough to know that those cosy bastards in Seddisvarr left us out to dry.'

There were grunts of agreement from soldiers sitting on either side of the compartment. 'Old Hungry,' hissed one. 'I never thought he'd finally do for the captain like that. Leastways, not so overt.'

'Emperor bless the White Boar for taking command and pulling us out like that,' said one. More grunts of agreement sounded over the rumble of the engine.

'All credit to the White Boar,' added another. 'The Pit-Dog's a great man, but I reckon he'd have stood his ground to the last. One's life for the Emperor and all that.'

'The Pit-Dog?' asked Karif in some confusion.

'That'd be Captain Sebastev, sir,' offered Trooper Akmir. 'Only, he doesn't like the name much, so I don't recommend using it to his face.'

Interesting, thought Karif, and appropriate.

Voices rose in heated conversation, and Karif listened carefully, eager to discover more about the men's mood. They continued to surprise him. While they'd been somewhat stony and indifferent towards him during the first few days, these Vostroyans now seemed surprisingly open and unguarded. The change was remarkable. Perhaps it was due to his fighting alongside them in Korris. He'd heard it was the way with the Firstborn.

'Madness,' growled a loud voice. 'One bloody company to hold the Eastern Front!'

'Not madness,' answered another, 'just plain, old-fashioned treachery!'

Others agreed, adding their anger and their disbelief to the cacophony. But then the voices were joined by a new sound, a rhythmic clanging that cut through all the noise. Karif turned with the others to face its source. A grizzled old sergeant, scar-faced, grey-haired and built like a Titan, was striking the steel floor at his feet with the gilded wooden stock of his lasgun.

When he had everyone's attention, and their silence, he looked Karif in the eye and spoke. His was the kind of voice, quiet and controlled, that forced other men to listen. 'You must forgive these lads, commissar, speaking out of turn like that. They mean no disrespect to the captain, the general or anyone else. But you must understand our frustration, sir. It's not easy to walk away from Korris. We fought near enough two years just to hold it. A lot of good men died for it. It's hard to watch the old foe just roll in. Vostroyan pride, see? In the end, it'll kill more of us than winter, orks and rebels put together.'

Karif let his eyes linger on the sergeant's stripes until the man took the hint.

'My apologies, sir,' said the sergeant with a short bow. 'Sidor Basch, sergeant, First Platoon.'

'Daridh Ahl Karif,' replied Karif with a smile and a bow of his own, 'commissar.' Aware of the attention on him, he added, 'Proud to serve with the Sixty-Eighth.'

Basch thumbed for a young trooper opposite to vacate his seat. Karif sat down. The compartment remained quiet while the rest of the troopers listened in.

'How long have you served with the Sixty-Eighth?' asked Karif. 'Twenty years? Thirty?'

'Thirty-five, sir. Longer even than Captain Sebastev, though he's twice the man.'

Karif wasn't foolish enough to express his doubts about that remark, not while these men were being so frank, at least. But he still couldn't reconcile himself with the boorish captain's solid reputation, so he said, 'General Vlastan doesn't seem to think very highly of the captain. Why such bad blood between the two?'

Basch grinned and said, 'That's a hard one for a chevek, sir. No offence intended.'

'Make me understand,' replied Karif with good humour, 'and I'll forgive the mild insult.' Glancing at the seated men, he saw some of them stifling a laugh.

'There are a lot of reasons why the general doesn't like our Captain Sebastev, sir. The obvious ones are the biggest. Vostroya's class divide is a proper chasm, and the higher ranks were always the province of the aristocracy. Most of them would like to keep it that way. Major Dubrin… well, it was the major's dying wish that Captain Sebastev take over company command. Colonel Kabanov honoured that wish. Since General Vlastan owes the colonel a life debt from their early years of service, I guess he felt obliged to let it be, at least for a while. General Vlastan probably figured life on the frontline would be short for the captain, that it wouldn't require any direct intervention on his part. Obviously it didn't work out like that.'

The old sergeant shook his head. 'Like the men were saying, Captain Sebastev wouldn't have pulled us out of there without direct orders. We still draw breath because the White Boar stayed behind to save us. It's not the first time he's done something like that. The general will spit fire when he hears about it. It's a right mess. Mind you, for us grunts, none of that should matter a damn.' The sergeant threw a pointed look along the rows of listening troopers. 'There's little else should occupy a good trooper's mind than orders, kit and the Emperor's blessing.'

Karif found himself quickly warming to the man. It seemed that Sergeant Basch had all the qualities of discipline, dedication and honour upon which the mighty Firstborn reputation was built.

'Well said, sergeant,' said Karif. 'Well said, indeed. I'm gratified to find that the ardour of the Vostroyan Firstborn is no myth. Solid discipline, martial skill and good old-fashioned grit: where these things abound, there is nothing we can't achieve in the Emperor's name.'

'For the Emperor and for Vostroya!' called one of the troopers. The rest immediately took up the cheer. Basch leaned out from his seat and said to Karif, 'It seems you have a way with words, commissar.' When the cheer died down, Basch addressed a young trooper at the far end of the row. 'Let's have a tune, Yakin,' he said, 'something to stir the blood a bit.'

The trooper, Yakin, began digging through his pack. After a moment, Karif saw him pull out a long, black case. He drew a seven-stringed instrument and a bow from it, and the troopers around him began making requests. It wasn't long before notes filled the air, clear and high over the rumble of the Pathcutter's fuel-guzzling engine.

Sergeant Basch smiled, sat back, closed his eyes, and nodded his head in time with the tune. 'Have you an appreciation for the *ushehk*, commissar?'

To Karif's ears, the music sounded like the screeching of a wounded grot. It grated on his nerves, and he was forced to stop himself from wincing openly. 'I hadn't heard it until this moment, sergeant,' he replied. 'I'll have to assume one grows to appreciate it over time.'

The skin at the sides of the sergeant's eyes wrinkled as he laughed. 'A very politic answer. Our Yakin isn't the most talented player, but he's better than nothing.'

That's debatable, thought Karif.

The Vostroyans linked arms where they sat and stamped their booted feet on the floor in time with the music. Their earlier anger had been chased away for the moment by the musical reminder of their kinship and their home world.

Karif found himself infected by the camaraderie they displayed. Despite himself, he began tapping a foot in time with their stomps. He might even have joined in but for the sudden change in Basch's expression. It caught Karif entirely off-guard, and that was a rare thing. The sergeant leaned close and said, 'Now that they're occupied, commissar, perhaps you'll be kind enough to tell me what in the blasted warp is really going on? All that stuff about orders and kit is right enough for the troopers. They needed to hear it. But any man with two stripes or more needs to know what he's leading his men into. Are we heading straight for another fight, or did the

White Boar pull us out on a simple pretence? If you know which, don't keep me in suspense.'

White Boar this, and Old Hungry that, thought Karif. And the Pit-Dog? What is it with Vostroyans and nicknames? Throne help the man who christens me with anything less than respectful.

'It's no secret, sergeant,' Karif replied. 'Nhalich is under siege. The Danikkin Independence Army has made its push and there have been attacks from within the city, either by agents of the secessionist movement or by sympathetic civilians. Commissar-Captain Vaughn reported heavy fighting before comms were lost. We've heard nothing from Nhalich since then. Perhaps the relay station was struck in the fighting. We'll know soon enough, I suppose. How a mere planetary defence force can hope to stand against the might of the Emperor's Hammer, with or without its damned civilian militias, is quite beyond comprehension. Are they mad?'

'We were fools who once believed so, sir' said Basch. 'Again, I mean no disrespect, but two thousand years of carving a life out in the deep winter, of struggling for survival without any aid from the Imperium... It changed these people. The Danikkin are a hard folk. That lord-general of theirs, Vanandrasse, is as black hearted and vicious as the winter night.'

Karif's jaw clenched. 'The man is no lord-general, sergeant. He has turned his people from the Emperor's light and doomed them to oblivion. Hard as ice, they may be, but the Emperor's Hammer will shatter them. To that end, I will be unrelenting in my duty, and so will all of you.'

Karif's righteous fury had done for him what the Vostroyan music could not; his blood surged and he felt his pulse beat in his clenched fists and at his temples. He longed to personally smash aside the traitors on this world. Orks were foul, benighted things, and must be decimated utterly, but they had never known the

Emperor's light and never would. To know it and to turn from it was the greatest crime in the Imperium, and the mere thought of it sickened Karif.

The worthless apostates, he thought, *they've brought death down upon themselves.*

Sergeant Basch nodded and raised his hands to his chest, pressing them there, splaying his fingers in the sign of the aquila. 'Inspiring words, commissar! They could have come from the lips of Commissar Ixxius himself.'

That was all it took, a few simple words, poorly chosen, to shatter the bridge Karif had felt building between himself and these men. He stood quietly from his seat, holding back his irritation and disappointment.

'Damn it, man,' he said to the confused sergeant through clenched teeth, 'I am your commissar now. I won't be constantly measured against the dead. Mark my words well, and tell your men.'

Then Karif walked away, steadying himself against the juddering motion of the Pathcutter with the overhead grips as he moved. Sergeant Basch stared after him, dumbfounded.

At the far end of the compartment, nearest the cockpit section, Karif hauled himself up the steep metal stairs to the top deck.

Trooper Yakin brought his tune to an end with a final quivering note.

SINCE LEAVING KORRIS, Stavin had been kept busy on the top deck of the transport while the commissar mingled with the men on the lower deck. He turned his head for only a moment when the music first began drifting up from the deck below. *The Eyes of Katya*, he thought with a smile. *Someone's playing The Eyes of Katya.*

'Focus, boy,' snapped Sergeant Svemir. 'I need you to put pressure here and here. Hold that in place while I stitch this up.'

Sergeant Svemir was a medic with Fifth Company's Second Platoon. His head was round like a melon, and covered with grey stubble that looked so coarse you could light a match on it. The line of his jaw was likewise covered, but the waxed ends of a long, salt-and-pepper moustache hung over it.

The first thing Stavin had noticed about the man was the absence of two fingers on his left hand. He tried not to stare. At least the loss of those fingers didn't seem to hinder the sergeant while he worked.

Though his eyes stayed on his wounded patient, Sergeant Svemir talked as he worked. 'I don't mean to snap at you, son. I appreciate you helping out, but you need to keep your eyes on your work. These brave fighters need our help.'

The upper deck of the Pathcutter transport was currently functioning as a rather inadequate surgery. Commissar Karif had loaned his adjutant to the sergeant, remarking that Stavin needed 'exposure to the grim realities of life in the Guard.' Stavin didn't mind. These bleeding men had fought bravely against the xenos. They deserved to live. If he could do something to help them, he would.

Sixteen of them, with wounds of varying seriousness, lay on bedrolls spread across the floor. It was no small relief that they were quiet now. The anaesthecium injections administered by Sergeant Svemir had really kicked in, bringing a welcome end to the groaning and the cries of pain. A few had needed flesh clamps, but most, according to Svemir, would get by with simple stitches. Stavin watched the sergeant carefully tug a long, black piece of shrapnel from a trooper's arm. Then he lifted a curved needle and deftly stitched the wound shut.

'This one got too close to a greenskin grenade,' said Svemir. 'That's a hard one, boy. Do you throw it back, or do you dive for cover? Half the time, the damned things are duds anyway.'

Stavin didn't take long to answer. 'If it was just the one, sir,' he said, 'I'd try for the return.'

Svemir looked up, having finished stitching. 'You're a strange one, shiny. The accent is from Muskha, but the looks say you're from The Magdan.'

There it was again: *shiny*. Stavin wondered how long they'd call him that. It didn't bother him all that much, but it was another barrier between him and acceptance. It was common knowledge that new things needed breaking in before they worked properly.

Then again, he thought, I don't really want their acceptance. I want to go home. I don't belong here at all.

'My mother is a Magdan, sir,' said Stavin. 'My father was Muskhavi. I grew up in Hive Tzurka.'

It was the first time he'd mentioned anything of his family since leaving Vostroya. No one had asked, not even the commissar. But something about Sergeant Svemir made Stavin want to open up. There was a strange comfort in the presence of a man who worked to save lives rather than take them. Stavin realised then that he was desperate to talk to someone, though he also saw the danger in that need.

It was dangerous because Stavin was a keeper of secrets, and his greatest secret was that he had come to Danik's World under false pretences. Basic training might have made him a soldier, but he'd never be true Firstborn on account of his older brother, the brother whose name he'd taken when he joined the Guard.

'Hive Tzurka, eh?' said Svemir, shuffling across to the side of his next patient. He waved Stavin over beside him. 'What was that like? I'm from Hive Ahropol in Sohlsvod. Never got out as far as Muskha.' He gestured for Stavin to raise the woozy trooper's leg so that the blood drenched bandages could be replaced.

Stavin wasn't sure how to answer. Words didn't seem adequate to the task of expressing the misery of existence in Tzurka's slums. So he pretended he hadn't heard the question, and tied off another fresh bandage in silence, noting how sticky his hands had become with the drying blood of other men.

Sergeant Svemir interpreted the young trooper's silence for himself. 'That bad, huh?' he said. 'I'd heard Hive Tzurka was rough. Trouble with anti-Imperial dissidents a while back, wasn't there? I heard they took over a bunch of old munitions factories. You know about that?'

Stavin nodded. His father had been a Civitas enforcer seconded to the local Arbites at the time. He'd been killed in the fighting. It was the turning point in Stavin's life, the dark, pivotal moment that had thrown his family into poverty and desperation. But these were private pains. Stavin bit back on them and said simply, 'That was eleven years ago, sir. They got them all in the end.'

'Good to know,' said Svemir with a nod, 'can't have bastards like that running around on Vostroya. Though I admit the home world's a fading memory to me these days. You'll get like that before long. Fighting on so many worlds… after a while, the battles all merge together. You feel like you've been fighting your whole life without a break. Makes it easier to keep going, I suppose. The regiment becomes home.' His voice grew quieter. 'Lost some good friends out here, sitting in the snow, waiting to finish this business. I'll be glad to get off this rock when the time comes.'

Stavin didn't like all this talk of long years in the Guard. It made him anxious to be away, eager to return to the mother and brother he'd had to leave behind. They'd watched helplessly as the Techtriarchy's much-hated conscription officers had dragged him off to their truck. It was for the best. They would have taken his brother, the real Danil Stavin, if they'd known about the switch of identity cards.

Then again, thought Stavin, maybe those officers didn't care who they took, so long as the numbers added up.

Iador Stavin, that was his real name, had a brother just two years older who'd been born with a learning

disability. Life in the Guard would have been brutal and
short for Danil. For years, Stavin had endured nightmares
about Danil being mistreated at the hands of xenos,
heretics, or even other troopers. Neither he nor his
mother could bear it. So Iador had become Danil, and
Danil had become Iador.

Now I fight the monsters from those dreams, thought
Stavin. I don't regret it, but I must find some way home.
I must get back to them, one way or another.

Sergeant Svemir had been lost in his own thoughts as
he worked on. He emerged from them now and ordered
Stavin to fetch a box of ampoules from the medical case
he called his *narthecium*. Some of the men were coming
round from the effects of their anaesthecium injections
and would need to be administered a second dose.

As he raised his injector pistol, Sergeant Svemir said,
'Twenty whole years in the Guard. Time pours through a
man's hands, by the Throne.'

Stavin must have looked horrified, because the sergeant
laughed and said, 'You think that's a long time? You think
I should have left after my ten?' He shook his head.
'You're fresh, son. Your memories of home are still sharp.
Give it time. Ten years from now, when the papers come
through, you'll tick the second box just like I did. When
you've given such a chunk of your life to the Emperor's
service, it doesn't take much to sign over the rest of it. A
little guilt will do it. I could never have left knowing my
brother Firstborn fought on. Retiring from the Guard is
the coward's way out.'

Stavin's jaw clenched.

I'll never tick the second box, he promised himself. If
that's what the Emperor asks of me, he can bloody rot on
his Golden Throne. They can call me a coward as much
as they like but, one way or another, I'll find my way back
to Vostroya.

'My family, sir,' said Stavin. 'I'll want to return to them.
When my term is up, I mean.'

Sergeant Svemir was readying to dispense another injection, but he stopped and met Stavin's gaze as he said, 'Family is important to a good Vostroyan. It's good that you feel this way. Think of the honour you do your family. What Vostroyan mother could be anything but proud to have her son serve with the finest regiment in the Imperial Guard?' He waved a hand over the wounded men that surrounded him and said, 'They all left their families behind. They all made the same sacrifice you did. After twenty years of service, the Sixty-Eighth is my family now. It's yours, too, though you're too fresh to know it yet.'

No, thought Stavin, I'm not like them. I'm no Firstborn son. My family is back in Hive Tzurka.

Footsteps rang on the metal staircase to the lower deck, and Stavin knew before he turned that Commissar Karif was ascending. A moment later, the familiar black cap appeared, followed by the rest of the tall, dark form as the man pulled himself up the metal railing and stepped onto the top deck.

For a brief moment, Stavin caught a look of cold fury in the commissar's eyes. Someone or something on the lower deck had made him angry. But the moment Sergeant Svemir looked over at him, the commissar masked his discontent. He threw the sergeant a half-smile and said, 'I hope my adjutant is proving his worth, sergeant.'

Svemir nodded, and then winked at Stavin. 'Rest easy, commissar. The lad has been most helpful. It'll take more than the sight of shed blood and broken bones to shake this one up. In fact, we're always short of medics, perhaps with some additional training—'

'Nice try, sergeant,' replied the commissar, 'but young Stavin has quite enough to do as my adjutant.'

That's right, thought Stavin, don't bother asking me what I think. He talks as if I'm not even here.

Stavin had thought he was getting used to the commissar's incredible arrogance, but it still irked him now and then. The man was mercurial, to say the least. At times, he was surprisingly friendly, almost parental in his level of concern. At others, he was ice-cold, with an absolute disregard for the feelings of others.

Still, Stavin supposed, *there are worse things to be than a commissar's adjutant, I'm sure. I could be cleaning latrines somewhere.*

'And what of these men?' asked Commissar Karif. He looked around at the men lying bandaged on the floor. 'How many can we count on should we find the battle at Nhalich still raging?'

Sergeant Svemir's face darkened. 'These are badly wounded men, commissar,' he said. 'Colonel Kabanov will receive my strong recommendation that none be called upon to perform in battle. If their wounds were to re-open…'

'I see,' said the commissar. 'However, sometimes even the wounded must fight. Let's hope the town is secure by the time we arrive.'

The transport suddenly lurched hard, almost throwing the commissar off his feet. His hand caught the steel banister at the top of the stairs, saving him from a fall. A number of the wounded groaned as their bedrolls shifted on the floor.

'We've stopped,' said Svemir. 'Something must be wrong. We can't be at Nhalich already.'

Commissar Karif raised one hand for silence and pressed the other to the vox-bead in his ear. His eyes widened. 'Stavin,' he said, 'get cleaned up. We're returning to the colonel's Chimera.'

Stavin nodded and rose to his feet.

'What's going on, commissar?' asked Sergeant Svemir.

Karif was already halfway down the stairs, his boots clanging on metal, but he paused before his head disappeared below the deck. 'Contact, sergeant,' he said. 'The colonel's driver just spotted las-fire in the woods up ahead.'

CHAPTER SIX

Day 686
161km West of Korris – 21:06hrs, -27°C

THE MOMENT THE Chimera's hatch crashed open, Sebastev felt the night air stabbing at his skin. He pulled his scarf up over his nose and stepped out, his boots crunching on the snow. Lieutenant Kuritsin followed a step behind him.

Low clouds muddied the sky, moving up from the south-east at speed, swallowing the bright stars as they came. The landscape had turned from moonlit silver to dark, icy blue. Bitter winds were picking up, driving north-west from the Gulf of Karsse.

All around, the air was filled with the impatient rumble of idling vehicles. The Chimeras had moved up on Colonel Kabanov's orders, arranging themselves in a tight wedge formation with autocannons, multi-lasers and heavy bolters aimed out into the night, ready to protect the more vulnerable Pathcutters.

The Pathcutters held back, arranged in a single column that extended out behind the Chimeras like the shaft of an arrow. The Danikkin machines were light on both armour and armaments. They'd never been intended for a frontline combat role. Maximum load capacity was their strongpoint.

Fifth Company's officers descended the ramps of their respective vehicles. All interior lights had to be switched off before they opened the hatches. Nhalich wasn't far away. It wouldn't do to be spotted. For that same reason, the vehicles had been pushing west all night without the benefit of headlights. The snow was bright enough, even now, for them to see where they were going.

Sebastev watched the silhouettes of his officers as they kicked their way through the snow towards him. Soon, he was surrounded by expectant men. In the darkness, the figure of Commissar Karif stood out from the others, his commissarial cap distinct among the tall fur hats.

Sebastev gestured for the men to step close, and they formed a huddle with their backs to the night air. 'About three minutes ago, Sergeant Samarov reported seeing lights up ahead,' he told them. 'Possible las-fire at a distance of about three kilometres. Nhalich is about twenty kilometres west of here. According to our maps, it should be visible from the next rise. It's possible that Samarov's lights were Vostroyan, but since there's been no further contact from Nhalich, I'm not counting on it.'

'You expect the worst, captain?' asked Commissar Karif.

'I'd say we've every reason to do so, commissar. Something should have gotten through to us by now. This lack of vox-chatter…'

The men were silent as they considered the implications.

'Regardless,' said Sebastev, 'our immediate objective is to investigate the lights that were spotted in the woods up ahead.' He turned to the First Platoon leader and said, 'Lieutenant Tarkarov, I want you to organise a reconnaissance. Draw scouts from each platoon and have them sweep in twos. The moment they find anything, I want to know about it. The rest of you, go back to your vehicles and prep your men for combat. We'll know what we're up against soon enough. Colonel Kabanov will let us know how he wants to play it.'

'I don't want to believe, sir,' said Lieutenant Severin of Fifth Platoon, 'that our own company might be all that remains of the Sixty-Eighth.'

'I don't want to believe it, either, lieutenant,' said Sebastev, 'but I won't lie to you. We have to consider it a possibility. The colonel always planned to pull us out of Korris. It's why he stayed. But I don't think he was expecting this. We'll proceed with all caution. Lieutenant Tarkarov, let's get those scouts out there. I want vox-chatter kept to a minimum. And one more thing: get your snipers up front with your drivers. I want our best eyes searching the darkness, not sitting in the back with the others.'

Before the men turned to disperse, Commissar Karif asked them to wait. With hands pressed to his chest in the sign of the aquila, he said, 'Emperor, grant us your blessing. Let us be the hammer in your hand, as you are our lantern in the dark. This, we beseech thee. Ave Imperator.'

'Ave Imperator,' replied the officers. Their tone was subdued. Sebastev could tell just how worried they were. The mood was grim as they moved off.

For a moment, he watched their shadows disappear up ramps and into hatches. Then, as he turned to re-enter the colonel's command Chimera, an unwelcome image came upon him: his officers walking, not into the hatches of their vehicles, but into the hungry mouths of a dozen crematory furnaces.

Troopers Grusko and Kasparov moved into the cover of the trees. A wide road cut through the woods, but it was well-buried under the drifts. Before the deep winter had come, the road had been a busy highway, well-used by trucks carrying Varanesian goods to the docks at Nhalich for export to other Danikkin provinces.

Only the biting winds travelled this road regularly now.

Grusko and Kasparov had been skirting the woods together when a noise – was it a human cry, or just the wind? – made them stop. They split up, intending to advance on the source from two different directions. They were close to the area in which Colonel Kabanov's driver, Sergeant Samarov, had glimpsed the lights, but there were no lights visible now.

Overhead, the wind whipped at the tops of the Danikkin pine, dislodging snow, and sending a rain of frozen flakes down to the carpet of fallen needles below.

Grusko was glad of the wind in the branches. It masked his footsteps as he pressed forward. Both he and Kasparov had been issued with low-light vision enhancers. The old goggles didn't offer true night vision, the best kit was always earmarked for the regiments that served on the Kholdas Line, but at least Grusko could see where he was going despite the all-consuming darkness of the woods. As he moved cautiously from trunk to trunk, he caught movement up ahead. The goggles showed him the figure of a man leaning against a tree with his lasgun raised. He was aiming at something on the ground a few metres away from him.

The man was dressed in a long, padded coat, with a light pack strapped to his back, and seemed to be wearing night-vision apparatus of his own. Unusual headwear, tall and pointed, sweeping backwards like the crest of a strange bird, immediately identified him as a member of the Danikkin Independence Army.

DIA filth! cursed Grusko. What the hell is he pointing his lasgun at?

Kasparov was nowhere to be seen. He should have been approaching from the left. Had he already spotted this figure? Grusko pressed forward, lifting his own lasgun, and taking careful aim.

By Terra, he thought, if I could just take the man alive...

Grusko stopped. Another shadow was moving towards the rebel soldier from the right. The thick woods made the approaching figure difficult to discern. Is that Kasparov, he wondered, or another rebel bastard?

He continued forward, but even slower now, placing each foot with a careful shifting of his weight. The second figure had almost reached the first, and Grusko still couldn't be sure if it was Kasparov.

As the mysterious figure finally emerged by the side of the first, Grusko saw that both men were, in fact, rebel soldiers. They began talking in hushed voices, but he could clearly make out the sound of harsh Danikkin consonants. So where in the warp is Kasparov, he asked himself? If I attack on my own, I'll have to kill both of them. I'm sure the colonel would appreciate the chance to interrogate one.

The first figure still held his lasgun steady, barrel pointed towards something that Grusko couldn't make out from his current position. From their posture and the smug, taunting quality of their laughter, Grusko felt sure they'd caught themselves a prisoner.

Emperor above, it must be Kasparov, he thought.

Grusko considered trying to circle around, get closer and find out, but any more movement at this range might cost him the element of surprise. There was nothing for it. He'd have to take the shot, and it would have to be a clean kill, because the moment he fired, the remaining rebel would know exactly where he was. If the rebels' prisoner was indeed Kasparov, Grusko hoped he'd have the sense to scramble for immediate cover.

He eased himself down onto the carpet of needles, careful to make as little noise as possible. The wind continued to cover what noise he did make. Once he was settled, he sighted along the barrel of his lasgun and slowed his breathing.

Right between the eyes, he told himself. One shot, one kill.

He placed his gloved finger on the trigger and gently began to squeeze it.

A single crack sounded in the night, echoing from the black trunks. The woods lit up momentarily with the flash of a single las-bolt.

The man with the raised lasgun fell to the ground, as suddenly limp and silent as a discarded marionette. The other stood stunned, gaping at his comrade's body. Grusko drew a bead on him, but the rebel soldier's training kicked in. He threw himself behind the nearest tree before Grusko could fire.

Grusko scrabbled to his feet, his heart pounding in his ears. He raced forwards, using the trees for cover as he moved. 'Surrender, rebel dog!' he called out.

There was a grunt of pain some metres off to his left. It was the prisoner the rebels had been taunting.

'Kasparov?' hissed Grusko. 'Is that you? Are you hurt?'

He was answered with more groans of pain.

'Hang in there, Firstborn,' said Grusko, trying to pick out the shape of the wounded man among all those trees and shadows. Then the wounded man moved, and Grusko saw him, lying on his back with one hand pressed to his stomach. The smell of blood and burnt flesh was strong on the air.

It wasn't Kasparov.

Fifth Company scouts rarely deployed with carapace armour. The heavy golden plates confounded any attempt as stealth. This wounded man wore full Vostroyan battle-gear.

'Another Firstborn,' said Grusko. 'Who are you? Can you talk?'

The soldier might have answered, but Grusko never heard it, because the surviving Danikkin rebel chose that moment to open fire. The first bolt seared the air just centimetres from Grusko's head and caused him to duck back down into cover.

'Damn you!' he yelled. 'Throw down your weapon in the name of the Emperor, Danikkin scum.'

More lasfire followed, carving deep black lines in the trunk that protected Grusko. But the firing stopped quickly, replaced by a chilling scream that echoed through the woods.

What now, thought Grusko? Is this a trick?

'Nice try, traitor,' he called, 'but I've used that one myself.'

A familiar voice came back at him from the same direction as the scream. 'Who are you calling traitor, Grusko, you grox-rutting *zadnik*?'

'Kasparov? Is that…?'

'Well it's not Sebastian Thor,' replied Kasparov, poking his head out from behind the thick, black trunk the rebel had used for cover. 'You can relax,' he said. 'This one has gone to answer before the Emperor for his treachery.'

Grusko stepped out and saw Kasparov tug his knife free from the rebel's corpse. 'Damn it, Kasparov,' he said, shaking his head. 'Couldn't you have taken him alive?'

Kasparov shrugged and wiped his knife on the dead man's coat. 'He was a traitor, you said it yourself. He didn't deserve to live. Besides, you weren't doing so great. You're lucky I was here.'

Through the lenses of his goggles, Grusko could see that the dead rebel was drenched in blood from a multitude of gaping wounds. Still shaking his head at the missed opportunity for a capture, Grusko turned and walked over to crouch by the groaning Vostroyan soldier. The steaming hole in the soldier's belly said he wouldn't be alive for much longer. 'We've got us a survivor here, Kasparov, but only just. We need a medic, fast.'

Kasparov came over and stood looking down at the wounded trooper. 'By the Throne!'

'We're out of vox-bead range. Get back to the vehicles and get old Svemir down here,' said Grusko. 'Sprint, damn it! Go now!'

Kasparov didn't waste time arguing. He turned east towards the transports and raced off into the darkness to get help.

Grusko rose and fetched the padded coats from the bodies of the dead rebels. He had to keep the soldier warm. He had to keep him alive. Colonel Kabanov, Grusko knew, would have important questions for this man.

LIEUTENANT TARKAROV LED Captain Sebastev and Lieutenant Kuritsin through the trees, risking the light of a torch on its lowest setting. Here, where the snow rested on the canopy overhead rather than on the ground, the men could move at a decent pace. Tarkarov and Kuritsin were long-legged men, but they carefully paced themselves so as not to overtake the captain. Up ahead, the low amber light of a hooded promethium lamp marked the clearing where Sergeant Svemir was already tending to the wounded man.

As the trio of officers drew closer, they saw two other figures moving about in the light: First Platoon scouts Grusko and Kasparov. Their restless pacing betrayed their agitation. Grusko was the first to see Sebastev coming, and marched forward to greet him.

'Sir, I'm sorry. We couldn't take the rebels alive.'

Kasparov moved up to stand by Grusko's side. 'It was my fault, sir,' he said. 'I got a bit carried away.'

Sebastev looked them in the eye. 'Did they have comms equipment? Did they get a vox-message off?'

'No, sir,' said Grusko, 'not to our knowledge. Neither man was carrying a vox-caster unit.'

'And neither of you were injured?'

'No, sir,' said Kasparov.

Sebastev nodded and pushed past them, saying, 'Never apologise to me for killing traitor scum. You did fine.'

The scouts saluted, but Sebastev didn't notice. He'd already turned towards the wounded man on the ground.

'Get back to the transport,' Lieutenant Tarkarov told his scouts. 'Get some hot ohx' down you. No rahzvod. I need you to stay sharp. Are we clear?'

'Clear, sir,' replied both men. They saluted their platoon leader, turned and jogged back towards the waiting vehicles.

'What have we got here, sergeant?' Sebastev asked the medic.

Sergeant Svemir was bent over a Vostroyan dressed in full battle-gear. The man's breathing was shallow, and his eyes were closed, but he continued to grip his lasgun tightly with one hand. Svemir lifted away the edges of two Danikkin coats to show Sebastev the extent of the man's wounds.

Sebastev grimaced when he saw what lay beneath. The armour that was supposed to shield the trooper's stomach had been melted through. It looked to Sebastev like the result of a full power lasgun blast at very close range. Beneath the hole in the man's armour, the flesh was burnt black and cratered. Steam rose from the wound.

As Sebastev got down on his knees, the soldier opened his eyes and looked straight at him.

'Hang on, Firstborn,' said Sebastev, 'our man will do what he can for you. Just hang in there, son.'

'This one's Eighth Company,' remarked Lieutenant Kuritsin. He pointed to the bronze motifs on the trooper's hat and collar, 'One of Major Tsurkov's men.'

The trooper's eyes shifted to Kuritsin. 'That's right, sir,' he croaked. 'Bekov, Ulmar, trooper, Eighth Company, Second Platoon.'

'Well met, Bekov,' said Sebastev, 'but don't talk, man. Save your strength.'

Sergeant Svemir turned and threw Sebastev a meaningful look. 'I think it would be all right if Trooper Bekov talked to you for a while, captain,' he said. 'You'll have to listen carefully, of course.'

Sebastev understood. There would be no saving Bekov. The man was dying where he lay. If he had anything to pass on to Fifth Company, it had to be spoken right here, right now.

'Trooper Bekov, my name is Captain Grigorius Sebastev, Vostroyan Firstborn Sixty-Eighth Infantry Regiment, Fifth Company. We're from the same regiment, son. I know Major Tsurkov well.'

'The Pit-Dog?' asked Trooper Bekov.

Sebastev winced. He hadn't had his nickname spoken to his face like that for quite some time. Most of the men knew better than to say it within earshot of him, but this man, dying slowly on the floor of these night-shrouded woods, had nothing left to fear.

'Aye,' said Sebastev, 'the Pit-Dog. You know me then, Bekov. You've got to tell me what happened, son. Where is the rest of Eighth Company? Where's Major Tsurkov?'

Bekov coughed. It was a harsh, rasping sound. His face creased in pain. Sebastev turned to Sergeant Svemir and raised an eyebrow.

'Very well,' said Svemir. 'I'll give him one more dose, but another and you won't get any sense out of him.' The medic slid a brown ampoule into his injector pistol and pressed it to Bekov's neck. With a sharp hiss, the liquid emptied into the trooper's veins.

Bekov's creased brow soon smoothed, and his breathing became a little easier. When he opened his eyes again, they were glazed, but he was better able to talk. Sebastev asked him again what had happened to the rest of Eighth Company.

'We hit Nhalich three days ago, sir,' said Bekov. 'No one was happy about leaving the Fifth back in Korris. You should know that. The Sixty-Eighth don't go anywhere without the White Boar. Major Tsurkov was livid. Said it was grox-shit, sir.'

Suddenly, something occurred to Bekov and he gripped Sebastev's arm. 'The colonel, sir. Does the White Boar live?'

It was Kuritsin who answered. 'Have no fear on that count, trooper. The White Boar still leads us. It will take more than filthy greenskins to beat him, by Terra!'

'Bekov,' said Sebastev, 'we need to know about Nhalich. The rebels: what's the situation?'

'The rebels!' gasped Bekov. 'Mad with hate for the Imperium, sir. There were spies in Nhalich from the start. The DIA hid people among the loyalist refugee caravans from the south-east. Don't know how they got past our checks. Once they were in they sabotaged our armour, our stores, everything. It was the bridge that hurt us most. We lost a lot of men on the bridge. Still, I'd rather have died in the Solenne than suffer the fate of the 701st.'

Behind Sebastev, Lieutenant Tarkarov cursed and struck a tree with his fist.

'What happened to the 701st, Bekov?' asked Sebastev.

'Blind, sir. The bastards got into their stores somehow. Tainted their food, their water. The troopers from the 701st couldn't see a thing after that. There was chaos at the barracks. Major Tsurkov ordered us back onto Guard issue meal bricks. No local food. The Danikkin armour had already engaged us by then. We tried calling Seddisvarr for help, but we couldn't get through. Nothing. And there was no answer from Helvarr or Jheggen. Some said they were jamming our vox.'

'Jammed?' asked Kuritsin. 'Could it be that we've blamed atmospheric conditions all this time, while the rebels…?'

A breath snagged in Trooper Bekov's throat and he began coughing. Blood flecked the sides of his mouth. His face screwed up with the pain.

'He's fading,' said Sergeant Svemir. 'You'll need to be fast, captain.'

'Not yet, son,' said Sebastev. 'Soon, but not yet.'

Bekov tried to smile through the pain. 'I'm trying, sir,' he said, 'but I reckon I can hear the Emperor's angels singing.'

'The White Boar,' said Sebastev, 'he needs to know about Nhalich. How many are there? What's the condition of the bridge?'

'It's gone. We tried to pull back across the bridge when the west bank fell to the enemy, but they came up from the south-east too.' He coughed again, blood bubbling on his lips. 'They caught us right on the bridge. Ordered us to surrender. Old Tsurkov wasn't having it. Galipolov, neither. Not to bloody rebels, sir. So the enemy shelled the bridge.'

If Sebastev had thought things could hardly get worse, that nugget of information proved him wrong. The bridge was gone, and with it, the company's most direct route back to Vostroyan territory.

'A handful of us–' Bekov's words were broken off as he began choking on his own blood. It ran freely from his mouth, soaking into his moustache. He gripped Sebastev's arm tight.

Bekov kept fighting to speak through the blood, and finally managed a few words, spoken more to himself than to those around him. 'The Pit-Dog,' he gurgled. 'Imagine that.' Then his lungs rattled and his chest sank for a final time.

The silence of the woods roared in Sebastev's ears. Gently, he pried the trooper's hand from his arm, and rose to his feet. 'Thank you for your efforts, sergeant,' he said to Svemir. 'Let's get a flamer out here to cremate the body, and make sure you bring his tags and lasgun back to the transports with you. I'll want to apply for a posthumous commendation on his behalf when we get back to Seddisvarr.'

Svemir bowed his head and replied, 'I'll take care of it, captain.'

'Good. Gentlemen.' Sebastev walked past Kuritsin and Tarkarov, heading back to the waiting vehicles. His lieutenants turned to follow him.

So it's true, thought Sebastev. Fifth Company may very well be all that remains of the Sixty-Eighth. What a burden to bear! We must survive at all costs. By abandoning us at Korris, Old Hungry unwittingly spared us to resurrect the regiment. Thank the Throne Colonel Kabanov stayed with us.

With their long strides, Kuritsin and Tarkarov caught up to Sebastev easily. As the three men stepped from the forest, back out onto the open snow, Sebastev looked up at a night sky thick with storm clouds. They stretched from horizon to horizon. The day was still some hours off, but it would bring the snows with it when it came.

'I'll never understand why you don't just embrace it,' said Kuritsin, and Sebastev knew immediately what his old friend was talking about.

'It is an insult,' he snapped. 'It was created to be such, and so it remains.'

'You're wrong. That snotty officer from the Thirty-Third may have intended it to be such, but our men use it as a term of great respect. It's a strong name, and it suits you. What does it matter who coined it? I've used it on occasion myself. Would I do so if I thought it was an insult to you?'

Sebastev didn't answer.

'Names have power,' continued Kuritsin. 'The White Boar revels in his. The men rally to it. Will you not let them rally to yours, also?'

Sebastev was occupied with far greater and darker matters. He didn't have time for this. 'Let them continue to rally behind the White Boar, damn it,' he growled. 'That has always been good enough for me.'

He put an extra burst of speed into his step.

This time, Kuritsin and Tarkarov let him pull ahead.

In a mood like this, the Pit-Dog was best left alone.

COLONEL KABANOV DIDN'T try to soften the blow. There was little point, the truth was the truth. Nhalich was in the hands of the Danikkin Independence Army. The 701st and the Sixty-Eighth, with the exception of this very company, were all but wiped out. The bridge over the Solenne lay as rubble beneath its deep, black waters.

To make matters worse, thought Colonel Kabanov as he looked at the anxious faces of his assembled officers, there's all this talk of rebel jamming abilities. We should have suspected it from the start. There's no doubt the Adeptus Mechanicus spoke the truth when they told us the atmosphere would interfere with our comms, but we should never have assumed all our problems stemmed from a single source.

Danik's World had never been known for technological developments. Up until the dawning of the deep winter, it had been a rather average world, civilised and fairly self-sufficient, but with little to distinguish it from a million other worlds in the Imperium. Then the eruptions on the southern continent had changed everything, plummeting the world into two thousand years of ice and snow. The people that had survived fled to the warmth of the hive-cities, hoping their descendants, at least, would one day be able to return to the land.

How would these people come by jamming technology? Some officers had commented on the possibility of outside support for the rebels. Trade with pirates and arms smugglers was typical of all rebel worlds. The idea that they might even be colluding with xenos sickened Kabanov, but couldn't be ruled out. Without proof, however, all of these things remained mere speculation.

In any case, thought Kabanov, such things are for others to attend. We've got enough trouble up ahead. Right now, these men need briefing.

Since this briefing required all officers, commissioned or otherwise, to attend, Kabanov had been forced to hold it in the belly of a Pathcutter transport. The men on the upper deck were being treated by a Second Company medic and couldn't be moved, but that was fine. The injured men had as much stake in the coming events as everyone else.

Let them listen if they wish, he thought.

Kabanov turned to Captain Sebastev, sitting on his right, and said, 'About the trooper in the forest, captain, were the rites observed?'

Sebastev nodded. 'They were, sir. Father Olov has formally commended the man's spirit to the Emperor.'

'Very good, captain,' said Kabanov. 'We must focus our attention on the fate of the living. There's a time to honour our fallen, but it's at the conclusive end of a crisis, not in the middle of it.'

Kabanov saw Captain Sebastev sit up a little straighter. 'It is as you say, sir,' he answered. But there was something in the man's eyes that Kabanov hadn't expected: anger. It wasn't anger against the enemy, but at Kabanov himself. Had Sebastev misinterpreted his colonel's words?

Perhaps I shouldn't have been honest with him, thought Kabanov. He didn't take it as well as I'd expected. I may be dying slowly, but I was sure he'd guessed as much for himself. It seems I was wrong. And this anger... Perhaps he blames me for the pressure he feels, knowing that the future of the regiment will soon pass into his hands. What a time to receive that responsibility! While I've still got some fight left in me, I'll do what I can to see this company through. But Sebastev, you'll have to face up to the truth soon.

Kabanov glanced at his adjutant and said, 'If you would, please, Maro.'

Maro called the men to order.

'Thank you, gentlemen,' Kabanov said when they had quieted. 'I want to start by making sure we're all on the same page. A young soldier from Eighth Company was found mortally wounded in the woods. Before he passed away, he was able to inform Captain Sebastev of the situation we face up ahead. I'm afraid his message was dire indeed. I can say with grim certainty that Fifth Company faces its greatest test yet. This company is all that remains of our proud regiment.'

Some among the officers shook their heads in denial, unwilling to believe that their fellows in the other companies were gone.

Twelfth Army Command had underestimated the Danikkin Independence Army, and the rebels were punishing them for it, but Vlastan's tactical council needn't shoulder all that blame themselves. Lord Marshal Harazahn and Sector Command were as guilty as anyone else. Proper reconnaissance could have made all the difference. If they'd only known that the orks were here.

The rebel leader, Vanandrasse, had played things surprisingly well for an ex-PDF upstart. He'd ordered his men to back away from the Vostroyans, fostering a belief among the Imperial forces that the orks represented a far greater threat. Then the rebels had watched and waited, and marshalled their strength. Their strike had been well planned, well executed, and superbly timed. Kabanov could admit that much.

'Nhalich is in enemy hands,' he continued, 'that much is certain. The hows and whys remain somewhat unclear. Trooper Bekov reported poisonings, sabotage of Imperial vehicles, and the advance of rebel armour columns on both sides of the Solenne, not just on the west. That means the second column slipped up behind us as we occupied Korris. Regardless of communication difficulties, our preoccupation with the orks is unforgivable. It has cost us dearly, and I intend for us to make amends during the coming day.'

The officers were silent, knowing better than to interrupt Kabanov, but perhaps also unsure of what to say given the enormous gravity of their situation. Kabanov let the silence hold for a moment. His throat hurt and he indicated to Maro that he required water. Maro handed him a canteen from which Kabanov gulped down a few mouthfuls. The cold liquid soothed his throat.

Commissar Karif, who was standing against the back wall, uncrossed his arms and raised a black-gloved hand.

'Yes, commissar?' said Kabanov. 'You wish to ask something?'

Karif touched a finger to the brim of his cap by way of apology for his interruption, and said, 'From the sound of it, colonel, you're committed to entering Nhalich, despite the fact that we almost certainly face an overwhelming force.'

'I dislike the word "overwhelming", commissar,' said Kabanov. He scanned the faces of his men as he spoke. 'We have little idea of the true size of the force entrenched in the town, save that it was large enough to overcome our kinsmen. A straight fight would have seen different results, I'm sure. From the words of the trooper we found in the woods, it's clear the rebels employed every bit of shameless trickery at their disposal. They fought without honour or pride. That will come back to haunt them, I assure you. As far as actual numbers are concerned... yes, we can expect heavy resistance, but the enemy on the west bank no longer concerns us. When they shelled our forces on the bridge, they cut themselves off from this side of the river. That was a big mistake. Whatever strength they have on the far bank will be staying on the far bank. We face only those units entrenched on this side. That evens things out a little, I'd say.'

Though not by much, he thought to himself.

'It's also a certainty that our brother Firstborn from the Sixty-Eighth and the 701st inflicted some damage on the invading force before they succumbed. We can be sure they took some of the bastards with them. We ride to deal with the rest. Fifth Company will have vengeance. Are you with me?'

They responded in the affirmative, strong but still unsure. It wasn't enough for Kabanov. The fires in their bellies had to be stoked. It was time to make them remember just who led them. He still held Maro's canteen. Lifting it high into the air, he hurled it at the metal floor of the transport and shouted, 'I said are you with me, warp damn it?'

The sudden motion caused pain to flare under his ribs, and his ears filled with the sound of his pounding heart, but he couldn't let it show on his face. Instead, he glared at each of them with all the intensity he could muster.

Every man in the back of that Pathcutter sat up straight under the burning stare of the White Boar. 'Yes, sir!' they shouted back at him.

Kabanov turned to Sebastev and said, 'I don't know what the hell's wrong with Fifth Company today, captain, but it'd better get sorted out fast. I'm the White Boar, by Terra, and my Firstborn are supposed to be the toughest damned killing machines in the Imperial Guard. This company will live up to its reputation. The Emperor demands it!' He turned from Sebastev, to face the rest of the assembly. 'If we die, we die in the Emperor's name. This company will not go down without a fight. Every man left in my regiment will do his duty. Is that under-stood?'

The voices were much louder this time, and filled with the kind of fire that Kabanov had needed from them. 'Yes, sir!'

As the men answered, Kabanov fought to hold back a fit of coughing. His lungs felt as if they were full of pine needles. He suddenly wished he hadn't thrown Maro's water on the floor. There was another flask, one contain-ing rahzvod, in the adjutant's pocket, but it wasn't strong alcohol that his body needed, it was rest.

When he'd overcome the need to cough, he addressed them again. 'That's better,' he said. 'Every day you've spent serving in the Guard, all of it, comes down to what you do now. The regiment mustn't end with us. We have to smash our enemies, live through this and rebuild. It won't be easy. With the bridge gone, we may be stuck out here, cut off completely from our own lines. The Solenne is too fast and too rough to be forded by Chimeras. The orks will be assaulting Grazzen in the north, in which case both of that city's bridges will have been destroyed, too. The ports to the far south are located in the rebel heartland, so a sea crossing is out. For now, at least, it looks like we're stuck on this side of the line, no matter what we do.

'I believe the biggest difference we can make is right here at Nhalich. I want the relay station and, if it exists, I want the Danikkin jamming device. If we can capture it, we can counter it.' He looked over at Enginseer Politnov, sitting at the back of the transport beside Commissar Karif and Father Olov. 'Is that not so, enginseer?'

Politnov lifted his head, hooded as always, and said, 'Obtain the device and the Machine-God will reveal its secrets to us. We need only observe the proper rituals.'

Kabanov nodded. 'I have absolute faith in that, and I don't need to tell you the difference we could make to this campaign by restoring full communications to the Twelfth Army. What a worthy task! If the damned thing is in Nhalich, Fifth Company are going to go in there and get it for me, aren't you?'

This time, Kabanov thought he felt the transport tremble at the sound of their voices. He couldn't fight the grin that spread across his face. He raised a hand to his long, white moustache and stroked one end. 'Excellent,' he said, 'that's what I thought you'd say.' Turning to Captain Sebastev, he said, 'It's time I turned the floor over to you, captain. Tell these fine officers just how we're going to dispense the Emperor's justice.'

'Aye, sir,' said Sebastev as he stood.

And I'll sit down, thought Kabanov, before I fall down.

CHAPTER SEVEN

Day 687
Nhalich, East Bank – 06:03hrs, -28°C

IN BETTER DAYS, Nhalich had been a hub of commerce, and a vital link between the Danikkin nations of Varanes and South Varanes. The city's massive bridge, straddling two and a half kilometres of deep, rushing water, was the primary conduit for trade between the two neighbouring countries. Vast loads of fruit and vegetables from the temperate south moved eastwards through the town, while timber and ore moved west. The citizens enjoyed life, gave weekly thanks to the Emperor in the local cathedral, and looked forward to many more years of the same.

Nhalich had been a bright, comfortable place to live back then.

None among its people had imagined that two thousand years of winter would destroy everything they knew, but it had. The Nhalich of today was a dead place. The streets and alleyways were choked with snow. Habs lay derelict, their doors and windows hollow and dark like the eye sockets of human skulls.

It was not, however, completely dead. Ghostly figures moved in pairs, slipping between the buildings, little more than shadows sketched on the dark canvas of the hour before dawn: Vostroyan shadows.

Sebastev's hand-picked team of saboteurs infiltrated the town, moving quickly and quietly, committed to the mission objectives that Colonel Kabanov had assigned them. Their first priority was to de-fang the snake: to cripple any rebel armour and render it useless prior to Fifth Company's imminent charge.

A freezing mist had risen as night gave ground before the coming day, aiding them in their work. Sebastev saw the Emperor's hand in it. The mist was a divine gift, cloaking his men from the eyes of the enemy as they worked to even the odds. Maybe his regular prayers were finally paying off.

The mist had also forced the Danikkin soldiers to rely on promethium lamps to light their way as they patrolled the town's perimeter, making it easier for Sebastev's men to avoid them. Defences seemed light, as if the rebels believed their east flank was secure now that the Vostroyan presence in the town had been eliminated. They hadn't counted on the arrival of Fifth Company.

Since the operation called for both stealth and technical knowledge, Sebastev had paired scouts with those troopers who had anti-vehicle experience. Since he qualified on both counts, having served as a scout in his early years and taken out his fair share of vehicles in later ones, he'd insisted on deploying, despite the protestations of Lieutenant Kuritsin. But there was another reason he'd included himself in the operation; by engaging in direct action, he hoped he'd be able to drown out the darkest of his thoughts. The sense of doom that had descended on him as the company had travelled from Korris was heavy, and he knew he had to shake it off.

Sebastev focused on his anger and on his hunger for the Emperor's justice, as he lay on his back under the chassis of a rebel Salamander. Cold seeped into his body from the frozen ground as he fixed small, high-yield melta-charges to points that shielded vital wiring and control mechanisms. The Salamander was a scout variant, but it shared much of its construction with the Chimera on which it was based. The underside was vulnerable. The charges would burn straight through when the time came, and another machine would be rendered useless.

He cursed silently as he worked against the clock. Who knew how old the Salamander was? It was certainly a former PDF machine, a leftover from the days of Danikkin loyalty, shipped from a nearby forge-world, probably Esteban VII, to serve in the Emperor's name. Perhaps its venerable machine-spirit had known great honour before it had been turned against the Emperor's forces.

Such a waste, he thought, a machine like this in the hands of fools. Mankind has enough enemies among the stars without these idiotic secessionist wars. Division weakens us, leaving us open to xenos attack. It has to be stamped out.

Sebastev dug another melta-charge from the pack lying at his side. It was the last of them. He'd already rigged two rebel Chimeras and a Leman Russ Demolisher to blow when the timers hit zero.

Even from under the tank, he could see that the mist was growing lighter as day dawned in the east. The greater part of the enemy forces would be waking soon. There would be civilians, too.

Most refugees that passed through the Vostroyan-held towns were loyalists eager to escape persecution by Lord-General Vanandrasse's agents. They numbered in the millions. They usually went west to the so-called *contribution camps* established by Old Hungry in the territories south of Seddisvarr. Once there, they were fed and housed, and put to work making coats, blankets and the like for the Vostroyan forces.

Since the camps were filled to bursting, the decision had been made to allow refugees to stay in the garrisoned towns, but the price of that decision was becoming all too apparent. Sebastev couldn't be sure how many non-combatants remained in Nhalich. If they stayed out of the coming fight, they'd live through the day, but if they insisted on joining the battle, Sebastev's men would cut them down without remorse.

Civilian or not, those who turned their back on the Emperor deserved no quarter.

The killing of misguided civilians was a grim duty, true, but it was hardly new to the men of Fifth Company. As Sebastev set the timer on the final charge, memories returned of the war on Porozh some thirteen years before. It had been a beautiful, lush world, warm with sunshine, covered in bright fields and orchards. On the face of it, the differences between Porozh and Danik's World couldn't have been greater. The women on Porozh had been so pretty, small and delicate like finely sculpted dolls with skin the colour of rich honey and hair the colour of chocolate. He remembered one, a young woman, her hat covered in flowers, who'd brought his men fruit while they patrolled the borders near her family's orchards. She had danced as she moved, smiling brightly as she handed each man a gift from her basket. Even the most jaded old veterans had smiled back, eyes alight as they followed her, taking in the swell of her hips and breasts, and the light playing on her hair. They thanked her and bit into the succulent fruits she dispensed.

She'd finally stopped in front of Sebastev, beaming at him and holding up a juicy local fruit called a *vusgada*. He'd accepted it from her with a nod of thanks. The bright yellow fruit was almost at his lips when one of his troopers began retching. Then the trooper began vomiting mouthfuls of blood onto the grass.

The girl didn't stick around to watch. She immediately threw down her basket and broke into a run. More of

Sebatev's men fell to the ground around him, groaning, clutching their bellies and puking blood.

He'd turned and killed her, of course, without even thinking about it: a single shot to the back of her head at about sixty metres. All that beauty, all that light, extinguished with a crack of his bolt pistol. The flowers on her hat burst like little fireworks, scattering pink petals on the warm afternoon air. Her body hit the ground so hard it flipped over. Sebastev remembered feeling hollow and confused.

Under all that beauty and light, he thought, Porozh was as sick and faithless as Danik's World, as all rebel worlds. Scratch the surface and they were all the same, dead the moment they turned from the rest of the Imperium.

Of the men who had bitten into the poisoned fruit, three died that day and six were permanently injured, requiring augmetic organs. The rest received medical treatment in time to avoid long-term damage. No one ate local food again.

The girl's family was burned to death for treachery. Commissar-Captain Vaughn had seen to that. Over the years, Sebastev had wondered about the girl. Had she even known the fruits were poisoned? He hadn't given her a chance to say.

New regulations on interacting with the local populace had come after that, but for many Guardsmen, it was too late. Thousands had caught terminal diseases from the local women. An official investigation concluded that the prettiest Porozhi had deliberately infected themselves before sleeping with as many of the occupation troopers as they could entice.

What a campaign that was, thought Sebastev. Those people turned everything they had against us. Why do all these traitors and heretics insist on sacrificing themselves for the ideals of madmen like Vanandrasse?

Sebastev had never forgotten the young woman's face, the pretty smile as she handed him her deadly gift, the way her wounded head blossomed in the air like a crimson flower.

'Are you done, sir?' hissed a voice from the side of the Salamander. 'The patrol will be returning any second.'

Sebastev finished up and slid out from under the vehicle. Trooper Aronov stood close by. Fifth Company scouts were generally small, lithe men, but Aronov was huge. He towered over Sebastev, turning his head this way and that, scanning the mists for any sign of trouble. 'Don't you think you're cutting it a bit fine, sir?'

'We're done,' whispered Sebastev. 'Think you can get us to the rendezvous point?'

'You know it, sir' replied Aronov. He tapped a finger on the side of his head. 'Pictographic memory. It's all in here. I figured that's why you partnered with me.'

Sebastev shook his head. 'Not a bit of it, trooper. I just needed the biggest, dumbest human shield I could find.'

'Pfft! Whatever you say, sir,' said Aronov. 'Let's move.'

They headed west through the back streets, still well-cloaked by the mist, but holding to the shadows regardless. There were only minutes left before Nhalich got a very special alarm call. Sebastev was surprised at how fast Aronov moved, and how quietly.

Damn it, he thought, this is what my commission has done to me. There was a time when I moved like that. Now I'm slowing this one down. By the Golden Throne, if I live through this...

They reached the corner of an intersection when Aronov suddenly dropped into a crouch. Sebastev halted immediately. With a blur of hand signals, the big scout indicated a patrol up ahead. From the mist, three men emerged, armed with lasguns, moving south to north along the street that bisected theirs. With more sign language, Aronov asked Sebastev how he wanted to proceed.

We can't wait for them to pass, thought Sebastev. We should get to the rendezvous point on the east bank before the charges blow, but if we attack and one escapes to raise the alarm, Colonel Kabanov will face heavy resistance on the way in.

Aronov's gestures became more urgent. The rebel patrol was getting closer.

How good is this trooper, Sebastev wondered? How good am I?

He made his decision. His hands cut three quick gestures in the air: *Take them out.*

'THIS IS CLOSE enough, sergeant,' said Colonel Kabanov to his driver. 'I can see lantern lights at the edge of the town. Any closer and our engine noise will give us away. Lieutenant Kuritsin, order the others to hold position.'

'Aye, sir,' said Kuritsin. He lifted a speaking horn from the wall beside him, using the Chimera's voxcaster rather than his own. He keyed the appropriate channel and said, 'Command to all units. Hold position on this ridge. Ready yourselves to charge on the colonel's order.'

Fifth Company's Chimeras ground to a halt in the snow. The Pathcutters pulled up into horizontal formation behind them, ready to disgorge their payloads of vengeful Guardsmen when the time came to storm the town. Fifth Company simply didn't have enough resources to launch attacks from multiple angles, so Kabanov had decided that they'd charge forward in a wedge formation, punch through the rebel line and engage them in a city fight. Urban warfare was a Firstborn speciality, after all.

'Let's hope the captain can ease our way in as planned,' said Commissar Karif.

The colonel turned to look at him. 'Have no fear on that count, commissar. Captain Sebastev's effectiveness is not to be doubted. By the time we descend on the rebel filth, there won't be a working piece of enemy armour on this side of the river. Not that their infantry will be a pushover, of course.'

'There it is again, colonel,' said Karif, 'a certain respect for the strength of the rebels. It's a stark contrast to the attitudes that seem to prevail in Seddisvarr.'

'Twelfth Army propaganda, commissar,' said Colonel Kabanov. 'They'd have you believe we're fighting hapless fools. I wouldn't put too much stock in it, if I were you. Good for morale, of course, but the greatest mistake a man can make is to underestimate his foe. The deep winter has made the Danikkin a hardy people. That they occupy the town up ahead should be ample proof of that. They're not constricted by any sense of honour or piety. They fight with desperation. It gives them strength. Perhaps our own desperation will do the same for us.'

'Perhaps,' responded Karif, 'but honour and piety will prove greater in the end. I expect Fifth Company to uphold both. A commissar can accept no less.'

The colonel nodded as he said, 'Honour means a great deal to the men of this company. You needn't worry about that. But their survival means a great deal to the future of the regiment. I believe that sometimes, in order to serve the Emperor better, honour must occasionally be sacrificed. Had we served Captain Sebastev's sense of honour and duty at Korris, Fifth Company would have fallen before the orks. You and I would both be little more than frozen bodies. Despite everything, Captain Sebastev wouldn't have disobeyed General Vlastan.'

Karif remembered the words of the troopers in the back of the Pathcutter. 'Which is, of course, why you stayed with us, is it not, colonel? Through your insistence on taking command, you managed to preserve both the company and the captain's honour, at least in the meantime.'

'That's your interpretation of events, commissar,' said the colonel testily, 'and you're welcome to it. But the Danikkin Campaign is not a simple one. Few men outside the Twelfth Army's tactical staff, including myself, have anything more than a rough idea of the whole picture. I can tell you this much: a man would have to look far back in the annals of the Sixty-Eighth to find days as dark as these.'

Colonel Kabanov flexed his fists as he continued. 'The history of the regiment is a chain unbroken for thousands of years. Despite countless wars and untold losses, there have always been survivors around whom the regiment could be restored. But the Danikkin... their hatred is a powerful thing. They don't take prisoners, commissar. Enemies of their secessionist movement are killed at once. I believe that Fifth Company is the last remaining seed from which the regiment might again grow. The coming day will bring one of two things: either the breaking of our proud tradition, or another victory to add to it.'

Karif sat quietly, digesting the colonel's words for a moment before he said, 'With your permission, colonel, I'd like my adjutant to man the heavy bolter as we ride in. The boy needs such experiences if he's to become a well-rounded soldier and aide.'

'No objections here,' replied the colonel. 'Send him up front. Sergeant Samarov will make good use of him.'

Stavin moved up as ordered. Karif heard Sergeant Samarov welcome the young man into the driver's compartment.

Lieutenant Kuritsin, sitting opposite Karif and next to Father Olov, lifted a gold-plated chronometer from his coat pocket and looked at it. 'Saints be with the captain. He should be at the east bank by now. We'll have our signal soon.'

Father Olov's gravelly voice sounded from under the matted tangle of his long, white beard. 'Rest easy, lieutenant. The Grey Lady watches over that one. You should know that well enough.' He looked over at Karif and said, 'Saint Nadalya, commissar. Patron saint of Vostroya. The captain is a man protected by his faith, mark my words.'

Karif grinned at the old priest and said, 'I know who she is, Father, but your words have reminded me of a matter I wished to discuss with you. I hope you won't think it presumptuous on my part.'

'Which means it is presumptuous,' grumbled the old priest, 'but go ahead, commissar.'

Olov's beard was so long that he could have tucked the end of it into his belt. Beside him, sheathed in a covering of brown leather, was his preferred weapon, the mighty eviscerator chainsword favoured by many a battlefield priest. Years of wielding it in practice and in battle had given the priest a broad physique. Karif hadn't missed the hints of thick muscle beneath Olov's robes.

'I confess to feeling a certain kinship with you, Father,' said Karif. 'We're both men of the Imperial Creed. Granted, our roles differ, but I hope you feel the same kinship in your own way. With that in mind...'

'Spit it out, man,' rumbled Olov.

Once again, Karif found the Vostroyan manner a source of no small irritation. He had to keep reminding himself that it was a cultural trait, one that clearly extended to both the officer class and members of the Ecclesiarchy. Suppressing a retort, Karif said, 'Very well. I'd like to make a battlefield reading to our men during the coming fight. I'm sure I can fortify their spirits and lend them some divine strength. What say you, Father?'

Olov's brow creased and his eyes narrowed. 'I handle the readings, commissar. That might not have been explained to you properly. Have done for almost eleven years with this particular lot.'

And from what I've heard, thought Karif, you've made a fine mess of it. The Septology of Hestor? It may be officially approved by the Ministorum, but it's widely held to have been written by madmen. It's time this regiment had a proper reading that will gird them for battle.

Karif didn't think it prudent to mention that Captain Sebastev had asked him to consider orating in the priest's place. Would the priest have believed him anyway?

Instead, Karif said, 'This company is lucky to have you, Father Olov, and they know it well enough. But as a newcomer, I'm eager to strengthen my presence among the men, get them acclimatised to me, as it were.'

Colonel Kabanov spoke up from his seat near the driver's compartment. 'I can see the logic in that, commissar' he said, 'but the decision lies with you, Father Olov. Would you have our new commissar try his hand?'

If Father Olov was at all influenced by the colonel's words, it didn't show on his face. 'What would you read, commissar?' he asked, still scowling.

It was time for Karif to play his ace. He drew a small blue tome from an inside pocket and raised it for the others to see.

Lieutenant Kuritsin's eyes flashed. 'Have a care, commissar,' he hissed. 'If you've taken that book with anything less than his express permission, he'll have your head, and all laws be damned.'

'Do you mean to say, lieutenant,' spluttered Kabanov, 'that the book is Captain Sebastev's own copy?'

'It is, sir,' said Kuritsin, 'unmistakably so.' He faced Karif. 'That book is the last memento the captain has of his father, commissar. I'm sure you didn't know, but perhaps you should give it to me. I won't tell him of this. It would be better for all concerned that he never find out.'

Colonel Kabanov nodded. 'That sounds best.'

Karif grinned, shook his head and returned the book to his pocket. 'I suppose I should be terribly offended, gentlemen, but you're reaction amuses me. Captain Sebastev insisted I read the book. I can assure you that I carry this copy with his express permission. I'd like to give a reading from it during the battle, provided the honourable father has no objections, of course.'

Olov's scowl had softened, but the man still looked less than friendly. 'The very worst orator in the Imperium could motivate Firstborn with a reading from the *Treatis*

Elatii. It's a safe choice, commissar, unoriginal, but safe. Go ahead with my blessing. I'll listen with interest.'

Karif bowed his head in mock gratitude. Conceited old grox, he thought.

Was it possible that the old man didn't know his own reputation? The men of Fifth Company thought him a far better soldier than a priest. His kill count was impressive and his faith in the Emperor inspirational. It was just a shame, said some, that Olov had been born a second son, rather than a first. He'd proven to them on the battlefield many times that he would have made an excellent sergeant.

Karif knew all this from his time among the troopers. The words of the officer class alone rarely painted accurate pictures. It was only by listening to the conversations of the rank-and-file that one could learn the truth as seen from ground level. He was confident that his reading would be well received, earning him a little more acceptance among the men. Today would be hard on all of them: a single company against Throne knew how many. Karif's chest swelled as he thought of it.

Commissars are made for these kinds of odds, he thought. Glory abounds on such days. Victory may bring decorations, medals and promotions. With luck, I'll receive the kind of recognition that will see me returned to a higher station, a station befitting my past achievements. Breggius may blame me for the shame his son brought upon him, but all his scheming will have been for nothing if I can restore my former status.

'...reading?'

Karif shook himself, realising that the colonel had addressed him. 'I apologise, colonel. I'm afraid I didn't catch that.'

'I asked, commissar, whether you believe you'll be able to fulfil your other duties while giving a battlefield reading.'

'Oh, without question,' said Karif with a broad smile. 'I won't be reading from the actual pages. I've already committed the entire volume to memory and made some preliminary selections. I'm sure you'll be satisfied.'

Father Olov's scowl deepened, but he didn't meet Karif's eyes. The priest was probably damning him for a braggart and a fool. So be it. Karif had indeed memorised the text using techniques of mental imprinting taught to commissars in scholams throughout the Imperium. He could hardly be blamed for the Ecclesiarchy's failure to promote such skills among its own servants.

Lieutenant Kuritsin mumbled something to himself, drawing Colonel Kabanov's eye.

'If you've something to say, lieutenant,' said the colonel, 'share it with the rest of us.'

Kuritsin's face reddened. 'Sorry, sir. I was just thinking that, in all my years serving with Fifth Company, I've never known the captain to let someone else handle his treasured book. I confess that it's got me in something of a spin, sir.'

Kabanov grinned. 'Dare we hope that Captain Sebastev is finally maturing? I don't mean as a man, of course, but as a commanding officer. Dubrin always insisted that it would happen eventually. Our current crisis may have been the catalyst he needed.'

'Change can be a painful thing,' said Father Olov. 'Captain Sebastev has always struggled with his responsibility for the company. I think he regrets his promise to the late major. But it's about time he stopped wishing he could be a simple grunt again.'

Lieutenant Maro, a man Karif had noticed was prone to quiet observation, surprised everyone by speaking up. 'Let's hope his acceptance of the role doesn't jeopardise the very qualities for which Dubrin selected him.'

Colonel Kabanov nodded. 'Sebastev can be bad-tempered, even for a Vostroyan, but Dubrin knew what he was doing. I'd trust Sebastev's instincts before I'd listen to any tactician in Seddisvarr.'

They do flap on about him, thought Karif. There are hard men on worlds throughout the Imperium. I wonder what they see that I don't.

Lieutenant Kuritsin again lifted his chronometer from his pocket. 'Sir,' he said, addressing Colonel Kabanov, 'the melta-charges should be just about–'

Explosions sounded from the direction of the town, a deep stutter so rapid it sounded like stubber fire. The walls of the Chimera trembled.

'That's our cue, gentlemen,' said Colonel Kabanov. 'Lieutenant Kuritsin, you know what to do.'

'Yes, sir,' said Kuritsin. He pulled the horn of the Chimera's vox-caster from the wall and said, 'All Chimeras, advance! Hold formation until you hit the streets. Follow your designated routes. Gunners are to provide continuous covering fire for our infantry squads. Visibility is low. Use caution. Friendly fire incidents will be logged and passed to Commissar Karif. Ride out, for the Emperor and the Sixty-Eighth!'

Colonel Kabanov's Chimera gunned forward. Within minutes, the sound of las- and bolter-fire erupted all around. The Danikkin rebels had awoken to the sound of explosions and the growl of advancing Chimeras. They were already firing out into the mist.

Sergeant Samarov shouted back from the driver's seat, 'Nothing to worry about, sirs. They're trying to zero their fire on engine noise. They can't see us worth a damn.'

'Maro,' said Kabanov, 'get onto that multi-laser and give our lads as much cover as you can. Trooper Stavin,' he called up to the front of the vehicle, 'make that bolter work for us. Bring the Emperor's punishment down upon them.'

Lieutenant Maro leapt from his seat, moved forward, and climbed up into the chair of the Chimera's turret.

As they raced nearer the rebel defences, Stavin opened fire on the rebel positions. The deep barking of the bolter began reverberating through the Chimera's frame. The sound was soon joined by the hum of the charging multi-laser.

'As soon as we reach the perimeter, gentlemen,' said Colonel Kabanov, 'this will become a street fight. And let me tell you, commissar, no one loves a street fight more than the Firstborn!'

SEBASTEV AND ARONOV threw themselves down the snow-covered bank as a drum roll of explosions ripped through the town. Shouting immediately sounded on the freezing air. Sebastev could hear rebel officers barking orders to their men in their harsh Danikkin accent. From some of the habs by the river, those boasting windows and cold-sealed doors, the muted cries of frightened civilians could be heard. They should have left when they had the chance, thought Sebastev. If they stay inside, they might just live through this.

He looked out into the mists. He could hear the rushing waters of the river close by. As he moved down the slope towards the sound, shapes resolved themselves. For a moment, Sebastev was sure he'd been misinformed. Hadn't Trooper Bekov said the bridge was shelled to rubble? He could see thick steel girders reaching out into white space. They looked undamaged. But as he moved closer, more of the framework revealed itself. The straight spars became twisted and then completely broken.

It was true; the bridge over the Solenne was gone.

'Captain,' hissed Aronov, 'over here.'

Sebastev walked over to the big scout's side. There was movement in the shadows under the bridge's truncated stump. Lieutenant Tarkarov was waiting there with the other saboteurs. 'Glad you finally made it, sir,' said Tarkarov with a grin.

'Are you saying I'm slow, lieutenant?'

'Perhaps we can settle on thorough, sir?'

There was a chuckle from some of the men. Sebastev managed a smile and said, 'We had a bit of trouble with an enemy patrol, but not much.'

Tarkarov gestured at Sebastev's greatcoat. 'I can see that, sir. What did you do, mop the blood up after you killed them?'

Sebastev looked down. Every fight seemed to end with him soaked in blood these days. 'Damn it. I'll have to give Trooper Kurkov an extra bottle of rahzvod.'

Kurkov of Third Platoon was the only man in the regiment of a similar stature to the captain. Since Sebastev's own coats boasted a little too much gold for stealth operations like this one, he'd borrowed Kurkov's. It was unadorned, and far better suited to the task. The men around him were likewise dressed in only the most basic kit. Their carapace armour remained with the rest of the company. With the exception of Sebastev, who'd brought his bolt pistol, each man carried a lasgun slung over his shoulder and a standard issue, Vostroya-pattern long knife sheathed at his waist.

For Sebastev, the knife had already proven its worth. When he and Aronov leapt on the surprised Danikkin patrol, Sebastev had rammed the cold, black blade straight up under the jaw of the nearest rebel, punching through the roof of the man's mouth and into his brain.

Then, with no time to yank the knife free, Sebastev had flown at the second man, grasping the collar of his quilted Danikkin coat, hoisting the man's body over his hip and slamming it hard to the frozen ground. The man's neck had twisted awkwardly as he landed. The sickening snap announced a quick end to the fight.

Aronov had choked the third man, holding him until his brain was starved of oxygen. Sebastev had watched the man's eyes roll up into his head. Then, they'd hidden the bodies and dashed west to the rendezvous at speed. Their melta-charges had ruined a great deal of rebel armour, and the Danikkin forces on this side of the river would be in utter chaos.

Colonel Kabanov was about to descend on them, and that meant it was time for Tarkarov, Aronov and the rest of the saboteurs to move into phase two of the operation.

'Right you lot,' said Sebastev, 'you know what you've got to do. Get into your squads. Lieutenant Tarkarov will take his squad and deploy at the rebels' backs. You'll give them a nasty surprise while they're engaged with our main force. Make sure our boys know exactly where you are. Save your surprises for the Danikkin scum. I don't want to hear the words "friendly fire".'

'Don't worry, sir,' said Tarkarov. 'We'll make sure our lads know exactly where all the help is coming from.'

Sebastev turned to the squad he'd be leading. 'While we've still got this mist to cover us, let's make the most of it. Our objective is the comms relay station south-west of the old cathedral. I want that building, Firstborn. Possible heavy resistance there, so you need to stay on top of things. Aronov knows the way, don't you Aronov?'

Aronov tapped the side of his fur hat with a gloved finger.

'Good,' said Sebastev. 'Let's move out. It's time we take our revenge for the Firstborn who died here.'

Fires blazed in the eyes of his men when they heard those words. Sebastev turned back to Lieutenant Tarkarov and said, 'Best of luck to you, lieutenant. Don't disappoint the White Boar.'

Tarkarov gave a sharp salute. 'I've no intention of doing that, sir. Best of luck with the relay station. I'll see you when it's over.'

'Yes, you will,' said Sebastev with conviction.

Tarkarov marched his men out from under the shadow of the broken bridge. Within moments, their forms melted into the mist.

Sebastev turned and nodded to Aronov. 'Lead the way, trooper.'

As his squad moved out, Sebastev heard the sounds of heavy fighting from the east. Colonel Kabanov had engaged the enemy. The battle for Nhalich raged.

CHAPTER EIGHT

Day 687
Nhalich, East Bank – 07:38hrs, -26°C

KARIF HELD ON tight as Colonel Kabanov's Chimera smashed through the rebels' outer defences, lurching over the rubble of shattered walls, and easily bridging old trenches that hadn't been manned since the Vostroyan frontline had moved east to Korris two years earlier. The colonel's driver, Samarov, held his speed steady so the vehicle didn't pull away from the infantry squad it was shielding. Each of the Chimeras was followed by a squad on foot, pounding the snow packed hard by the broad treads of the thirty-eight tonne behemoths.

Karif peered out from a firing port in the Chimera's rear. It was difficult to properly assess the strength of the rebel defences in the glowing mists, but it was clear to him that the enemy hadn't expected any kind of assault on their east flank. Between the rebels' over-confidence and the weather, Fifth Company had caught the so-called Danikkin Independence Army completely off guard.

Lethal beams of energy cut bright ribbons in the mists, and the air resounded with the staccato of cracking lasguns and chattering bolter fire.

Damn it all to the warp, thought Karif. Now that we've breeched the town, I wish the mist would lift. If I can't see the enemy, how can I be expected to kill him?

Colonel Kabanov called out to Maro and Stavin as the Chimera shuddered and jounced. 'Don't waste ammunition firing blind. Trace their fire back. Give them something to think about before our infantry breaks cover.'

Sergeant Samarov shouted something from the driver's compartment. Karif had to focus hard to catch his words over the angry buzz of the Chimera's multi-lasers.

'Colonel, sir,' called Samarov, 'this is as far in as I can take you. There's tank wreckage all over the road. It looks like armour from the 701st, sir.'

'Understood sergeant,' said Kabanov. 'Maro, stay on the multi-laser. Cover our men as they move forward. Try to keep the enemy's attention on the Chimera. The rest of you, get ready to deploy. Lieutenant Kuritsin, inform Squad Breshek that I will be joining them. Make sure they're ready when I drop that ramp.'

Lieutenant Kuritsin immediately relayed the message to Squad Breshek.

Karif fastened his black fur cloak over his shoulders. Apart from his usual robes, Father Olov's only concession to the biting cold was a pair of brown leather gloves that he tugged over his hands. Karif eyed him incredulously.

'Should you not don something more substantial, Father?' asked Karif.

'I'm cloaked in my faith, commissar,' rumbled the old priest. 'It's always been enough.'

'Is that so? Then perhaps the fires of your holy zeal are warming you from within.' Karif's tone was snide.

'Almost certainly true, commissar,' rumbled Olov. 'Speaking of holy zeal, I'll be listening closely to your reading.'

'Then I'll be sure to give my best.'

Lieutenant Kuritsin finished helping Colonel Kabanov ready himself to lead the men. The colonel presented a striking image of Vostroyan military nobility. Under the white fur, Karif saw shimmering golden carapace armour that was finely embossed with images of the Imperial eagle, the winged skull of the Imperial Guard and the ancient icon of the colonel's noble family, House Kabanov.

On command, Stavin abandoned his position up front and moved to join his commissar in the troop compartment.

Lieutenant Kuritsin stood admiring the colonel. 'It does me good to see you like this, sir,' he said. 'The men will fight all the harder for the presence of the White Boar among them. I know they're looking forward to making you proud.'

Colonel Kabanov nodded once. Karif thought the man seemed a little embarrassed by the appreciative stares of the others. This was confirmed when he faced Karif and said, 'I'm not usually prone to such ostentation, commissar. Perhaps I'm like our Captain Sebastev in that respect. But today we visit revenge on those that murdered our kinsmen. I want our men to see me leading them in.' His gaze moved to the others. 'We are the Emperor's hammer, gentlemen. Let us fall on these traitors and smash them asunder. Open the hatch, if you would, commissar.'

'At once, colonel,' said Karif.

'Aye,' said Father Olov. He hefted his massive eviscerator. 'Open it up and let me out. I've apostates to punish.'

'For the Golden Throne,' said Karif. He slammed the heel of his hand against the hatch release glyph. The Chimera's rear hatch crashed heavily to the snow, and cold air rushed in. He emerged from the Chimera behind Colonel Kabanov.

Squad Breshek snapped to attention; ten men in two ordered rows. They stood unflinching as enemy lasbolts slashed through the mist around them. When Colonel

Kabanov stepped forward, Sergeant Breshek and his men saluted as one. Then Breshek marched forward and presented himself. 'Squad Breshek awaits your orders, colonel,' he said.

'Thank you, sergeant,' replied Kabanov.

Sergeant Breshek moved to stand by the colonel's side.

'We will press forward through the enemy positions,' said Colonel Kabanov, addressing the squad, 'eliminating opposition as we go, moving with all available speed to Reivemot Square. We will secure key structures at that location. I'll update your orders once we have the square.'

'For the Emperor and Vostroya,' shouted Sergeant Breshek.

'For the Emperor and Vostroya,' shouted his squad.

Colonel Kabanov turned to Breshek and added, 'By the Emperor's grace, sergeant, some of our brother Firstborn may yet live. Given past experience with DIA forces, I realise the likelihood is slim, but still… If there are Firstborn prisoners here, we must liberate them. I want the town taken with all available speed. No quarter is to be given to the Danikkin traitors. Is that understood?'

'No mercy, sir,' said Breshek. 'My fighters are with you all the way.'

'I know they are, sergeant,' said Colonel Kabanov. 'Now let's form up and move out.'

SEBASTEV DUCKED BACK behind the hab wall as another torrent of stubber shells tore into the stonework, chewing the edge to pieces only inches from his face. 'Son of a grox!' he growled as he was showered in flakes of stone. 'Keep to cover all of you.'

His squad had reached the relay station just minutes earlier, surprising and easily overcoming the patrolling rebel guards they'd encountered in the streets nearby. But Sebastev's objective of gaining control of the station was a very different matter. Two good men were already down, killed while dashing to forward cover. They'd been chewed up by the heavy stubbers that poked from dark apertures about fifteen metres up each face of the building. With the chill mist still hampering visibility somewhat, it seemed the rebel gunners were targeting his men by thermal signature. They fired with deadly accuracy. The bodies of troopers Ravsky and Ilyanev attested to that. They lay in the middle of the street, leaking steam into the air from each of the fist-sized exit wounds in their backs.

Wait till I get my hands on the bastards inside, cursed Sebastev.

'Any ideas, sir?' asked Aronov behind him.

Sebastev's men were looking at him expectantly. They didn't like hanging back. Two of their number had gone down right in front of them and, just like Sebastev, they wanted to punish those responsible.

'The defenders will have called someone in to flank us,' said Sebastev. 'We've got to move fast. If we can get inside and interfere with the rebel comms, our main assault force can really start to carve them up. We just need a way past those damned heavy stubbers.'

Sebastev risked another glance out from his position. He could clearly see the main entrance to the relay station through the thinning mist. It was about fifty metres away. He squinted up at the muzzles of the west-facing stubbers. There were two of them. From his position, Sebastev judged that the guns' vertical firing arcs were limited by the stone sills beneath them. It looked as if the guns wouldn't be able to fire on targets any less that fifteen or twenty metres from the base of the wall.

Suddenly, the guns spat again, stitching the wall that shielded him with bullets. He whipped his head back into cover. 'Warp damn and blast them!'

'They can't take all of us out, sir,' said a blue-eyed trooper crouching behind Sebastev. It was Vamkin. He'd been a Ministorum choirboy before his entry into the Firstborn. It was hard to picture it now; his face was a mess of scar tissue and grafted skin, hardly the image of purity and perfection the cathedrals liked to present. But the young man's eyes were still clear and bright. 'I mean, if we all ran together, sir,' continued Vamkin, 'I think most of us would make it to the door.'

Acceptable losses again, thought Sebastev with a scowl. Do I have a choice?

Others voiced their agreement with Vamkin's suggestion. Aronov was among them. 'I counted five streets that open onto this side of the building,' he said. 'I think if we all rush forward from different corners at the same time, we'll at least buy ourselves a better chance, sir. As you said, sir, time is against us.'

'It sounds like—'

Sebastev was interrupted by the sound of doors being kicked open, followed by orders being shouted in a thick Danikkin accent.

He carefully peeked out from cover.

A rebel squad had spilled from the main entrance. They were taking up positions around the building. As always, the heavily accented Gothic was difficult to comprehend, but there was something else too. The rebel sergeant sounded worried. Could it be that he's heard his forces are falling in the face of the colonel's assault, hoped Sebastev?

'He's unsure of himself,' he told Aronov.

'Sir?' asked the scout.

Sebastev faced him. 'That rebel bastard, the sergeant, he's nervous. I can hear it. They weren't expecting anyone to get this far into the town. Warp damn them, they actually thought they'd secured the whole region. I've just heard him tell his men to stay calm, that the heavy stubbers will protect them. It sounds like we're facing civilian militia, not former PDF. What do you think, Aronov? Willing to gamble on it?'

'Well, sir,' said Aronov, 'if there's a case of rahzvod in it, you can count me in. But I'd give you much better odds if we didn't have to face both the stubbers and the guards. We'll suffer if we try to charge straight towards both.'

Sebastev nodded his agreement, thought about it for a second, and said, 'We could send two troopers around to feint an attack from the east. I don't think it will be hard to draw the rebels away from the entrance if they think they're needed on the building's east side. That would just leave the stubbers. Once we're under their vertical firing arcs, we can take care of the militia-men as they come back around the sides of the building.'

'It sounds like a plan, sir,' replied Aronov.

Sebastev's eyes lingered over the bodies of Ravsky and Ilyanev for a moment. Each man lay in a pool of dark blood frozen mirror-smooth. The steam from their wounds had stopped. The bodies were quickly freezing solid. He knew he'd lose more before the relay station was firmly back in Vostroyan hands.

'Ulyan!' said Sebastev. 'Gorgolev! Get your backsides up here.'

Two troopers shuffled forward, eager not to step out too far from the safety of the wall. Ulyan was the older of the two. He was grey-eyed, slim, and a damned good shot with a lasgun. Gorgolev, on the other hand was brown-eyed, broad-faced and mean: a trouble maker. That made him a good choice for what Sebastev had in mind.

'Get yourselves into cover on the other side of the target. Use the back alleys to get there. Don't let the stubbers draw a bead on you. When you're in position, I want you to unleash hell on the station. You don't need to hit anything specific. I just need you to draw the rebel guards away from this side. They need to believe a concentrated attack is coming from the east. It shouldn't be too difficult. The rebels defending the base are militia, I'm sure of it. Feel free to engage them once they move to your side of the building. Are we clear?'

'A feint, sir,' said Ulyan.

'Count me in, sir,' grinned Gorgolev.

'Good,' said Sebastev. 'What are you waiting for? Go.'

The two troopers moved off to begin their circle to the other side of the relay station. Sebastev faced the others and said, 'The rest of you know what we've got to do. It'll be a dangerous sprint over open ground. Spread out. Find cover along this side and be ready to run like the warp. The signal to move will be a single shot from my bolt pistol. Understood?'

'Yes, sir,' replied the men.

'Go,' said Sebastev. He watched his men scatter.

May the Emperor smile on us, he thought. With numbers like these, there was no such thing as acceptable losses.

KARIF MOVED THROUGH the streets with Squad Breshek, his boots crunching on the snow between tall tenement-habs of blue-grey stone. His eyes flashed to every shadow and cranny as he pressed forward.

Almost every building they passed showed some degree of damage from the conflict of the previous day. Stone pillars had spilled halfway across the road from a colonnade that had collapsed, blasted by stray cannon-fire. Hab walls on either side of the street had been ripped open by artillery. Dark, gaping wounds with ragged brick edges testified to the power of each impact.

The roads themselves were littered with twisted, black wrecks. A small number of machines still blazed, pouring black smoke into the air above. These machines were casualties from Captain Sebastev's sabotage operation. Karif couldn't help but be grateful for the thoroughness of the captain's men. Thus far, not a single enemy vehicle had rolled out to challenge them. But rebels kept appearing among the rubble to fire their lasguns at the advancing Vostroyans.

Colonel Kabanov organised Squad Breshek into two fire-teams in order to flank enemy positions. This way, Squad Breshek managed to gain ground quickly.

In the lee of two barely recognisable Leman Russ battle-tanks, the men took a moment to reload. Danikkin rebels continued to pour fire at them from further up the street.

Karif looked down at the young man crouching on his right. 'How are you doing, Stavin?'

'Fine, thank you, sir,' replied Stavin. Steamy breath rose from the adjutant's scarf where it covered his mouth. 'But I can't really see well enough in this mist to fire effectively, sir.'

'Just do as the colonel suggested,' said Karif. 'Trace our enemies' fire back to them. Exercise your judgement. Don't waste ammunition if you've no shot. The air is definitely clearing. Now that we're pushing deeper and the streets are getting narrower, the pace of the battle is sure to change. Things will get close and bloody. How many charge packs have you got?'

'Two in my pockets, sir,' said Stavin. 'One up the spout with the counter reading half.'

'That's plenty for now,' said Karif. Beneath the warm fabric of his muffler, he grinned.

I don't mind admitting, he thought, that this lad's aptitude for war has genuinely surprised me. His diffidence and youthful appearance belie a fighter's constitution. I should have expected as much. The Vostroyans, by the very nature of their curious conscription system, must prepare their children for war from a very young age.

Karif felt a hand grip his upper arm. He turned and saw Colonel Kabanov beside him, breathing hard. 'I'd say it's about time, commissar, that you started your oration. Our men are right in the thick of things. Give them some words to fight by, as you said you would.'

'Yes,' barked an impatient Father Olov from the corner of the burnt-out tank. 'Get to it, commissar. I would've started by now. Let's see what the Schola Excubitos taught you about oration.'

The wild old priest had been in a foul mood since they'd left the Chimera. There was a blood-thirsty quality in his eye that Karif found unusual for a Ministorum man. Zeal was one thing, but animal savagery? Olov had, as yet, been unable to make use of his massive chainsword. This was still a fire fight for the moment. His patience was clearly being tested.

'You're right, of course,' said Karif. 'It's time I began.'

Karif raised a finger to his vox-bead, keyed an open channel, and said, 'Hear me, Firstborn sons of Vostroya. This is your commissar, Daridh Ahl Karif. I fight beside you in the name of the Emperor, and for the Imperium of Man. Our lives for the Emperor! Let these words from the Treatis Elatii of Saint Nadalya inspire you to victory over our wretched and unworthy foe.'

Even as Karif said the words, fresh waves of lasfire slashed out from the rebel held hab-stacks, hissing and sending up steam where they laced the snows. The volley was answered a second later by Vostroyan retaliatory fire. Karif dedicated part of his awareness to his memory of the text. 'Have faith in the Emperor, said the Grey Lady, and you may abandon fear. Abandon fear, she said, and you may do your duty unhindered. By this alone will you earn your place at the Emperor's side.'

Screams sounded from rebel positions in the street to the south as Squads Severin and Vassilo moved up to flank entrenched enemy infantry.

'The Grey Lady did not stay long on Vostroya,' continued Karif, 'but she set foot in each of the seven states, and their capitals swelled to bursting with those that wished to gaze on her.'

Colonel Kabanov addressed Squad Breshek as Karif gave his reading. 'Move up. I want two pairs of sweepers clearing each building as we go. Leave nothing alive to fire on our backs.'

'There are civilians in some of the habs, sir,' replied Sergeant Breshek as his squad moved out from behind the shelter of the ruined tanks.

'I said leave nothing alive, sergeant,' barked the colonel. 'The rebels will have already killed those who joined our brother Firstborn in defending this place. Those still alive are either traitors, or bystanders that did nothing to prove their loyalty. Apathy and cowardice are as bad as treachery in my book. The Emperor will judge their souls. We send those souls before him.'

Over the vox, Karif continued. 'On the day of her leaving, the lady blessed the Techtriarchy with a gift. Into the air, she released a great two-headed eagle, symbol of the Imperium, and told them that the Emperor would watch Vostroya through the eagle's eyes. Toil hard in the factorums, she said, for where would the Imperium be without its machines? Fight hard on the battleground, she said, for where would the Imperium be without the endless sacrifice of its sons?'

Heavy bolters and stubbers added to the las-fire. The rebels had built a hasty barricade on the road ahead and were bringing out their heavy weapons. Sandbags and razorwire stretched across the street, from one corner to the other, and the colonel's men were forced into the shelter of the side alleys.

In the middle of his reading, Karif heard a Danikkin sergeant shouting orders from nearby. Three rebels rounded the corner of a building on his right, clearly intending to flank the Vostroyans while their fellows provided suppressing fire. Before Karif had time to mentally process what he was seeing, his hand rose of its own accord and fired off a lethal hail of laspistol shots.

The first of the Danikkin flankers was knocked from his feet, his face a smoking black oval.

Trooper Stavin slew another with two solid hits to the chest in rapid succession. He hit the last man in the shoulder, enough to spin him and cause him to scream out, but not sufficient to kill him. Karif remedied that by rushing forward with his chainsword raised high. He swept the man's head from his neck.

Lasguns cracked all around as Squad Breshek returned fire on the roadblock ahead, but it did little good. From the other streets, screams and shouts filled the freezing air. Karif returned to his oration.

'The lady left Vostroya with one hundred regiments of Firstborn in her charge. Many said she favoured her Vostroyan fighting men above all others, for they were grim and hardy, and they sold their lives dear for the honour of their world and for the Imperium they had sworn to serve.'

While Kabanov and his squad were pinned down, more rebels moved up, eager to make the most of the Vostroyan loss of momentum. High above the street, the Danikkin announced themselves by shattering ice encrusted panes of glass. They began firing down on the Vostroyans from tenement windows. Stavin loosed a trio of shots into the shadows of a high window on his right. Seconds later, a lifeless rebel body tumbled from the empty sill. It hit the street below with a crunch of breaking bone.

Members of Squad Breshek turned the muzzles of their lasguns upwards and pushed the rebels back into cover, but it was becoming too dangerous to hold their position. Colonel Kabanov opened the command priority channel on his vox. It meant his words would cut across Karif's reading, but it was necessary. No man who offered battlefield oratory expected to do so free of interruption.

Kabanov's voice sounded in the ears of every man in Fifth Company. 'Use your grenades on occupied buildings. We mustn't lose momentum, and someone flank that damned roadblock up ahead.'

It was easier said than done. A squad of Danikkin rebels, ten heads by Karif's count, charged round the left-hand corner, firing wildly at the Vostroyans as they ran. Karif dived for cover as las-bolts slashed the air around him. A derelict hab on his left offered the most immediate respite. 'Stavin,' shouted Karif as he threw himself through the door, 'to me, boy. To me!'

Stavin didn't wait around. He darted through the gaping doorway just as another searing volley strafed the walls. Someone screamed outside: one of Breshek's men, cut into burning chunks by enemy las-fire.

The hab interior was absolutely black with shadow. Karif's feet kicked broken furniture as he moved to peer from a broken window. He could see Colonel Kabanov, Lieutenant Kuritsin and the others. They were completely pinned down in the shelter of a broken wall that wasn't going to offer cover for much longer. The enemy heavy bolters began rattling, chewing the wall apart.

'We're out-flanked, warp-damn it!' roared Colonel Kabanov. Even from across the street, the colonel's rage was palpable. Karif saw Father Olov stand up, eviscerator in hand, as if readying to rush the rebel positions singlehanded. But the powerful form of Sergeant Breshek wrestled the crazy old priest back into cover.

'Damn it, Stavin,' spat Karif. 'Those rebel flankers are getting ready to move up. Squad Breshek has nowhere to go. They'll be massacred.'

Stavin scrabbled to his feet in the dark. 'Maybe there's a back door, sir. I'll check.'

Karif had been looking outside where the snow was bright. When he turned to face Stavin, he couldn't see a thing, but he could hear frantic movement in the back of the derelict hab. 'Damn this all to hell and the warp,' he growled. 'Stavin, are you all right? What have you found back there?'

There was a crash and cold daylight spilled in from the rear. 'I found it, sir,' chirped Stavin. 'There's a narrow alley running all the way along.'

'By Terra!' exclaimed Karif. 'A chance to make a difference. Good work, trooper. We move.'

Karif joined Stavin at the back door and poked his head out to scan for activity. 'You weren't joking about it being narrow,' he said. 'We'll have to move sideways. Follow me.'

They moved out from the doorway, heading south, lifting their feet high to clear the deep, hard snow. Stavin tried desperately to keep his armour from scraping the walls, but it couldn't be helped. The sounds of battle were softer between the high walls of the old tenements. By contrast, every noise they made sounded unusually loud to the commissar's ears.

They soon reached the corner where the narrow alley opened onto the street. Karif peered around the corner and raised a hand for Stavin to halt. About twenty metres up the street, leaning out from their positions of cover to loose barrages of las-fire, Karif could see the rebels that had moved up to flank Squad Breshek and the colonel's men.

'Two against ten,' he told his adjutant in hushed tones. 'It won't do to engage directly. Hand me one of your grenades.'

'Yes, sir,' nodded Stavin. He plucked a frag grenade from the fixings on his belt.

Karif took the grenade with a grin. 'This is the Emperor's work, by Throne! How's your throwing arm, Stavin?'

'I'm sure it's not as good as the commissar's, sir.'

'Patronising, but well said. Let's find out. I'd say two of these ought to clear those fools right out. Think you can put one right in amongst them?'

'You point, I throw, sir.'

'Right then,' said Karif. 'Pull that pin and get ready. Throw on three.'

Stavin nodded. Both men pulled the pins from their grenades. 'One…'

Side by side, they stepped out of the alley and into the street. 'Two…'

Karif leaned back, careful not to tense, but to keep his muscles loose. 'Three! Damn all traitors to the warp!'

Whipping their arms forward, Karif and his adjutant hurled their grenades towards the unwary enemy squad. Some of the rebel soldiers spotted the motion, but it was too late. Both grenades landed within metres of each other, close to the enemies' feet.

'Good throw,' said Karif as he shoved the young trooper back into cover. The grenades detonated with a sharp boom, sending a shower of snow and icicles down on them from the rooftops above.

Loud screaming filled the air. Those few rebels who hadn't been killed outright by hot shrapnel fell to the snow with gushing wounds. 'Move up,' said Karif, and he broke from cover to sprint towards the wounded men.

'No mercy, boy,' he called over his shoulder. 'The graveyards are full of merciful men.'

Stavin pounded up the street after the commissar, skidding to a stop when they reached the wounded rebels on the ground.

Together, the commissar and his adjutant fired lasbolts into the writhing bodies at their feet. Each shot silenced another howling man.

It was murderous work. Karif couldn't deny it. He wondered how Stavin felt about it. To the young soldier's credit, he'd done exactly as ordered at every turn.

'Don't you dare pity these men, Stavin. They turned from the Emperor's light. They put themselves above every other man, woman and child in our great Imperium. Never forget that.'

Stavin nodded silently.

Karif turned from the smoking bodies and looked up the street to where Kabanov's squad still huddled behind their covering wall, harried by the bolters and stubbers at the roadblock on their west side. The colonel was poking his head out, trying to see just what the hell was going on, but his tall fur hat confounded him, announcing his every movement.

'Colonel,' voxed Karif, 'your south flank is secure, sir.'

'About bloody time,' the colonel voxed back. 'Now move up that street and flank that khekking roadblock, if you would, commissar.'

'You're welcome,' grumbled Karif to himself. 'Come on, Stavin. It seems even the famous White Boar needs someone to save his backside now and then.'

SO FAR, SO good, thought Sebastev.

The diversion had begun. Repeated las-fire sounded from the far side of the relay station, answered by the chatter of the east-facing heavy stubbers. As Sebastev had fervently hoped he would, the rebel sergeant became flustered. Loud booms joined the sounds of las- and stubber-fire. Troopers Ulyan and Gorgolev were using the few grenades they carried to draw the attention of the relay station's defenders.

It worked.

At the sound of the explosions, the rebel sergeant became convinced that the Vostroyan attackers had circled east and were throwing themselves into a full assault against the east side. He ordered all but two of his men to follow him and took off at a run.

'You ready, scout?' Sebastev asked Aronov.

'Ready, sir. First man to the door gets a case of the good stuff, right?'

'Right,' said Sebastev as he raised his bolt pistol. 'I'll pay for it myself when we get to Seddisvarr.' All along the street, hidden behind stone walls, his squad crouched ready to rush the building.

Sebastev's pistol barked and spat a brass shell casing, and the Vostroyans exploded from their cover, zigzagging as they ran forward, desperate to throw off the guns.

Sebastev sprinted hard, not daring to glance left or right to see how his men were doing. He saw muzzle flashes flicker out of each of the dark apertures positioned high in the relay station walls. 'Khekking run!' he yelled at his men. He put everything he had into pumping his legs, powering forward as fast as he could. His muscles started to burn, and the cold air rushed into his lungs, making them feel like they were on fire.

The stubbers sent a blizzard of shells whipping down around him, but nothing hit. There was no pain, no battering impact. Then someone to Sebastev's left cried out. Sebastev couldn't look round. Pausing for just a moment meant certain death.

'Keep moving!' he bellowed. In his peripheral vision, he saw a number of troopers moving forward, outpacing him in their race to the safety of the relay station's walls.

Torrents of lead continued to pour from the stubbers. Bullets churned the snow and bit into the frozen rockcrete beneath. Some of the shells punched into living meat. Screams sounded from Sebastev's right. Someone behind him shouted, 'No!'

Five metres! Four... Three...

Sebastev passed under the stubbers' field of fire, moving so fast he couldn't stop. He threw himself down onto his right side, skidding to a stop just as one of the remaining rebel guards fired off a las-bolt at him. The bright beam scorched the air above him, missing by centimetres. Sebastev looked over in time to see Aronov impale the offending rebel on his long knife. The man was still screaming when the big scout hoisted him into the air with his free hand and yanked his knife out. That cut the scream short.

The crack of a lasgun marked the death of the other rebel that had been left to guard the entrance. Sebastev rose to his feet and brushed the snow from his coat. He looked back at the street they'd just crossed. Two fresh bodies lay bleeding on the snow. One of them was still moving, still groaning, calling out weakly for help. It was Blemski, a young trooper from Fourth Platoon.

Trooper Rodoyev, also from Fourth Platoon, followed Sebastev's gaze and saw his comrade lying wounded out on the street. He dropped his lasgun and made to rush to his friend's aid, but Aronov's massive hand caught him by the wrist. 'Don't be a fool, trooper,' hissed the scout.

'Aronov's right,' said Sebastev. 'The guns will chew you up the second you run out there. Blemski wouldn't want that, and I can't lose another man. Think about it.'

'But he's not dead, sir,' said Rodoyev through gritted teeth.

Perhaps Blemski heard those words because, at that moment, he struggled to his knees, fighting the agony of the horrific injuries he'd sustained. The movement was enough for the rebel stubbers. They spat another stream of shells. Blemski's body shuddered as it was chewed apart by a score of impacts. Then it fell forward on the blood spattered snow and lay perfectly still.

Rodoyev howled. His face reddened and his eyes bulged. He snatched up his lasgun. 'Where are they? I'll kill them. I'll kill them all.'

Sebastev grabbed him by the collar and hauled him downwards so that they were almost nose to nose. 'Pull yourself together, Firstborn. I need you in control of yourself. If you can't give me that, you're no damned–'

Sebastev broke off in mid-sentence. He could hear orders being shouted from the other side of the relay station. The rest of the rebel guards were coming back.

'To the corners, all of you,' he hissed, letting go of Rodoyev. His men rushed to either edge of the building, some following Sebastev to the north-east corner, the others moving with Aronov to the south-east.

When the rebel guards appeared, the Vostroyans gave them time to commit themselves. When the rebels were halfway around, beyond easy reach of any solid cover, Sebastev gave the order to open fire.

Bright beams stabbed out, punching holes in the thick, quilted coats of the rebels and cutting deep, charred pathways into their flesh. Screams filled the air. Bodies crumpled to the snow, some thrashing in pain from wounds that weren't immediately fatal.

'Move up and put them out of their misery,' ordered Sebastev. He threw Rodoyev a pointed look. 'Remember that you are Firstborn, not torturers. You're here to represent the Emperor. I want the wounded rebels dispatched quickly. No toying with them. Firstborn fight with honour.'

As his men moved forward to do as he'd ordered, Sebastev walked back around to the west entrance of the relay station. It was sealed tight from the inside. He was standing in front of the door when Aronov joined him.

'Are they dead?' asked Sebastev.

'Aye, sir.'

'The door is sealed. Any melta-charges left?'

'I haven't got any,' said Aronov, 'but I think Rodoyev and Vamkin are still carrying, sir.'

'Rodoyev… is he all right?'

'They were good friends, sir. He took Blemski under his wing when the lad joined Fourth Platoon. Both men were from Hive Slovekha.'

Sebastev thought of Dubrin and Ixxius. He remembered watching Dubrin's life ebb away as he lay on a stretcher. He remembered seeing Ixxius's body disintegrate in a burst of shrapnel from an ork grenade. 'Understood,' he said to Aronov, 'but the time for mourning is after the battle. Words from the White Boar himself.'

Aronov nodded. The others joined them at the entrance. There was a fierce look in their eyes, a look of absolute focus on the work in hand. It was just what Sebastev wanted to see.

'Get a melta-charge on this door,' he told them. 'Once we're in, we move in pairs, sweeping each level. The gunners are still inside. We'll make them pay, by the Throne. But there may be others, comms officers and the like. Keep your eyes open. They know we're coming in, so no mistakes. Watch each other's backs. Are we clear?'

'Clear, sir,' said the troopers.

'Like good rahzvod, sir,' said Aronov.

CHAPTER NINE

Day 687
Nhalich, East Bank – 11:21hrs, -20°C

KABANOV STOOD IN Reivemot Square. It was a terrible sight. The corpses of good men, men of the Sixty-Eighth and 701st, lay in heaps like stacked timber. The Danikkin rebels had stripped them of anything useful and piled them up. Now the bodies were frozen together, as cold and hard as blocks of ice. His heart filled with anger and regret as he looked at them. He ordered Sergeant Breshek to organise a search of the corpses, looking for Commissar-Captain Vaughn and Major Galipolov. He was sure they lay somewhere in the square, but it was still hard to believe that these uncompromising men were truly dead.

The remains of a statue that had once been dedicated to the Emperor stood in the centre of the square. Who knew what it was supposed to be now? It stood headless, limbless, wrapped in razorwire and splashed with vivid red paint. A dedication, perhaps, to that misguided notion of independence that had brought war to this world. Some damned fool rebel had written *DIA – No*

Emperor, No Slavery in the same red paint on the base of the statue.

The occasional crack of lasguns still sounded in the air as Fifth Company troopers continued to discover and eliminate rebel stragglers hidden in buildings on this side of the town, but the greater part of the fighting was over. Nhalich East was back in the hands of the Firstborn, for now. Kabanov could do nothing about that part of the town that sat on the west bank.

No matter what we achieved today, he thought, *the DIA has taken control of South Varanes, the orks are dominating in the north-east, and Fifth Company has little hope of getting back to the relative safety of our own lines. By Holy Terra, have Lord-Marshal Harazahn and Sector Command completely forsaken the Twelfth Army? General Vlastan may be unsuited to this campaign, but one can hardly lay all the blame at his feet. In his own way, he must be struggling as much as we are.*

Vostroyan squads moved through the town, herding frightened groups of Danikkin civilians into temporary containment facilities. They'd be locked up until it was decided what to do with them. Many had been killed during the battle, but there had been little need for more slaughter once the town was properly secured. The survivors simply had nowhere else to go. Nhalich might be a battle zone, but it was the only shelter for many kilometres. The nearest town had been Korris until Fifth Company sappers had razed it.

Kabanov wondered how much damage the power plant explosion had done to the orks. How many had survived? Would they follow Fifth Company out here?

With the losses we took today, he thought, *we couldn't hold this town for a full hour. The headcount isn't in yet, but I saw enough men fall in my proximity to know the numbers aren't going to be good. We won, and the regiment lives on, but only just. If there are over a hundred* men left by the time the headcount comes in, I'll be genuinely surprised.

A light snow was falling. Tiny flakes alighted on Kabanov's hat and cloak, becoming invisible against the thick, white fur. Around him, Lieutenants Maro and Kuritsin, Father Olov, Enginseer Politnov, Commissar Karif and his adjutant stood awaiting orders and surveying the activity in the square. Sergeant Breshek's squad searched the bodies methodically. Kabanov didn't envy them their grim work.

A voice crackled over the vox. 'This is Captain Sebastev. The relay station is secure. I repeat, we have the relay station.'

Kabanov lifted a finger to his vox-bead, hit the transmit stud and said, 'Colonel Kabanov here, captain. Message received. We're on our way.'

'Very good, sir,' replied Sebastev. 'We await your arrival. Sebastev out.'

Kabanov turned to the others. 'Gentlemen,' he said, 'let's not keep the captain waiting.'

SEBASTEV STOOD UNDER the buzzing lights of the relay station's basement, bolt pistol drawn. The gun's muzzle was trained on a man dressed in black, a rebel officer, who sat on the floor, back pressed to the cold, stone wall.

To Sebastev's left, banks of security monitors hissed and crackled, leaking acrid, blue smoke into the air. The rebels charged with protecting the relay station had been supervised from this room. They'd all been killed when Sebastev and his men had stormed the building. Only one man remained alive. Sebastev didn't plan to leave him that way for much longer, but he wouldn't execute the man before Colonel Kabanov gave his permission. There'd be an interrogation first.

Trooper Aronov stood behind Sebastev, also looking down at this killer of Vostroyan Firstborn. The other troopers had been posted to defensive positions around the building, but Sebastev knew from voxed reports that the fighting on this side of the river was essentially over.

Trooper Rodoyev had needed to be physically wrestled from the room after rushing forward with his knife drawn, yelling that he would flay the prisoner alive. He was outside now, posted to the east entrance. Sebastev was torn between Fifth Company's current lack of manpower and his need to see Rodoyev disciplined. The man was setting a bad example for the other troopers and he couldn't go unpunished. Sebastev decided he'd consult with Commissar Karif on the matter when they both had time. Other matters took precedence.

The body of Trooper Vamkin lay in a corner of the basement, another man lost in the effort to secure this place. As Vamkin had entered the room, the rebel officer had surprised him, stabbing him once in the stomach with a wickedly serrated blade. The knife had been coated with a deadly neurotoxin. Vamkin's lungs had stopped working almost immediately. He'd died of suffocation long before he could bleed to death.

Trooper Petrovich, a scout from Second Platoon, had been following right behind Vamkin. Petrovich, who'd lost an ear in a knife fight a few years back, was well known for his cool head. He'd shot the enemy officer in the thigh, crippling him and sending him to the floor, but sparing him to face the colonel's wrath.

For his part, the rebel seemed strangely unconcerned that he'd been taken alive. He sat nursing his wounded leg, occasionally raising his eyes to meet Sebastev's gaze. There was something in his look that disturbed Sebastev greatly, but it was impossible to define. Sebastev felt deeply uncomfortable around the man. He wished Colonel Kabanov would hurry up.

The captive was dressed surprisingly similar to an Imperial commissar. He wore a long, black coat with gold brocade and buttons. His face was clean-shaven. The greatest visible difference was in his headwear. While commissars across the Imperium proudly donned the peaked, black cap of their station, these rebel officers wore tall, pointed hats that swept backwards like the dorsal fin of some sea mammal or shark.

How will Commissar Karif react when he sees this man, Sebastev wondered? I've heard a lot about them but, to my knowledge, this is the first time a so-called officer-patriot of the Danikkin Special Patriotic Service has been taken alive. They usually take suicide capsules prior to capture. Why didn't this one do so when we took the building?

The men and women of the Special Patriotic Service were hated and feared by their own people. Here was an agent of the secession whose task it was to purge Imperial loyalists from the populace, and to ensure absolute dedication to Lord-General Vanandrasse among the forces of the Danikkin Independence Army. They were reputed to be masters of torture and intimidation.

Not only do they look like commissars, thought Sebastev, but they share much of the same remit.

To some extent, however, the limits of their authority differed. The Danikkin officer-patriots had power over both civilian and military conduct. The history of their organisation, going back only a few decades according to Imperial intelligence reports, was bloody and brutal.

Booted footsteps sounded on the ferrocrete floor. 'Cover him, Aronov,' said Sebastev. Aronov raised his lasgun. Sebastev holstered his bolt pistol, turned, and saluted Colonel Kabanov. Kuritsin, Maro, Politnov and Commissar Karif filed into the room.

'Solid work in taking this place, captain,' said Colonel Kabanov. 'I had no doubts whatsoever that you'd manage it. Now tell me, who do we have here?'

'I'd like to make the introductions, sir' replied Sebastev, 'but the bastard hasn't told me his name yet.'

'I see,' said Kabanov. He faced the patriot-officer and said, 'Your attire says you're an officer. Act like one. Tell me your name and rank. My own name is–'

'Colonel Kabanov of the Vostroyan Sixty-Eighth Infantry Regiment,' interrupted the rebel with a grin, 'formerly stationed at Korris, now occupying Nhalich East with the barest remnant of your force.' Lifting his hand slowly, he adjusted his fin-shaped hat. 'I know who you are, colonel. I know your reputation. Had I realised you were not among the dead of yesterday's battle, you might have found breaching our defences a lot harder than you did. Still, you won't hold the town for long with so few men, and no help will come. Your Imperium has forsaken you just as it did the people of Danik's World.'

'By Terra,' spat Sebastev, 'you don't have to listen to this, sir. Just say the word–'

Kabanov held up a hand. 'In due course, captain, in due course. The man was just about to tell me his name.'

'Very well,' said the rebel. 'I am Brammon Gusseff, a patriot-captain attached to the Danikkin Eleventh Mobile Infantry Division.'

'Patriot-captain, my eye,' hissed Commissar Karif from Kabanov's right. 'You are a faithless traitor to the Imperium of Mankind.'

Gusseff actually laughed at that. 'The similarities between us offend you, commissar. That is most amusing. What is your name? You're no Vostroyan.'

'There are no similarities between us, traitor.'

Sebastev looked over at Karif and saw his face twisted with hate.

'So you say,' replied Gusseff before returning his attention to Colonel Kabanov. 'It seems, colonel, that there's no shortage of Imperial slaves in this room who'd bloody their hands on your behalf. Perhaps they should fight amongst themselves for the privilege. That would provide some fine entertainment. Of course, if you do kill me, you'll never open the case the machine-man is so interested in.'

Gusseff inclined his head towards the far corner, where Enginseer Politnov was occupied with something. The enginseer had spotted the case while the others were talking and was about the business of trying to open it. Despite his mastery of all things mechanical, he was having some difficulty.

'What do you have there, enginseer?' asked Colonel Kabanov.

Politnov turned his hooded head and said, 'The case contains something of significant weight. There is a mechanism to avoid forced entry. If I attempt to open it without the relevant codes, the mechanism will destroy the contents. I believe there is a high probability that this case contains something of strategic importance.'

'Can't you bypass the mechanism somehow?' asked Colonel Kabanov.

'Not with the equipment at hand, colonel. A number of the devices I require can be accessed at the Mechanicus facility in Seddisvarr.'

'What makes you think we give a damn what it contains?' growled Commissar Karif, stepping forward, ready to draw his chainsword. Colonel Kabanov put a hand on his shoulder and halted him.

'Case or no case,' said Gusseff, 'I'm the first officer-patriot your idiotic forces have ever taken alive, and I expect to stay that way. Contact your superiors in Seddisvarr and inform them of my capture. You'll find establishing contact somewhat easier than before.'

Lieutenant Kuritsin stepped forward. 'Do you mean to say that you've disabled the jamming device? Where is it?'

'Jamming device?' asked Gusseff sardonically. 'I really couldn't say. Just call your superiors. I might be the only hope you have of getting back behind your own lines.'

'Enginseer,' said Colonel Kabanov, 'do you judge that case adequate to hold a possible jamming device?'

'I do, colonel. It would need to be attached to a large vox-array in order to be effective, but such a device could be built to fit this case.'

'Is the device in the case, patriot-captain? Don't play games.'

'I'll say no more on that, colonel. Contact Seddisvarr, unless you want your men to die here when the next DIA armour columns come rolling into town, as they soon will.'

'Fine,' said Colonel Kabanov. 'Enough of this. Where is the main communications console? I want to speak to Twelfth Army Command at once.'

'The console is on the uppermost floor, sir,' said Sebastev. 'I can take you there.'

'Very good, captain' said Kabanov. 'No one is to kill this prisoner without my express consent. Any soldier who attempts to do so will be executed by Commissar Karif for disobeying a direct order.' Kabanov fixed his gaze on Patriot-Captain Gusseff and added, 'We'll find out soon enough, faithless wretch, whether you live or die.'

LIEUTENANT KURITSIN SAT down at the console on Colonel Kabanov's orders and began adjusting dials as he called into the vox-mic, 'Six-eight-five to Command HQ. This is six-eight-five calling Command HQ. Are you receiving?'

There was nothing but the hiss of static and whining tones that rose and fell but never gave way to speech. Kuritsin adjusted his dials and tried again, but with the same results. He turned to Kabanov and said, 'I don't know what to think, sir. It could be the weather, I suppose. Even with an array like this, sir, the atmosphere of the planet could still be playing hell with long-range signals. Things aren't too bad at our end, but I can't vouch for the weather over Theqis.'

Just as he finished his sentence, a tinny voice sounded through the console speakers. '...Command... eight-five...'

Kuritsin hurriedly adjusted the dials, desperate not to lose the signal before he could lock onto it. Soon, the voice at the other end was coming through loud and clear. Kabanov let a look of great relief show on his face.

'This is Command HQ. We are receiving you, six-eight-five. Name and rank.'

'Command HQ, this is Lieutenant Oleg Kuritsin, speaking on behalf of Colonel Maksim Kabanov, commanding officer of the Firstborn Sixty-Eighth Infantry Regiment. The colonel is present and wishes to communicate directly with General Vlastan.'

'Very good, Lieutenant Kuritsin. My encryption glyph is lit. Please confirm that your own is also lit.'

Kabanov watched Kuritsin scan the console for the glyph that said comms encryption was active, securing the content of their transmission from enemy comprehension. There, on the left of the console, the glyph shone with a green light.

'Glyph is lit, command. I can confirm encryption is active.'

'Understood, lieutenant. I've got a standing order to patch any communications from regiments in your sector straight through to General Vlastan's personal staff. Await further instructions.'

After a moment of relative silence, a different voice spoke. 'This is Lieutenant Balkariev of the general's communications staff. The general is on his way. In the meantime, please report your status.'

Kuritsin looked up at Colonel Kabanov, who nodded for him to proceed. 'Fifth Company is currently occupying Nhalich East. Forces of the Danikkin Independence Army are entrenched in Nhalich West. The bridge between the two halves of the city has been destroyed by the enemy. We are unable to proceed across the river at this location. Our forces are down to...' Kuritsin pulled a piece of parchment from his greatcoat pocket and read, 'Down to one-hundred and eleven men, eighteen of those seriously wounded. The rebel presence on this side of the river has been eliminated. Civilians are present in the town, currently being kept under guard. We have also taken a prisoner who claims to be a member of the

Danikkin Special Patriotic Service. He claims to have something of strategic importance to both sides.'

'Have you… One moment, lieutenant. General Vlastan has arrived and wishes to speak directly with Colonel Kabanov.'

Lieutenant Kuritsin stood and offered Kabanov his seat. Kabanov sat down and immediately felt his body settle into the chair. He hadn't realised just how fatigued he was. Now, with his legs able to rest for the first time in hours, he dreaded having to haul himself out of it. His muscles ached and he longed for sleep. He forced himself not to let it show in front of the others.

'This is Kabanov.'

A wet, wheezy voice sounded from the console speakers. Even through the distortion of long-range vox, General Vogor Vlastan sounded a lot like he looked: a physical ruin of a man kept alive artificially.

'Maksim, Maksim,' he said, calling Kabanov by his first name, greeting him as an old friend. 'Praise the Emperor you're still alive. Damn this world and its bloody storms. We heard the DIA were moving up from Ohslir, but I knew the White Boar would see them off.'

'I regret to report, general, that we didn't exactly see them off. The 701st and most of the Sixty-Eighth were lost in a major DIA offensive. The rebels managed to occupy Nhalich, blowing the bridge in the process and isolating the east and west banks. Our losses were… grievous, sir.'

'But you're alive, Maksim. The White Boar lives on. You weathered the ambush and beat them back. There'll be medals for this.'

'Please, general, you misunderstand me. The rebel ambush was a complete success. They wiped out every single Vostroyan company under my command but one. I only survived by the grace of the Emperor and because I arrived after the event with our rearguard company, Fifth Company, sir.'

The vox-speakers went silent for a moment. The only sound was the background hum and crackle of dead air. Then Vlastan spoke again. 'At least you're alive, Maksim.' The blustery tone had gone from the man's voice, 'And you're holding Nhalich. That's something.'

Damn you for an old fool, thought Kabanov. We couldn't hold this place now if we tried. Half a company against Throne knows how many more orks or rebels? Don't be insane.

'There's more, sir,' Kabanov continued. 'We've taken a captive, sir.'

'You surprise me, Maksim,' said Vlastan. 'The Twelfth Army doesn't take prisoners in this campaign. You know that. We're stretched too thin already without worrying about detainees.'

'We believe he's a member of the Special Patriotic Service, sir. He was apprehended in the relay station, coordinating the rebel defence of the building. He seems to think his life is of some significant worth to the Twelfth Army.'

Vlastan seemed to hesitate for a moment before saying, 'A name, Maksim. Has he furnished you with a name?'

'He calls himself Patriot-Captain Brammon Gusseff, sir, attached to the Eleventh Danikkin Mobile Infantry Division, if I heard him correctly. His accent is very thick.'

Again the vox-speakers went silent. Kabanov had the distinct impression that General Vlastan was engaged in urgent discussions with others at his end. After almost a full minute, the speakers crackled to life again.

'Stay by your comms unit, Maksim. Just stay exactly where you are and await further communication.'

'Understood, sir.' Kabanov turned from the microphone. 'Damned strange, all of this. It doesn't feel right to me at all. Have any of you something to say?'

Atypically, it was Lieutenant Maro who spoke up first. 'He recognised the traitor's name, sir. I'm sure of it. He sounded unusually anxious. Throne knows why.'

Commissar Karif nodded and said, 'I must agree with Lieutenant Maro, colonel.'

'Very well,' said Kabanov, 'but I'm not sure what that suggests. We're talking about a man directly responsible for the death of Vostroyan Firstborn. I don't want to believe Twelfth Army Command is willing to deal with this devil.'

'The man did seem extremely confident that his life would be spared,' said Lieutenant Kuritsin. 'Could he have pre-arranged his own defection on the promise of handing over the alleged Danikkin jamming device?'

Sebastev shook his head. 'He's not defecting. Why would anyone switching sides kill Vostroyan Firstborn? Something is wrong in all of this. I've got a very bad feeling about the man. Part of me thinks killing him would be a kindness.'

A sharp burst of static preceded Vlastan's return to the airwaves. 'Are you there, Maksim?'

'I am, sir,' replied Kabanov.

'Good. Listen carefully, old friend. I have new orders for you. They must be followed to the letter.'

Old friend he calls me, thought Kabanov, but would I have saved his life all those years ago if I'd known times like these would follow?

Kabanov ordered his adjutant to record the general's words. Maro dug a battered old data-slate from a side pocket and began writing on the screen as General Vlastan said, 'You are to take what's left of your force, excepting anyone that can be expected to slow you down, and head north immediately to the town of Grazzen. When I say immediately, Maksim, you can be sure I mean exactly that. According to the most recent transmissions, our forces at Grazzen are under heavy attack from the greenskin horde. The orks have launched a major offensive there. If they reach either of Grazzen's bridges, our Thirty-Fifth Armoured Regiment have been ordered to destroy them. I'll send additional forces to Grazzen as

soon as we've finished talking. That should help to keep
the corridor open a little longer, but you must hurry. If
you don't reach Grazzen in time, Maksim, you and everyone with you will be stranded in Varanes. You will be lost
to us. No further support will be available.'

Kabanov shook his head in disgust. What kind of support have you offered up until now. he thought?

'Grazzen is over three hundred kilometres from our
current position, general, and we'll be lucky if the orks
haven't already taken the mountain pass. Just how long
do you think we have?'

'It's impossible to say, Maksim. You've got as long as
the Thirty-Fifth can hold out against the odds. This is
your only way home. You say the bridge at Nhalich is
gone. I say Grazzen is your last chance. The DIA will roll
more armour up from the south now that you've ousted
their people from the relay station. Nhalich West will
already have put a call out for support on the east bank.
Fifth Company should leave at once.'

'Very good, sir. Unless there's anything–'

'One second, Maksim. I'm not finished. It is vitally
important that the prisoner, Brammon Gusseff, remains
completely unharmed, likewise, the case that accompa-
nies him. You are to spare nothing in ensuring that both
prisoner and case reach Command HQ here in Seddisvarr. This objective is your highest priority and supersedes
all other considerations. The life of every last man under
your command is secondary to the achievement of this
task. I repeat: the prisoner and case are to be delivered
intact to Command HQ on Seddisvarr. Is that clear?'

'Sir…'

'These are my orders, Maksim. If there were any other
way…' There was a pause before Vlastan said, 'You know
I've always been grateful for–'

The general's voice was cut off as the entire relay station
shook. The walls and ceiling cracked and rained dirt down
on the heads of the men in the communications room.

'Artillery,' shouted Sebastev. 'They're hitting us from the far side of the river. Get the khek out of here now! All of you!'

Kabanov felt Sebastev's powerful grip on his upper arm as the captain hauled him out of his seat and pulled him after the others, just in time. Another artillery shell smashed into the relay station, bringing massive chunks of the shattered roof crashing down on top of the communications console. Kabanov saw enough in the moment he was yanked through the door to know he'd have been crushed where he sat were it not for Sebastev's reflexes.

The captain still had a grip on Kabanov's arm as they raced down the stairway followed closely by a thick cloud of choking, grey dust. Lieutenant Kuritsin was descending at the head of the group, shouting to the rest of the soldiers in the building as he went. 'Everyone outside now! Assemble on the east side of the building.'

Sebastev and Kabanov hit the bottom of the stairs and raced out into the open air as another artillery round thundered into the building, shaking the ground under their feet. The thick ferrocrete structure collapsed in on itself, transforming into a vast pile of rubble with a rumble and a great cough of dust and smoke.

'Not Basilisks,' shouted Kabanov over the noise of more shelling.

'No, sir,' replied Sebastev as they ran. 'One of their own machines. An Earthshaker would have snuffed us all out with the first shot.'

'I need to know, captain,' said Kabanov, 'did we get the prisoner out in time?'

Sebastev grunted. 'Look up ahead, sir.'

There, among the Firstborn assembled on the street, Patriot-Captain Brammon Gusseff of the Danikkin Special Patriotic Service stood eyeballing Trooper Aronov. The big scout had his knife pressed to the prisoner's neck. Kabanov could see the trooper was itching to use it, too.

'No one must hurt him,' said Kabanov as he slowed his pace. 'Orders are orders, captain, no matter how damned irregular they are.'

'I know that, sir,' said Sebastev, the distaste plain in his voice. 'The prisoner won't be harmed. I'll see to it myself.'

Kabanov was quiet as they walked. His body was screaming at him to rest, but there wasn't time for that. Once Fifth Company was under way, he'd lie down and close his eyes for a while. A mug of hot ohx' wouldn't be a bad idea either.

Just before he and Sebastev were within earshot of the other men, he turned to the captain and said, 'Thank you for pulling me out of there, Grigorius. Damn this body of mine. I'm trying to hold out as long as I can, but it's getting harder. Fifth Company must make it through. For the honour of the regiment, you understand.'

Sebastev didn't meet the colonel's eye. 'For the honour of the regiment, sir,' he said. 'But the White Boar is the only man who can see us back to Seddisvarr. You've got the Emperor's work still to do, I tell you. I'll assist you in any way I can.'

As they rejoined the others, Kabanov said, 'Very well. You can start by getting us out of Nhalich.'

CHAPTER TEN

Day 687
Nhalich, East Bank – 15:58hrs, -21°C

BEHIND SEBASTEV, THE sound of the Danikkin long guns could still be heard raining heavy shells down on the east side of town. The shelling was sporadic. The rebels weren't trying to level the place; their own forces were already on their way up from the south-east with the intention of taking it back. Fifth Company didn't plan to be there when they arrived. More Vostroyan wounded had already been loaded into one of the Pathcutters and were being administered to once again by Sergeant Svemir. The able-bodied men, barely a hundred of them now, were busy loading weapons and gear into another of the heavy transports. With so few men left to ride in them, two of the Pathcutters would be left behind, scuttled so the advancing Danikkin couldn't make use of them.

Lieutenant Kuritsin stepped up beside Sebastev. 'I've got some bad news, sir.'

'What is it, Rits?'

171

'One of our spotters reports Danikkin armour approaching the town, coming up the southern highway, strength unknown. At their current speed, they'll be here within the hour.'

Sebastev was about to respond when a call came in over his vox-bead. 'Tarkarov to Captain Sebastev. One of my men watching the east reports movement, sir. It looks like orks, a lot of them. They're still some distance away, but they appear to be covering ground quickly.'

'Orks and rebels at the same time,' said Sebastev. 'Someone really doesn't like us. Tell our men to speed things up. Anything not loaded within the next ten minutes gets left behind.'

'Sir,' said Kuritsin. 'Colonel Kabanov ordered a squad to salvage provisions from the town. Our own stocks are running dangerously low. Sergeant Breshek took a few men from Fourth Platoon and went to take care of it. They're on their way back with supplies, but with time running out, perhaps we should send extra men to assist them.'

'Fine, send the extra men. The longer we wait, the more chance we'll get entangled with either or both of the oncoming foes. In fact, our chances of getting away clean aren't looking good.'

Tarkarov's voice came back over the vox. 'Could we perhaps organise some kind of diversion, sir?'

'I don't think we can afford to leave without one. We don't want our flanks harried all the way to the mountains. We mustn't get sucked into another fight. Our chances of crossing at Grazzen erode by the minute. I'll consult Colonel Kabanov.'

As Sebastev walked towards the colonel's Chimera, vox-reports came in from his platoon leaders. The essentials had been loaded up. The men were, for the most part, ready to move out on the colonel's command. Sebastev ordered them to stand by.

Sebastev knocked on the sealed hatch of Colonel Kabanov's Chimera to announce himself. The hatch was opened by Lieutenant Maro, who ushered Sebastev in quickly and closed the hatch behind him. Father Olov, Enginseer Politnov, Commissar Karif, and the prisoner, Gusseff, sat in the back of the Chimera, still clothed in full outdoor kit. Gusseff's hands and feet were bound tight and his mouth had been taped.

Sebastev spared him only the briefest glance before he faced Colonel Kabanov and said, 'Sir, we're almost ready to move out, but it doesn't look like we're going to get away clean. Danikkin armour is rolling up from the south and orks are coming in from the east. Even if they don't see us, without some kind of distraction they'll pick up our tracks all too quickly.'

Colonel Kabanov indicated a seat and Sebastev took it. No one, it seemed, was particularly eager to sit next to the traitor. The seats beside and opposite him remained empty, despite the otherwise cramped conditions. 'This is grave news, captain. A distraction would need more time to organise than we can spare.'

'We could stand and fight,' rumbled Father Olov.

'As much as I believe that a glorious death should be the final wish of every man, father,' said Commissar Karif, 'I'm also reminded that General Vlastan gave very specific orders. There's little glory in a death that leaves important tasks unfinished.'

'The commissar is right,' said Kabanov. 'Besides, I've no intention of seeing this company meet its end in Nhalich. Twelfth Army Command wants this traitor, and they're going to get him. We must be away at once. Captain, are the men loaded and ready to move out?'

'We await the last few, sir. They're bringing essential provisions. We're running very low, as I'm sure you know.'

'How long before the men return to us, captain?'

Sebastev voxed the question over to Lieutenant Kuritsin, who was still outside, overseeing the final preparations to move out. When the answer came back,

Sebastev relayed it to Colonel Kabanov. 'They've just returned, sir. The provisions are being loaded up.'

'Good,' said the colonel, 'but that still leaves us the problem of a diversion. I blame myself, of course for the oversight. We should have rigged the power plants here like we did at Korris. There just hasn't been time. I don't suppose we could…'

'I think it's too late for that, sir,' said Sebastev, 'unless you're willing to sacrifice the few troopers we have left with any demolitions experience. And they'd need one of the Chimeras to get them to the target area in time. Enginseer Politnov would have to accompany them, too.'

The enginseer swung his cowled head in Sebastev's direction. His metallic voice sounded from somewhere in his chest. 'I have no qualms about remaining to lead such an operation. My life, such as it is, belongs to the Omnissiah.'

Sebastev nodded, but Colonel Kabanov held up a hand. 'No, enginseer,' he said, 'I appreciate your willingness, but we've suffered enough losses. Fifth Company can't afford to leave anyone behind.'

'My own analysis of the situation, colonel,' replied Enginseer Politnov, 'tells me that you will lose some men, or you will lose all. Certain losses will be necessary if Fifth Company is to evade pursuit. I have a proposition that I think will help to minimise those losses.'

In the close air of the Chimera, Sebastev found himself very aware of the mysterious clicks and hisses that emanated from the enginseer's body. Politnov always wore the same voluminous red robes. Oil-stained and torn in places, they were utterly inadequate for life in the deep winter, even more so than Father Olov's robes, but the enginseer seemed impervious to the lethal cold. He had little left in common with mortal men. Over hundreds of years, most of his organs and extremities had been replaced or upgraded. Perhaps he had more in common with the Chimeras and the Pathcutters that he worked constantly to maintain.

'Two of our Pathcutter transports are surplus to current requirements,' said Politnov. 'I believe it was the captain's intention to scuttle them prior to the arrival of the advancing rebels. Confirm, please.'

'It still is my intention,' replied Sebastev.

'Aside from my own distaste at the destruction of any machine, captain, I feel you would be in error to do so. My servitors and I are quite capable of driving both of the machines south-east. At a point between both ork and rebel parties, we will generate the sounds and visual signs of an engagement. This will almost certainly draw the attention of the orks. Those among you who have read Anzion's works will already be aware that orks cannot resist a battle. They crave the opportunity to grow in size and strength. It is like a drug to them. I know from your strategy at Korris, Colonel Kabanov, that you understand this well.'

Colonel Kabanov looked displeased but, when he spoke, his tone was one of resignation. 'You intend to draw the orks onto the rebels, enginseer. It's an audacious plan. I'd even call it foolhardy.'

The enginseer was quiet for a moment, but a slight motion of his shoulders suggested to Sebastev that the old machine-man was chuckling to himself. 'It has a reasonable probability of success, colonel. Far greater than an uncovered retreat, I assure you.'

'You and your servants are non-combatants,' said Kabanov, 'I can't order you to do this.'

'It would be a great and noble sacrifice,' said Commissar Karif, 'but who will appease the machine-spirits of our vehicles if you do this thing?'

'The machines will take you as far as you need to go, commissar. This planet has made them fickle, it's true. Offer due obeisance and they will get you to Grazzen. As for my life and the lives of my staff, they belong to the Omnissiah, as they always have. I have lived a very long time. In recent years, I have slowed. Processing takes more time. My functions include more frequent errors. My biological systems are finally collapsing centuries beyond their natural lifespan.'

Sebastev saw a meaningful look pass between the enginseer and Colonel Kabanov as the enginseer continued. 'These are matters I have kept to myself, though Tech-priest Gavaril detected the truth easily enough. I have watched and waited for the moment that my life might be spent for greatest gain. I suspected it would come during these dark times. I was correct. For the honour of the Machine-God, I am ready to face my death.'

Each of the men in the vehicle, with the exception of the gagged rebel prisoner, stared at the old enginseer with silent respect. His offer to stay epitomised the kind of honour and nobility to which every Vostroyan officer aspired.

I always regarded this man as little more than a functionary, thought Sebastev with no small sense of shame. When did I forget that he is a man of Vostroya? Here, he proves himself the equal of our very best, in spirit if not in combat prowess.

'Enginseer,' said Colonel Kabanov, 'you may take everything you need and go about your plan. May the Emperor as Omnissiah ensure your success for all our sakes. Your sacrifice will be remembered in the annals of this regiment.'

The enginseer bowed his hooded head. 'Then, if you'll excuse me, I will attend to the matter with all haste. The Omnissiah's blessings upon you, gentlemen.'

Enginseer Politnov didn't wait for permission to leave. He simply rose from his seat in the Chimera, opened the hatch and clambered out into the cold afternoon. On impulse, Sebastev rose and followed him outside. The enginseer was walking away in the direction of the Pathcutters, his red robes whipping around him in the bitter wind.

'Enginseer,' called Sebastev.

Politnov stopped and turned to face him. 'Captain?'

Sebastev said nothing. Instead, he raised his hands to his chest, made the sign of the aquila, and bowed deeply.

Politnov's laugh was audible this time: a dry, toneless sound like metal scraping on metal. He turned away and continued trudging through the snow. 'Get back inside the Chimera, captain,' he voxed, disinclined to shout over the noise of the winds. 'Flesh is so weak against this cold. Yes, flesh is weak, but the machine… The machine is indomitable.'

KABANOV'S CHIMERA GAVE a throaty growl as it pulled into position behind the lead Pathcutter. Fifth Company's vehicles moved away from Nhalich in single file, three Chimeras and two heavy transports in a loose column, making the most of the broad channel the Pathcutter's plough carved in the drifts. The setting sun fought its way through thick clouds, casting a bloody red glow over the western horizon and throwing long shadows out across the open snow.

Enginseer Politnov was beyond vox-bead range, but Lieutenant Kuritsin caught a final communication from him on the Chimera's vox-caster. Politnov reported success in drawing the orks south-west from their original path. As he signed off, he was pulling them straight towards the Danikkin armour column in the south.

Kabanov offered a silent prayer of thanks, commending the enginseer's soul to the care of Saint Nadalya so that she might speed its journey to the Emperor's side. Politnov had offered his life to aid them without a second thought, sure that the time was right for him to step up and make a difference. Kabanov could identify closely with that, particularly now, as Fifth Company sped towards its probable doom.

There seemed little hope that the Thirty-fifth Regiment would hold Grazzen long enough for Fifth Company to cross with the prisoner. It was far more likely they would arrive to find the place overrun with orks, and the bridge destroyed from the Vostroyan side. A few seconds too late might as well be a year too late for all the difference it would make.

Such grim thoughts were cut off by a sudden pain in his lungs. Kabanov scrabbled for one of his handkerchiefs and coughed into it wetly.

The others looked over at him, concern apparent on their faces, but said nothing. Kabanov threw back a weary smile as he stuffed the handkerchief into his pocket, keen to hide the red splotch that he knew would be there.

Kabanov's age wasn't considerable when compared to many high-ranking Imperial officers, but, unlike the others, General Vlastan included, he'd never opted to undergo expensive and often excruciating rejuvenat treatments. He had money enough to pay for them – House Kabanov had more than its fair share of investments on Vostroya and its neighbouring worlds – but he'd always trusted that the Emperor would take him when it was time.

That time isn't far off, thought Kabanov. *Will it be on my terms, I wonder? Or will I be denied my last grand gesture?*

Winds picked up, driving across from the east, buffeting the sides of the Chimera. Kabanov's body ached for sleep. 'Excuse me, gentlemen,' he said, 'but we've a hard fight ahead of us – our hardest yet, I've no doubt. It's been too long since any of us had adequate rest. So long as we take turns to keep an eye on the prisoner, I suggest we try to get some sleep. The mountain pass is some hours away.'

Captain Sebastev nodded his agreement, looking immensely tired himself. 'We've been running on ohx' for too long. Get some rest, colonel. That goes for the rest of you, too.' He was referring to Father Olov and Lieutenants Kuritsin and Maro. Commissar Karif, barely able to restrain himself in the presence of the captured traitor, had opted once again to ride with the troopers in one of the Pathcutters. 'I'll keep an eye on this rebel bastard for now.'

It was clear to Kabanov that Sebastev needed sleep as much as any of them, but the stubborn captain wouldn't be argued with. Someone else could relieve him later, he supposed.

'If anyone needs extra blankets,' said Kabanov, 'Lieutenant Maro will provide them.'

Father Olov shook his head, lifted a flask of rahzvod to his lips and took a deep draft. Before anyone else had even settled down, he was snoring like a cudbear.

As the others closed their tired eyes, Kabanov nodded to Sebastev and said, 'Wake Maro in a few hours, captain. He'll take over and give you a chance to rest. That's an order, by the way.'

'Yes, sir,' said Sebastev. 'I'll do that.'

COMMISSAR KARIF COULDN'T stand to be near the so-called officer-patriot, Brammon Gusseff. Breathing the same air as a man who had turned from the Emperor's light filled him with righteous fury. He wanted nothing more than to shove his chainsword into the man's belly and watch his life pour out.

At the same time, Karif had to acknowledge that the prisoner was worth far more alive than dead. If the interrogations were handled correctly, what secrets might the rebel give up? The codes to the case that accompanied him? Details of rebel deployment? Perhaps more besides.

Aware that his self-control was being sorely tested, Karif had excused himself from Colonel Kabanov's Chimera and opted to ride in the Pathcutter at the back of the column. Since he'd only been among Fifth Company for a matter of days, he expected to find a few faces that were new to him. But with Fifth Company reduced to less than a hundred men crammed into just a few vehicles, he soon found himself sitting among familiar figures. Directly opposite him, just as he had been on the journey west from Korris, sat Sergeant Sidor Basch of Second Platoon.

'Glad to see you're still with us, commissar,' said the veteran sergeant.

'Likewise,' said Karif. 'Did you take many losses during the assault?'

Basch shook his head. 'Two from my squad. They'll be missed. Considering the odds, though, I'd say we didn't do half bad.' The sergeant paused as if choosing his next words carefully. 'Commissar… if I offended you last time we spoke… I intended the comparison with Commissar Ixxius only as a compliment, I assure you.'

Karif raised a hand. 'I meant no particular disrespect to the late commissar. I merely dislike being the subject of comparisons, sergeant. I'm my own man with my own merits and, no doubt, my own flaws. I'll be measured by those alone if I'm to be measured at all. But let's have no more talk of it.'

'As you say, commissar.' Changing the subject, Basch asked, 'How did you enjoy that pict-slate?'

At first, Karif was at loss. He couldn't recall any pict-slate. He'd been with Fifth Company for only six days, but so much had been compressed into that time, he felt he'd been among them for weeks. Then it came to him; he'd confiscated a porn-slate discovered by two troopers searching the bodies in Reivemot Square in order to avoid fighting among the men.

'Naturally I destroyed it, sergeant,' he said. 'A man of the Imperial Creed wouldn't sully his eyes looking at filth like that. He'd have to flagellate himself.'

'We've got a different word for it on Vostroya, commissar, but I'm sure the meaning is the same.' The sergeant enjoyed a laugh, his infectious mirth spreading to the men seated on either side of him.

Karif had lied, of course. He had examined the images displayed on the cracked screen of the device. He'd been stunned that such unflattering and clumsy pictography could represent a source of entertainment to anyone. The subjects were unattractive to begin with.

The Emperor alone knows how you Vostroyans can find delight in such sturdy, thick-fingered women, he thought. Then again, they say Vostroya is a cold place. Perhaps the value of such women is in the heat they generate. And they look like hard workers. I suppose that counts for something.

Stavin, sitting by Karif's side as usual, was being engaged in conversation by a kind-faced soldier with a long, brown moustache and a patch of burnt skin below his left eye. The burn was probably the result of a near miss back at Nhalich. Las-bolts could still singe flesh if they passed close enough without hitting.

'I saw you fighting back there,' said the soldier to Stavin. 'You got guts for a shiny. What's your name, then?'

'Stavin. What's yours?'

'I'm Kovo, Fourth Platoon. My squad came in from the north-east and joined up with your lot at the crossroads, remember? I saw you drop the two traitors manning that bolter.'

'Oh,' said Stavin simply.

'Aye, good kills. Some of the others said you're from Hive Tzurka. That right?'

Stavin nodded.

'Me, too, the Merchant's Quarter. Can't say I miss it much. Anyway, don't worry about the others ragging on you. All the shinies get it. Just so you know, we saw how you toasted those rebels. You're bloodied now, proper Fifth Company. You won't get any grief from us.'

'How long have you been with the regiment, Kovo?' interjected Karif.

Stavin jumped as if he'd been stung, and only just realised that the commissar was listening to their exchange.

Kovo gave a shallow bow before answering. 'I've been with the Sixty-Eighth for over eight years, commissar. I'm

proud to serve under the White Boar. Never thought we'd
be hit this hard. Curse Old Hungry for the fat bas–'

Suddenly reminded that he was talking to a political
officer, Kovo's cheeks flushed, but he held Karif's gaze.

Karif let his smile put the trooper at ease. 'I haven't met
the man myself, but I've heard he could do with a few
laps around the compound, so to speak.'

A few of the soldiers listening offered polite laughs, but
Sergeant Basch leaned forward, elbows on his knees, and
said, 'It's a common misconception, commissar, that the
name Old Hungry refers to the general's physical appearance. It doesn't. Captain Sebastev never intended for the
name to be taken like that. He calls the man Old Hungry
on account of all the Vostroyan lives his career has
needed to sustain itself. Look under "attritionist" in a lex-
icanum and you'll see a picture of General Vogor Vlastan.
I won't deny he's a wretched figure of a man, mind you,
but that's hardly his fault. We were fighting dark eldar
pirates on Kalgrathis twenty-five years ago when an assas-
sin managed to slip poison into his food. Together, the
Medicae and the Mechanicus managed to save his life.
Whether they should have bothered is open to debate, I
reckon.'

A trooper with a face criss-crossed by white scar tissue
spoke up from Karif's left side. 'If it weren't for Vlastan's
political connections with the Administratum and the
bigwigs out of Cypra Mundi, he'd never have made general in a million years.'

Someone on the right, hidden from Karif's eyes by the
press of bodies, decided to add a few comments of their
own. 'Man's a bloody fool. We should have swept on the
hive-cities as soon as we made planetfall.'

'Hestor's balls!' another called out. 'Who knew the
orks were here, too? If you ask me, it's hardly the general's fault. The Twelfth Army was undermanned from
the start. Look to the Lord-Marshal if you want to blame
someone.'

More voices chipped in. 'Khek off! It was Old Hungry ordered us to hold Korris when the rest pulled out. Nhalich might have been a different story for the rest of our regiment and the 701st if the White Boar had been there to lead them.'

'You really think he could have saved them?' asked someone.

'Nothing saved Vamkin,' said a man with First Platoon insignia.

'Or Blemski,' added someone else, 'or Makarov.'

Other voices joined in, adding to the cacophony, half of the men battling to be heard, the other half shaking their heads in silent anger at the loss of their brother Firstborn.

Vostroyan truculence, thought Karif. Is this to happen every time I sit amongst them? Their battlefield discipline is impeccable, but the moment the enemy is overcome, they turn to arguing with each other. Well, I've got my own way of dealing with such things.

He took his laspistol from the holster at his hip and aimed the barrel at the floor of the passenger compartment. A sharp crack rang out, killing the raised voices in mid-sentence. The odour of ionised air and metal reached out to every nose in the cramped space. Wisps of smoke rose from a circular scorch mark in the floor.

Karif spoke quietly, knowing it would force the men to concentrate just to hear him. 'Before I joined this company,' he said, 'I heard many great things about Vostroyan discipline. I heard of victories other Guard regiments could scarcely imagine. I heard of a fighting force dedicated to the Emperor's service in every way.'

He turned his head and saw every eye on him. Those farthest from him, near the hatch at the back, craned forward to watch him as he spoke.

'I was honoured to be placed among you. As we fought in Nhalich, I was honoured to recite words from the *Treatis Elatii* to spur you on. But twice I've sat with you in the back of these transports, and twice your discussions have degenerated into disordered shouting. I wonder if I should feel quite as honoured as I did before.'

Karif looked to his left and met Sergeant Basch's hard eyes as he continued. 'You are the last hundred men of the Sixty-Eighth Infantry Regiment, and on your shoulders rest the future of the regiment and the honour of both Captain Sebastev and Colonel Kabanov. You owe the very best you can give to these men dedicated to leading you through this struggle. You owe them unquestioning loyalty, just as every man here owes it to the Emperor. Recent arrival I may be, but I have pledged to see this thing through. Fifth Company has fought hard and will need to do so again before this is finished. One last fight to secure our passage to safety. One last fight to fulfil your duties and preserve the honour of the regiment.

'What say you? Will you join me in asking the spirits of our fallen comrades to aid us, to galvanise our hearts for the coming fight? On your damned knees, every last one of you.'

All the troopers in the transport shuffled their backsides off the benches and knelt on the hard, steel floor facing Karif. Some were slower than others, but a glare from Sergeant Basch enlisted even the most reluctant.

Standing before them, Karif made the aquila on his chest and watched the men before him copy the gesture. 'In the name of the Holy Emperor, Majesty Most High, saints we beseech you.'

'Ave Imperator,' came the response.

'For the glory of the Imperium and the tireless efforts of all who sustain it, we beseech you.'

'Ave Imperator.'

'He who gave his life, He who suffers the eternal agonies of undeath that we might live, to Him we pray. Let the souls of our brothers be commended to His side, to offer their essence in death as they did in life.'

'None die in vain that die in His name,' intoned the soldiers as one.

Karif smiled inwardly.

They're a bloody-minded rabble when left to their own devices, he said to himself, but see how pious they are when the moment calls for it. I had thought there would be trouble, a struggle between their loyalty to the Cult Mechanicus and their faith in the Imperial Creed. But no. Over the millennium, they've found a balance between both. It's remarkable.

'Let us commend the souls of the fallen faithful to His side by naming them.'

Between them, the men present made sure that not one fallen soldier from Fifth Company was forgotten in their prayers.

IN THE EARLY hours of the morning, in the darkness, the driving snows and the howling winds, Fifth Company's vehicles began their steep climb up into the Varanesian Peaks.

The massive Pathcutter at the front of the column hugged the mountainsides, following the pass that connected the Valles Carcavia in the north with the lowlands in the south. The pass was buried under metres of snow, but it was well mapped and had been marked out with beacons placed at regular intervals. The beacons repeatedly transmitted short bursts of noise that could be followed using a standard cockpit auspex. Even so, between the black of night and the relentless snowfall, visibility was extremely poor, and there was no margin for error.

After hours of treacherous climbing, the road finally levelled out. Fifth Company had reached the apex of its journey through the pass. Soon they'd be heading downhill into the valley and straight towards Grazzen.

Trooper Gavlin Rhaiko, the driver of the lead vehicle, gave a sigh of relief when he noticed that the sky over the mountains was beginning to grow lighter. For the first time in long, stressful hours, he could see beyond the plex bubble of his cockpit. He still needed the auspex to guide him through the falling snow, but every few moments, he raised his head from the green monitor screen to peer outside. It was while doing so that he noticed irregular, flickering lights on the road up ahead.

A firefight!

His finger was halfway to the vox-bead in his ear when a bright red rocket flashed straight towards him, smashed through the plex bubble and detonated, killing him instantly.

SEBASTEV WINCED AS shouting erupted from his vox-bead, sending a jolt of pain into his left ear. 'Get your khekking transports off the road, warp-damn it. You're wide open out there.'

The voice over the vox had the sharp tone of a Vostroyan officer, but Sebastev didn't recognise it. The man wasn't one of his.

'This is Captain Sebastev, Firstborn Sixty-Eighth Regiment, Fifth Company. Identify yourself at once.'

'Captain, get your men out of those bloody transports and off the road now! You're gift shots, the lot of you.'

Sebastev turned to look at Colonel Kabanov. The colonel had jumped awake at the sound of the explosion up ahead. 'I repeat,' he voxed to the stranger, 'identify yourself at once.'

'This is Captain Yegor Chelnikov, Thirty-Fifth Regiment, Second Company. I have orders from Twelfth Army Command to rendezvous with your company and accompany you into Grazzen.'

The sound of gunfire rattled from the snow covered road ahead, loud even through the hull of the Chimera. 'You must get your men out of those transports, Captain Sebastev. It sounds insane, I know, but the orks are fielding a type of guided missile. You… you won't believe it until you see it.'

Colonel Kabanov gave Sebastev a nod and the captain turned to Lieutenant Kuritsin. 'Rits,' he said, 'get our lads out of the transports and into cover. This is a combat zone. There are orks ahead on the road.'

'Aye, sir,' said Kuritsin and voxed the order across to the others.

'I think, captain,' said Kabanov as he stood, 'that we'd better lead by example.'

Maro was already helping the colonel don his fur hat and cloak. Everyone else in the Chimera began readying themselves to disembark as fast as they could. Sebastev looked down at their Danikkin prisoner. 'What about this idiot?' he asked.

'Cut the bonds at his ankles,' said Colonel Kabanov. 'Maro, keep your laspistol at the prisoner's back. There's nowhere for him to go. If he tries to run, the orks will get him. If they don't, the deep winter will.'

Brammon Gusseff, still gagged and with his hands tightly bound, stood at a gesture from Lieutenant Maro. A few moments later, Lieutenant Kuritsin cracked the rear hatch open and they dashed out into the snow, one after the other.

Sebastev raced to the side of the Chimera the moment his boots hit the snow, eager to assess the situation up ahead. The lead vehicle poured roiling black smoke into the sky. Vostroyan Firstborn poured down the ramp in the damaged Pathcutter's belly, shaken by the impact, but unharmed thanks to the shielding between the cockpit and the troop compartment.

Sebastev could see Commissar Karif at the rear of the column, ushering other Firstborn down the ramp of their last operational Pathcutter. The troopers moved in pairs, immediately taking up covering positions to allow the rest of their squads to deploy safely.

Gunfire sounded close by. Ork shells began to zip past. The lead transport rattled with the impact of fat metal slugs from ork stubbers. On either side of the road, rising up the snow covered slopes, thick forests of pine seemed to offer some shadowy cover.

'Get our fighters into the trees, captain,' ordered Colonel Kabanov. 'I want to push up as fast as possible. Perhaps we can flank the orks while their attention is centred on our vehicles.'

'To the trees, Firstborn,' yelled Sebastev into his vox. 'Flanking manoeuvres on both sides of the road.' Then, to Captain Chelnikov, he voxed, 'Captain, we're moving up under cover of the trees. What's your status?'

'I've got two squads with me. We're pinned down between the treeline on the east slope and a depression by the side of the road.' Sebastev could hear the rapid crack of Vostroyan lasguns in the cold evening air as the squads from the Thirty-Fifth fought for their lives.

He was about to respond to Chelnikov when another explosion shook the lead Pathcutter. The giant vehicle erupted into a roaring ball of flames. Sebastev fought the urge to rub his eyes. It was difficult to believe what he'd seen just before the rocket hit.

For just a fraction of a second, he'd glimpsed a little green figure sitting near the nose of the rocket before it smashed into its target. The creature's face was twisted and insane with glee, baring needle-like teeth in mad laughter as it raced towards death.

They're using gretchin to guide their rockets, thought Sebastev.

Colonel Kabanov was leading men into the trees on the left of the road, huffing clouds of breath into the air as his boots kicked through the deep drifts. Men from Second and Fourth Platoons took up defensive positions around him.

Kuritsin was by Sebastev's side, unwilling to move off without his captain. Another rocket screamed past the smoking transport, heading towards their unprotected position. Both men instinctively ducked, but Sebastev had a much better view this time. His eyes met those of the mad gretchin pilot. The diminutive ork cackled and yanked hard on its guidance levers, but it was too late to adjust the rocket's trajectory enough to hit the vulnerable Vostroyans. Sebastev thought he could hear the frustrated scream of the mad pilot as the rocket blazed a smoky trail over their heads and disappeared into the screen of falling snow.

'Damn us for fools, Rits,' he barked, angered by the close call. 'Let's get our backsides into the cover of those trees, right now!'

They dashed off, using the tracks gouged in the snow by the other men to add speed to their steps. Just as they reached the treeline, chilling screams erupted from both sides of the pass.

'Those are human screams,' gasped Kuritsin.

'What the hell is going on?' voxed Sebastev desperately. 'Someone report at once.'

'It's the woods, sir,' voxed a breathless soldier from the trees up ahead. Cries of agony, shouted orders and the crack of lasguns sounded from between the black trunks.

'What about the damned woods?' snapped Sebastev.

'They're infested, sir,' replied the trooper, 'with squigs!'

CHAPTER ELEVEN

Day 688
Varanesian Pass – 08:42hrs, -26°C

KARIF YELLED INTO the cold air as he swept his growling chainsword left and right, chewing through the multitude of brightly coloured spherical bodies that leapt towards him. Thick orkoid blood soaked the carpet of pine needles that littered the ground beneath the trees. For every ten squigs he carved up like pieces of fruit, twenty more poured forward to snap at him with jaws rimmed by long yellow fangs.

There was a powerful smell of ork spores, like rotting flesh, from the mass of squig corpses that were piling up. It had begun to crowd out the scent of the pine. Knowing the woods meant close combat, the Firstborn had fixed bayonets to the ends of their lasgun barrels and were sweeping the deadly mono-molecular-edged blades through the tide of strange foes.

The vicious little beasts were knee high and hopped forward on short, powerful limbs. The jabbering noises they made assaulted the senses. There were too many of them to count.

Karif, Stavin and a trooper called Rubrikov had pressed their backs together, emulating the small knots of troopers nearby, eager not to leave their flanks naked to the savage swarm.

Sergeant Basch of Second Platoon wasn't far from Karif's position, just a little ahead and to the left, partially hidden from view by the trees. 'Keep fighting, you lot,' he yelled. 'We're thinning them out. Press forward!'

It was true, Karif realised. The squigs were still attacking in force, but the space between each round body was widening. More of the blood-sodden ground was showing through with each passing moment.

An orange ball of fungal flesh with a face from a child's nightmare leapt into the air in front of Karif and opened its cavernous mouth, eager to sink its rows of razor sharp teeth into his face. It was a close thing, but the commissar's swordsmanship had been tested by many foes both deadlier and more cunning. He swept his whirring blade upwards with both hands firm on the hilt, shearing straight through the orange body. Two symmetrical pieces flopped to the ground and lay there, quivering. A spray of stinking blood spattered Karif's clothes.

Before he had a chance to curse, searing pain raced up his leg.

He called out in agony and Stavin twisted around to face him, ramming the point of his bayonet into the slimy, pink sphere that had fixed itself to the commissar's lower leg.

'Son-of-a-grox,' roared Karif. Even dead, the squig's jaws were shut tight. There was no time to prise the corpse's teeth from his screaming calf muscle. More of the hopping fiends surged towards them.

Immediately behind Karif, so close it almost deafened him, an agonised scream sounded from Trooper Rubrikov's lips. Karif and Stavin both spun away at the same time, turning to face the howling man who'd been covering their backs.

Rubrikov's face was hidden from view by a fat yellow squig. Blood streamed from the troopers head where the beast's fangs had punched through flesh and into bone. Blinded by the creature, Rubrikov couldn't see to defend himself from the other squigs that crowded him, leaping up to bite great mouthfuls of warm flesh from those parts of him that were unarmoured.

A bright green squig closed its mouth over Rubrikov's flailing left hand, severing it completely. The trooper's horrifically shortened arm spouted a river of steaming blood as he stumbled to the ground, thrashing hopelessly at the swarming orks.

Karif did the only thing he could for the man. He pulled his laspistol from its holster and fired a single powerful shot into the body of the squig that was clamped to the soldier's face. The bolt burned straight through the squig's body and ended the trooper's suffering instantly.

Karif and Stavin quickly slaughtered the rest of the squigs that had fixed themselves to the dead man's body. 'Keep on!' shouted Sergeant Basch from up ahead. 'The squigs are almost beaten, but the herders are just up ahead.'

'Ulitsin is dead,' shouted a trooper at the rear.

'Vanady, too' shouted another.

From the corner of his eye, Karif caught Stavin staring at him and turned to face the boy. 'What would you have had me do? It was an act of kindness, by Terra. Could you have saved him from his agony?'

Stavin shook his head in silence.

'Then cover my back, damn you. We move up as the sergeant suggested.'

Karif turned from his adjutant and started moving through the trees, pacing himself with the Firstborn around him. The light of day was getting stronger, but the clouds were heavy and black, and the shadows beneath the snow covered branches of the trees were thick. Still, the Vostroyans knew better than to give their positions away with lamps. The sounds of battle could still be heard from beyond the treeline.

Captain Sebastev's voice broke through the static in Karif's ear, calling to Second Platoon. 'Sergeant Basch, where are you? Have you flanked those damned rocket launchers yet?'

'We're working on it, sir,' replied Basch. 'Had some trouble with squigs.'

'Understood, sergeant. 'Same on this side of the road. But you have to get moving. Captain Chelnikov's men are in trouble. They're pinned down. You need to draw ork fire away from them so they can get to the trees.'

Karif could see open snow between the dark trunks up ahead. Sergeant Basch was the first to the treeline and gestured for his men to take cover at the base of the thickest trunks. Karif and Stavin hurried forward to join the sergeant.

Out in the open, in the middle of the road, a Vostroyan Chimera lay overturned. Black smoke billowed into the air from its rear hatch and firing ports. A large ork, its silhouette a confused mass of cables and squared edges, tore at the bared underside of the vehicle with some kind of massive augmetic claw. Vostroyan las-beams blazed out at it from a shallow bank at the side of the road. Karif thought that must be where Chelnikov's men were trapped.

'Who's firing on that ork mech?' barked Captain Sebastev over the vox. 'You're wasting your damned time. Lasfire won't penetrate armour that thick. I want a heavy bolter on him, now. Where the hell is Kashr?'

'Here, sir,' growled a deep voice on Karif's right. 'I'm with Sergeant Basch in the trees to the east of you.'

Karif looked over at Trooper Avram Kashr. He was a huge Vostroyan, so large that he looked ready to burst out of his bronze-coloured cuirass. The fabric of his greatcoat was stretched tight over arms swollen with muscle. As the big trooper hefted his heavy bolter in readiness to fire on the augmetic ork, Karif could see just how he'd built such a massive physique. The oversized gun was usually fielded by a two-man team. Kashr wielded it alone.

'I have the shot, sir,' voxed Kashr.

'Take it,' voxed Captain Sebastev.

'Cover your ears, Stavin,' said Karif.

As Kashr opened fire, the thunderous noise of the heavy bolter shook snow from the laden branches overhead. The gun's muzzle flame lit the woods in every direction.

Karif watched intently from cover. He saw the big augmetic ork shudder as bolt after bolt struck its armour plates. Blue sparks flashed into life with each impact, vanishing just as quickly. Then the stream of bolts found a weak point – the armour was thinnest on the monster's sides. The ork began roaring and howling as explosive rounds punched through metal and deep into the green flesh beneath, detonating within and causing massive internal damage.

Kashr stopped firing. The ork looked down at its tattered torso in apparent disbelief for a moment before tumbling forwards from the top of the ruined Chimera onto the snow below.

'Well done, that man,' voxed Captain Chelnikov. 'You just took out the leader of this damned mob. That should make the others easier to deal with.'

'I still need Second Platoon to move up and flank those ork launchers,' voxed Captain Sebastev. 'Are you listening, Basch?'

'I'm on it, captain,' replied the sergeant. 'Second Platoon, forward at once!'

Karif and Stavin rose and raced forward with the soldiers of Second Platoon, making for the incline at the side of the snow-covered road. Up ahead, several bizarre ork machines – shoddy-looking red trucks that were difficult to classify until one noticed the launchers mounted on top – fired occasional rockets towards the cover that protected Captain Chelnikov's men.

'We're behind their launchers now, captain,' voxed Basch.

Commissar Karif could see gretchin crews manning the vehicles, working in teams to lift more heavy rockets into the launch slings. Among them, small mad figures leapt and chattered excitedly, apparently eager to climb onto the backs of the rockets and launch themselves to an explosive death.

Do not attempt to understand the mind of the alien, he thought to himself, quoting a section he recalled from the *Tactica Imperialis*. *Let your curiosity perish in the blazing light of your unquestioning faith.*

He turned to Sergeant Basch and said, 'How do you plan to take them out, sergeant?'

'Explosives, commissar,' said Basch. Something in the man's voice suggested to Karif that he was grinning beneath his scarf. 'I think it's time we blew these mindless bags of filth into the next life, don't you?' He turned to his men. 'How many of you dogs are carrying demo charges?'

Five responded in the affirmative and moved up beside their sergeant.

'Five charges, four ork launchers. That's good. Krotzkin, you stay back here as a reserve. You others, set your timers to five seconds. The moment you slap your charges on the back of those heaps out there, I want you to sprint back to the cover of this incline at full speed. Is that understood? Don't stop to engage the enemy. The rest of us will lay down a covering barrage. Your job is to plant the charges and run like khek.'

'Aye, sir,' answered the four men charged with the attack.

With the attention of the orks held by a continuous stream of fire from the Firstborn on the other side of the pass, Second Platoon readied for their attack on the launchers.

'Now!' barked Sergeant Basch. Four Firstborn raced off over the crest of the rise at a full sprint. Each man had been assigned a specific launcher to target. Karif watched without blinking as each of the Vostroyans slapped their charges against the sides of the launchers, hit the arming switches and bolted straight back to cover. The gretchin crews, alerted by the clang of metal on metal, turned and opened fire with their crude pistols as the men ran back to the cover of the slope.

'Open fire,' yelled Basch. His troopers loosed a blazing volley of las-bolts that cut half of the wicked-faced green-skins down. One gretchin managed to shoot the last of the returning troopers in the leg and the man went down screaming just a few metres in front of Karif.

Karif didn't hesitate. He leapt out from cover and grabbed the wounded man by the collar of his great-coat, hauling him back towards the others. The gretchin turned their pistols on him. Shells struck the ground around him, sending up white puffs of snow. The trooper Karif was trying to help cried out as a number of shots found their mark. He saw the man's eyes roll up into his head. There was no point helping him now.

He turned to leap back behind the cover of the slope, but at that moment, the demolition charges went off with a deafening boom. For a second, the world disappeared in an almighty white flash. He threw himself face down onto the snow as the heat from the exploding launchers flashed past him.

A moment later, hands grasped his coat and pulled him back into cover. It was Stavin. 'Are you all right, sir?'

Karif shook himself. 'I'm fine. Thank you, Stavin.'

Captain Sebastev was shouting orders to his Firstborn over the vox. 'Move in, now. Basch's squad, flank them from the rear. Use the smoke from those burning wrecks to cover your advance. I want all other squads ready to close in.'

Karif scrambled to his feet and took position with Stavin among the men of Sergeant Basch's squad. He drew his chainsword from its scabbard.

'The Emperor protects,' he told his adjutant.

Stavin gripped his lasgun tight. 'The Emperor protects, sir,' he replied.

'Firstborn, charge!' shouted Sergeant Basch.

THE ORKS FALTERED at first, surprised by the assault on their rear, but that didn't last long. They turned at once to engage the Vostroyans who charged through the smoke of the burning vehicles.

As soon as the orks turned to engage Basch's men, Captain Chelnikov of the Thirty-fifth Regiment's Second Platoon ordered his men up and into a full charge at the ork flanks. Colonel Kabanov ordered the rest of Fifth Company forward at the same moment, sure that their best hope of a swift victory lay in surrounding the orks on all sides and throwing everything at them. There was no time for anything else. Every second wasted brought Fifth Company closer to being stranded behind enemy lines.

If the Vostroyans had thought their earlier elimination of the augmetic ork leader would hamstring the orks in some way, they quickly found out just how wrong they were. The fighting was close-quarters and intense. At such close range, the orks didn't need accuracy to score with their oversized pistols and stubbers. Vostroyan men were blasted backwards as they tried to move in, their chests smashed open by the impact of the massive ork slugs.

All too quickly, the Vostroyan attempt to surround the orks degenerated into a chaotic melee as the orks surged forward to meet their attackers. The orks threw empty pistols aside to engage the Firstborn with cleavers, axes and clubs. The Vostroyans fought back, slipping under the ork blades to stab at them with bayonets. The Vostroyan officers carved their way through the orks with glowing power sabres. Each Firstborn had been trained well in the *ossbohk-vyar*, and their skills at hand-to-hand combat were outstanding, but the sheer power of the orks couldn't be denied. Where the crude ork weapons connected with flesh, men fell dead to the ground, their bodies broken open, spilling hot blood over the snow.

Commissar Karif's voice sounded over the vox, pouring words of inspiration into the ear of every man as he fought, inuring them to fear and panic with words from the *Treatis Elatii*. Even so, despite the Vostroyan prowess with blades, the orks were impossibly strong. The Vostroyan body count was rising at an unacceptable rate.

It was Father Olov, gripped by a berserker rage, who turned the tide of battle. He ran forward with the men of Lieutenant Vassilo's First Platoon the moment Colonel Kabanov ordered the charge. The priest swung his mighty eviscerator chainsword in broad circles above his head and it quickly became necessary for Vassilo's troopers to move away from him, leaving him to stand somewhat isolated against the orks that charged towards him. Olov laughed and his eyes took on a thousand-metre stare as he walked forward to meet his enemies. When he reached the press of ork bodies, he attacked with a savagery that rivalled that of the greenskins.

Again and again the purring eviscerator chewed its way through ork flesh and bone, sending massive bodies to the ground in so many pieces. Occasionally, the teeth of the blade bit into plates of ork armour and Olov had to physically wrestle the sword free, but his powerful body was more than up to the task. He forced his way forward, carving a wide channel through the greenskin mass.

The orks fought back with everything they had, but Olov's kills tipped the balance heavily against them. The greenskin numbers dropped rapidly. The Firstborn saw this and rallied behind Olov, surging forward in his wake, hewing orks apart with their bayonets.

'Keep the pressure up,' voxed Colonel Kabanov. 'We're breaking them.'

SEBASTEV STAYED CLOSE to Colonel Kabanov throughout the fighting, eager to protect him should he tire and falter, but it never happened. The colonel charged forward with the rest of the men, determined to fight by their side and urge them to a swift victory. Perhaps it was adrenaline, or perhaps it was zeal, but the colonel fought with a skill and speed that surprised Sebastev. In the heat of combat, he seemed not to have aged at all.

When the battle was won, however, Colonel Kabanov's age and condition settled back onto him with a vengeance. His breath rasped in his lungs and he was forced to excuse himself, moving back to the trees where Lieutenant Maro waited with his laspistol pressed to the head of the Danikkin prisoner.

Kabanov ordered Sebastev to take temporary command of the situation. It was imperative that everyone return to the vehicles as quickly as possible. Fifth Company had to be under way.

On the road, the last of the orks fell, hacked apart by three troopers from First Platoon, one of whom Sebastev recognised as Aronov.

Good to see you're still with us, scout, thought Sebastev.

'Captain?' said a voice at Sebastev's shoulder.

He turned and greeted Captain Chelnikov. The man was younger than Sebastev by a good few years. He was taller, too, but his body was lean and his cheeks were sallow. He looked as tired as Sebastev felt.

Of course he's tired, thought Sebastev. What must Grazzen be like right now?

Commissar Karif strode across the snow towards them, wiping the links of his chainsword on a rag and sheathing it in the ornate scabbard at his waist. The commissar's adjutant followed a few steps behind.

'The last ork is down,' said the commissar, 'and the men are trying to calm Father Olov. By the Throne, what a fighter!'

'Aye, commissar,' said Sebastev. 'Olov's mother should have borne him first. This, by the way, is Captain Chelnikov. He was sent to guide us into Grazzen.'

Commissar Karif acknowledged the man with a smile and a short bow. 'Then we'd best be on our way as soon as possible. What's the situation in Grazzen?'

The polite smile fell from Chelnikov's face as he said, 'Not good, commissar. When we left a few hours ago, the entire length of our defences was under heavy siege. I'm not talking about the usual rabble, either. This is the most organised attack I've ever seen from greenskins. They're clearly following a pre-established strategy.'

'What do you mean?' asked Sebastev.

'Well, captain, they began by launching a systematic series of probing assaults along our defensive line, fielding just enough of their force to make us reveal the extent of our strength at each defensive position. Subsequently, they launched concentrated attacks on the outposts farthest from our supply depots. Since then, they've pushed through our defensive line and converged on the city centre from several breaches. This side of the river is a warzone. Optimistic estimates have total ork domination of Grazzen's east bank in less than two hours from now.'

'And the pessimistic estimate?'

'A pessimist would tell you it's already too late, captain.'

'Which are you?' asked Commissar Karif.

Chelnikov shrugged. 'So long as the Emperor sits on the Golden Throne of Terra and cares about the men who serve Him, I'd say there's always hope. Wouldn't you? But the Thirty-fifth is hanging on by a thread.' He turned to Sebastev and added, 'The sooner you get that prisoner of yours across the bridge, the sooner my men can destroy the damned thing. Let's be on our way at once, captain. What's the status of your vehicles?'

'We lost one of our heavy transports, but we've another and three Chimeras intact.'

'It'll be cramped,' said Chelnikov. 'Some of my men will have to squeeze into your Pathcutter, but it's not far from here to Grazzen. We need to leave now.'

'As you say.'

Sebastev raised a finger to his vox-bead and transmitted orders to his platoon leaders. 'Get everyone back into the vehicles at once. I want the wounded on the Pathcutter. Bring their weapons. Leave nothing here that we might use when we hit the ork lines at Grazzen.'

As the affirmations of his officers came back to him, Sebastev turned in the direction of the trees. Colonel Kabanov stood with his back to a black trunk, coughing into a handkerchief. Lieutenant Maro stood close by, still covering the rebel prisoner, but looking at his colonel with obvious concern.

Just a little longer, colonel, thought Sebastev. Hang on until we reach Seddisvarr, damn it. The medicae will fix you up.

CHAPTER TWELVE

Day 688
Valles Carcavia – 10:21hrs, -22°C

As FIFTH COMPANY descended the north side of the Varanesian Peaks, Sebastev could feel powerful winds hammering against the side of Colonel Kabanov's Chimera. The mountains that rose up on either side of the Valles Carcavia channelled strong weather-fronts from the east, punishing the length of the valley with heavy snow, battering the city of Grazzen with storms.

Colonel Kabanov sat under two blankets, coughing wetly into another handkerchief. Lieutenant Maro seemed to have brought an endless supply of them from Korris.

Captain Chelnikov fumbled in his greatcoat pockets for something. After a moment, he smiled with relief and pulled out a sheaf of papers. 'Here they are: tactical maps of Grazzen. The situation may have radically changed in the few hours since I left, but these should give you some idea of where things stand.'

The men in the Chimera leaned forward in their seats, eyes on the maps that Chelnikov spread out on the floor of the vehicle.

Much like Nhalich, Grazzen was split in two, straddling the broad, black waters of the Solenne. Unlike Nhalich, however, Grazzen was a major city that had once been home to over two million Danikkin people. Two great bridges spanned the river, linking the eastern nation of Varanes with Theqis in the west.

Sebastev was looking at the southernmost of the two bridges, thinking it would be their quickest way through, when Chelnikov said, 'I'm afraid the south bridge was destroyed early this morning. The orks pushed up from the south-east edge of the city. Major Ushenko ordered the bridge blown before the orks gained access to the west bank.'

'Leaving only the north bridge intact,' said Colonel Kabanov as he wiped his mouth and returned the handkerchief to his pocket. 'From your map, captain, it looks like we've quite a distance to go once we hit the edge of the city.'

Chelnikov nodded. 'True, sir, but once we're back behind our own defensive lines your vehicles can ride the highway straight up the riverbank to the bridge. It hasn't been mined yet. We still need the highway to move our armour.'

'How much armour?' asked Sebastev.

'The Thirty-fifth has twelve tank platoons guarding all the main roads towards the bridge. General Vlastan sent out five further tank platoons to support us. They arrived last night. I wish I could believe the general would have offered that support in any case, but I'd say that decision had everything to do with ensuring the delivery of your package, captain.' As he said this, Chelnikov nodded towards the bound form of Patriot-Captain Gusseff. Once again, the man had been tied tightly in his seat.

'I don't know what's so important about that bastard, sir,' said Chelnikov, 'but Twelfth Army Command is going to great lengths to get him. It's not like General Vlastan to send armour detachments out from his precious defensive regiments at Seddisvarr. I can't tell you what it did for morale when our men saw all those Leman Russ tanks and Basilisk artillery platforms rolling over the bridge from the west.'

Sebastev glanced at Brammon Gusseff. The rebel sat staring into space as if in a trance. The more time Sebastev spent around the man, the more unsettled he became. From time to time, Gusseff's body would shake with muscular spasms that he seemed unable to control. It wasn't due to the cold, because the shakes were often localised to a single limb. Then there were the man's eyes, one moment, sharp and calculating, the next, filled with panic, flashing from left to right like those of a trapped animal.

'I don't know what's special about him either,' said Sebastev, 'but I'll tell you this: the man is damaged goods. There's something wrong with him, aside from being a traitor to the Imperium, I mean. He's suffering from some kind of mental problem.'

'He'll suffer a lot more than that when the interrogators start working on him,' spat Commissar Karif. The commissar had opted to ride in the colonel's Chimera on the way into Grazzen. Every available space was needed in the remaining Pathcutter now that Chelnikov's men had joined them.

'I suggest we focus on how we're going to get through the ork lines, gentlemen,' said Colonel Kabanov. 'The prisoner's worth is a matter for others to assess. All we need to know is that we've been tasked with his delivery. Captain Chelnikov, since you're familiar with the city, perhaps you've got some ideas?'

'Well, sir,' said Chelnikov, 'no matter where we try to push through, it isn't going to be easy. Major Ushenko has fought orks on a dozen worlds, sir. Before Danik's World he had a reputation as something of a specialist, as I'm sure you know.'

'I know it well,' replied Colonel Kabanov with a smile. 'I was lucky enough to fight alongside him during the skirmishes on Qietto and Merrand. Throne, that was a long time ago.'

'Major Ushenko says he hasn't seen greenskin leadership like this before, sir,' continued Chelnikov. 'We don't know who this ork warlord is, but he's unusually well organised and consistent.'

Chelnikov pointed to the eastern half of the city and said, 'When I left to rendezvous with your company, the orks had already encircled our forces, pressing us back towards the river, forcing us to give up most of the territory beyond the industrial belt. As you can see, this highway cuts through the city between the industrial and residential sectors; that's where we were holding when I left. The highway has proved an excellent killing ground. It's too broad for the orks to cross without getting chewed up by our heavy bolter nests, and their vehicles can't cover the open ground without taking fire from our tanks, Sentinels and lascannon batteries. The result is an impasse all along this road. I'm hoping it's still holding, but we're heavily outnumbered and, as I left, I heard that the orks were consolidating their forces for a big push. Major Ushenko believes the ork warlord will place himself at the head of a major charge. If that's true, it could provide a rare chance to eliminate him. Of course, Fifth Company has other matters to contend with. I apologise for digressing, colonel.'

Colonel Kabanov shook his head. 'Not at all, captain. I wish Major Ushenko good hunting. But, from what you've said, we'll have to push straight through the ork lines and cross the highway on our journey to the north bridge. Correct?'

'Correct, sir. It'll will leave our backs open to the orks, and it will put us directly in the firing zone of both sides, but Major Ushenko has planned a little welcoming party for us.'

'Just what kind of party are we talking about, captain?' asked Sebastev.

'We should follow this road here from the south-west edge of the city, heading north-east towards the bridge. There are ork infantry squads entrenched in buildings on either side of the road, facing north-east across the highway, engaged in a firefight with platoons from my company. What the orks don't know is that we have Basilisk artillery in the city parks here, here and here.'

Chelnikov pointed to open areas on the map not far from the Vostroyan defensive frontline. 'On receiving my signal, our Basilisks will begin shelling this part of the city. It should wipe out most of the ork infantry assembled in the area. If it doesn't kill them, it'll force them to keep their heads down, at the very least.'

Kabanov nodded for the young captain to go on.

'A moment later, the guns will stop firing. That will be our cue to race for the open highway. I emphasise the word race, gentlemen. We need to cross the killing ground at top speed. My comrades on the far side can only afford to hold their fire for a very short time. We can't give the orks a chance to cross and engage at close quarters. As for our crossing, I'm hoping the weather will cloak us from plain sight.'

'Once again,' said Colonel Kabanov, 'this damned winter is both a blessing and a curse.'

Chelnikov nodded. 'Once we're safely behind our own lines, my men and I will rejoin our company. You'll be assigned a guide to take you to the north bridge and get you across to Theqis as quickly as possible.'

Colonel Kabanov scrambled for his handkerchief again and began spluttering into it. Sebastev spoke on his behalf. 'Thank you, Captain Chelnikov. So long as the artillery barrage clears our path, it sounds like we've every chance of getting through.'

'By the Emperor's grace,' said Commissar Karif. 'Let us hope the balance of the fighting hasn't shifted in the time you've been away, captain.'

Chelnikov turned to face the commissar. 'I fear the same thing, but I can assure you that our orders from Seddisvarr left no doubt concerning the general's commitment to receiving your prisoner. My company has been ordered to lay down their lives, if necessary, to ensure that this man reaches Twelfth Army Command. You should have heard Major Ushenko's reaction to that. We've got men from the underhives in our company who'd never heard language like that.'

'I can understand the major's feeling well, captain,' said Sebastev. 'Not one of my troopers is stupid enough to believe the corridor back to Theqis would have been kept open for us if we hadn't secured the prisoner in Nhalich. The Emperor smiled on us that day.'

Colonel Kabanov had regained control of his breathing and asked his adjutant for a flask of hot ohx'. The smell of the salty drink filled the compartment as he drank. 'Throne, that's better,' he said. 'Would any of you like some?'

Sebastev felt he could use a mouthful, but before he could say so, Sergeant Samarov began shouting from the driver's seat of the Chimera.

'I have a visual on Grazzen,' he yelled over the noise of the engine. 'We're getting close, colonel. The city is… the city is burning, sir.'

AND SO IT was. As Fifth Company's vehicles rolled onto level ground at the bottom of the Varanesian foothills, reports started coming in from each of the drivers. The city of Grazzen was lit from end to end with raging yellow flames. The thick snowfall and the violence of the howling winds did nothing to put the fires out. The latter actually seemed to be fanning them and pushing them westward.

Kabanov's command Chimera pulled up at the front of the column. The rear hatch dropped and Sebastev clambered out, quickly followed by the others, all dressed for the freezing cold.

'What the hell...?' gasped Lieutenant Kuritsin at Sebastev's side.

'Emperor, no!' said Captain Chelnikov. 'Are we too late?'

'Very clever,' said Commissar Karif, 'incredibly so for a mere ork, don't you think?'

'I'm not sure I follow, commissar,' said Lieutenant Kuritsin.

Commissar Karif stood with his hands in his greatcoat pockets. 'It seems the ork leader needed a little something extra to motivate his troops. We all know that orks are rarely as stupid their reputation suggests. The ork infantry would've been reluctant to cross the highway without any cover. From what Captain Chelnikov has told us, the heavy bolters of the Thirty-Fifth were waiting to chew them up. Their losses would have been very heavy. So how does one force a reluctant army to charge an entrenched enemy? Excluding the employment of commissars, of course,' he said, smiling.

Colonel Kabanov nodded. 'Light fires behind them.'

Everyone gazed at the burning city. The flames lit the low bellies of the clouds with an angry orange glow.

'Big fires,' said Sebastev.

'Very effective,' said Commissar Karif with a nod. 'Not only does it push the troops forward en masse, but it cuts off any notion of retreat at the same time. I'd call that a very strong motivator indeed. I'd consider employing it myself under extreme circumstances.'

'The Thirty-Fifth must be getting hit hard out there,' said Chelnikov through gritted teeth.

'Perhaps, captain,' said Colonel Kabanov, 'but at the same time, the fires have pushed the orks into the open.

The highway you spoke of will be waist-deep in their dead, I'll wager. There's still everything to fight for.'

'What about us?' asked Lieutenant Kuritsin. 'What does this do to our plans?'

'We keep heading for the highway,' said Colonel Kabanov. 'If we can get through those fires safely in our transports, we can keep heading for our own lines along the same north-west road. We may have to fight through the ork lines without Basilisk support, but we'll be coming from the rear. The element of surprise is still with us.'

Sebastev couldn't share the White Boar's optimism.

The Thirty-Fifth will be retreating towards the north bridge even as we stand here, he thought. Prisoner or not, Major Ushenko will have orders to blow that bridge before the orks can gain a foothold in Theqis.

'Back to the Chimera,' ordered Colonel Kabanov. 'Time's running out.'

CHAPTER THIRTEEN

Day 688
East Grazzen – 12:07hrs, -19°C

THE VOSTROYAN OCCUPATION of Grazzen had at least kept the roads fairly clear of snow. The major arteries of the city were well-used. Fifth Company made good speed through the outskirts. Sebastev watched through a firing port in the side of the Chimera as isolated habs surrounded by open land gradually gave way to clustered buildings. Before long, the streets were crowded with tall tenements in the Danikkin style, their walls crumbling from two thousand years of climatic punishment.

Up ahead, getting closer with each passing second, a solid wall of flame roared and crackled as it danced in the gusting wind. In the light from the fire, Sebastev saw ork corpses littering every blood-slicked street and alleyway. The buildings on either side bore the scars of artillery bombardment and lascannon fire. The Chimera began to buck as it sped over bodies lying on the open road.

'Sergeant,' called Kabanov to his driver, 'give us all you've got. We've got to break through those flames at speed. I know they're well shielded, but I don't want our promethium tanks blowing up when we're right in the middle of that inferno.'

'Maximum speed, colonel,' replied the driver. 'I'll get us through it, sir.' The Chimera gunned forward, diving into the blazing heat and light.

Even through the heavy shielding of the Chimera's hull, with his cloak and hat removed and his greatcoat unfastened, Sebastev felt like he was being baked alive in an oven.

Sebastev doubted Sergeant Samarov could see where he was going. The flames were blindingly bright. He prayed they wouldn't get snagged or smash into a building before they'd cleared the far side of the blaze.

The other drivers reported that they too were racing across the burning ground. Just then, alarms sounded from the front of the vehicle. 'By Holy Terra,' shouted Samarov. 'It's as you feared, colonel. Much more of this and the tanks will blow.'

One of the Chimera's treads began to rattle, and Sebastev felt the vehicle pull to the left. There was a sudden decrease in speed. 'We've lost the left track,' shouted the driver. 'We're khekked!'

There was a deafening boom from below. Sebastev had time to yell, 'Brace yourselves!' before the Chimera flipped over and slammed to the ground on its back, the right track still running fast, clawing at thin air as if desperate to keep running.

'Throne above!' shouted Commissar Karif. 'Tell me we made it out of the flames.'

'The temperature is dropping in here,' said Lieutenant Maro. 'We must have just cleared them.'

Inside the rear of the Chimera, everyone hung upside down from their seats, saved from serious injury, perhaps even death, by their restraints. Sebastev looked over at Colonel Kabanov and saw blood running from the man's mouth and nose. He immediately hit his belt release, crashing to the ceiling, which had now become the floor, and said, 'Are you hurt, colonel? Answer me. Are you all right?'

Colonel Kabanov opened one eye, and then the other. He coughed, and a fine spray of blood misted the air. 'Damned stupid question, Sebastev,' he rasped. 'I'm hanging upside down. Of course I'm not all right.'

Sebastev moved forward to help the colonel. 'Maro, help me get him down.'

Lieutenant Maro hit his own belt release and dropped gracelessly to the floor, groaning as his head struck the metal. But he was up just as fast and moved to aid Sebastev in getting the colonel down. 'You work the belt release,' said Sebastev. 'I'll lift him down.'

Behind them, Commissar Karif, Lieutenant Kuritsin and Captain Chelnikov dropped to the floor with varying sounds of complaint. Maro worked the colonel's seatbelt off and Sebastev gently lifted the man down.

By the Emperor, thought Sebastev, he's so light. All his muscle, all his vitality… This world has stripped it from him. If the Twelfth Army ever pulls out of this campaign, I'll take some consolation in the knowledge that the Imperial Navy will bomb the damned planet to dust.

Kabanov began shouting as soon as his feet hit the floor. 'Hell blast and damn! I'm not some infant to be put over your shoulder, Sebastev. Unhand me, man. The indignity of it, by the Throne!'

Sebastev stepped back, his eyes fastened to the blood that streaked the colonel's face and clothes. 'You're bleeding, sir.'

'There's nothing wrong with me,' barked Colonel Kabanov, challenging the others with his intense stare. 'I'm the White Boar and I'm still in command of this regiment. You'll damned well do as I say, all of you.'

'Orders, sir,' said Lieutenant Maro. 'What are your orders?'

'Get the bloody prisoner down for a start,' snapped Kabanov, pointing a shaky finger at Gusseff. The man hung from the upturned seat into which he was still firmly strapped. Gusseff didn't even look at them. He simply sat upside down, his legs dangling in front of his chest, his expression as blank as a servitor.

'I'll get him down,' said Lieutenant Kuritsin. He stepped over with his knife drawn and cut the prisoner's ropes. Sebastev would have let the rebel drop to the ground, but that wasn't Kuritsin's way.

Do you pity him, Rits, wondered Sebastev? After what he did at Nhalich? Broken-minded or not, this man turned from the Emperor's light. How can anyone pity him?

Kuritsin looked up at Sebastev, almost as if he'd heard the captain's thoughts. 'If we're beyond the flames, sir, we'd better get moving. For all we know, the orks might have noticed us already.'

Colonel Kabanov spoke. 'Get your kit on, all of you. I want that hatch open at once. Sergeant Samarov, join us outside please.'

There was no answer from the colonel's driver. 'Sergeant, did you hear me?'

Sebastev moved forward towards the driver's compartment. What he saw made his shoulders drop. Sergeant Samarov's blackened body hung upside down. Small tongues of flame still fed on his flesh and clothes. The plex window of the forward view-port had cracked and broken in the heat of the crossing. Even while he was burning alive, the Vostroyan driver had pressed on, guiding their Chimera through to the other side. Sebastev had never heard the man scream once. He had died like a true Firstborn, and he had saved them.

'Samarov is gone. If we make it though this, I want him put forward for the Honorifica Imperialis.'

Colonel Kabanov's jaw clenched as he struggled with his sadness. Samarov had served as his driver for twelve years. Rather than voice his sorrow, he faced Sebastev and said, 'Open the rear hatch please, captain. Maro, help me to clean this blood off my face, would you? The troopers mustn't see me like this.'

'Yes, sir,' said Maro.

Sebastev stepped to the hatch and struck the rune that should have released it. Nothing happened. The rune wasn't even glowing. The Chimera had lost all electrical power. He'd have to work the hatch free manually. He put all his strength into the effort, throwing his weight against the manual release lever. The metal lever groaned and started to bend, but the locking bolts didn't move. The hatch was stuck tight.

'What's wrong, captain?' asked Commissar Karif. He lent his strength to the effort, but the lever simply bent a little more. 'I hope to Terra the damn thing isn't welded shut on us. Does anyone know exactly where on this door the locking bolts are?'

Lieutenant Maro stepped forward. 'There are two, commissar,' he said, 'here and here. Both are well shielded and made of titanium. If you're thinking of blowing your way out, I would remind you that any type of blast will almost certainly kill most, if not all of us.'

'I was hardly suggesting that, lieutenant,' said the commissar sourly. 'I'm not entirely sure that my chainsword could manage the task, but couldn't a power sabre slice through the bolts? Would anyone care to try, or are we to sit in this metal coffin until the orks cut us out?'

Sebastev immediately drew his power sabre and hit the activation rune on its hilt. The blade hummed to life, glowing and crackling with dangerous energy.

'Move back, gentlemen,' he said as he pressed the point of the blade to the seam where the hatch met the frame of the Chimera and pushed forward. The machine-spirit of the power sabre protested, changing its hum to an angry buzz as it slowly carved a path through the thick metal. Smoke drifted up and sparks showered the toes of Sebastev's boots.

'May the machine-spirit of this great vehicle forgive us,' said Lieutenant Kuritsin.

After a few moments, Sebastev lurched forward suddenly. His blade had punched straight through to the outside of the vehicle, severing the first of the bolts. The sword gave a last loud crack as the charge cell in its hilt died.

'That's one of the bolts cut,' he said. 'I'll have to swap cells before I tackle the other.'

'Here,' said Lieutenant Maro, 'let me take care of the last one.' He stepped forward with his own blade drawn, hit the activation rune, and began carving his way through.

Sebastev moved back and switched the cell in his sword. Maro gave a triumphant laugh a few moments later as his blade sliced through to the far side of the hatch. The last bolt was severed. 'Let's get out of here,' he said. He pushed the hatch open and climbed out.

As Sebastev followed, he saw that the remnants of Fifth Company had taken up defensive positions around the colonel's ruined Chimera. The crump of artillery echoed down the street. The fighting sounded heavy in the north of the city. Sergeant Basch and Lieutenant Tarkarov stepped forward to greet him. Father Olov, standing with men from Second Platoon, smiled over at him with obvious relief and bowed his head in thanks to the Emperor.

'Good to see you're all right, captain,' said Tarkarov. 'We considered using one of the melta-guns as a last resort, but it might have cooked you all. How is the colonel?'

Sebastev turned to see Colonel Kabanov clamber out from the hatch. Maro had made sure there was no trace of blood on the colonel's face, but his clothes still bore telltale stains.

'The colonel is... fine,' said Sebastev. 'He's eager to get us over that bridge. What's our status?'

Commissar Karif moved past them, calling for his adjutant. Trooper Stavin had been riding in the last Pathcutter with most of the other troopers. Now he dashed forward to stand before his commissar, relief plain on his face.

Lieutenant Tarkarov dropped his gaze as he said, 'One of the Chimeras didn't make it through, sir.' His voice was heavy with sorrow, close to breaking as he added, 'It's Fifth Platoon, sir.'

Lieutenant Kuritsin's voice sounded from over Sebastev's shoulder. 'Captain,' he said, 'Lieutenant Severin is asking to speak with your, sir. He… he doesn't have long. Vox-channel delta.'

Sebastev keyed the appropriate channel and said, 'This is Captain Sebastev. What the hell is going on, Severin?'

Severin's voice, when it came, was strangled as if he fought back screams of agony. 'Caught on wreckage, sir,' he voxed, 'tracks mangled. We're really cooking in here.'

'Emperor above,' roared Sebastev at the lieutenants standing close by. 'We've got to get those men out of there!'

'We're in deep, sir,' voxed Severin, 'pulling pins now. Grenades will be quicker. Make it easier on the… just wanted to tell you, sir…'

'Severin!' shouted Sebastev over the vox.

'And Colonel Kabanov… honour to serve…'

'Severin! Throne damn it, man!'

There was no answer. A muffled boom sounded from somewhere within the wall of flames. The vox at Severin's end went dead. Sebastev roared into the air.

That's no way for heroes to die, he raged to himself. Grey Lady, grant me dire vengeance on the orks. By the Golden Throne, I'll visit such a slaughter on them…

All around, the men of Fifth Company shifted uncomfortably. They'd heard Sebastev's half of the voxed exchange. With the absence of Severin's Chimera, it wasn't hard to work out what had happened. There were troopers among them who belonged to Severin's platoon. They'd come across the flames in the Pathcutter transport with most of the others. As the full weight of the situation struck them, they looked ready to drop. Sebastev knew how they felt.

That was when Colonel Kabanov stepped up to his side and laid a hand on his shoulder. 'Focus, captain,' he said quietly. 'Remember what I told you: the time for mourning comes after the battle. We have to get across that bridge. Time's running out on us. Don't let the sacrifices of brave men go to waste.'

The colonel stepped forward and addressed the men. 'Stand strong, Fifth Company. We've got a hard fight ahead of us. I want you organised into squads at once and ready to move out on my command. We've got a mission to complete for the honour of the regiment.'

As the men jumped to it, the colonel returned to Sebastev's side and ushered Captain Chelnikov forward. 'How far from here, captain?' he asked.

'Half an hour if we double time it, sir,' replied Chelnikov, 'much more if we meet resistance. And trust me, sir, we will meet resistance.'

'The way I'm feeling,' growled Sebastev, 'I hope we do. I'll soak my hands in ork blood before we're done, Throne help me.'

Colonel Kabanov shook his head. 'We all feel the same, captain, but it's a feeling you'll just have to get a damned grip on. Our sole objective is to deliver Gusseff. This regiment's revenge will not interfere. My word is law on the subject. Make sure you understand it well.'

Sebastev held the colonel's blistering gaze as he nodded.

'Good,' said Colonel Kabanov. 'Are all our men assembled? This is it?'

'This is it, sir,' said Lieutenant Kuritsin. 'We've got sixty-three men, excluding the wounded on the top deck of the Pathcutter and the survivors of Captain Chelnikov's squad.'

'Sixty-three,' replied the colonel. 'By Terra, let's not lose any more.' Though the bloodstains were bright on his golden armour and the collar of his greatcoat, he seemed to have regained control of his breathing. His coughing had stopped for the moment. 'And the vehicles, lieutenant? The Chimeras?'

Kuritsin shook his head. 'The heat caused irreparable damage to their treads. Ours is the only one that suffered a fuel tank incident, but the others are practically fused to the road. The Pathcutter is still operational, but it suffered heavy damage. It can manage little more than a crawl. Its width restricts it to travelling the open highway. We'll be much faster on foot, but that doesn't help our wounded.'

'By the saints, that's grim,' sighed the colonel. 'We need all the speed we can get. I want all able-bodied men moving forward on foot. We can't slow ourselves down. The Pathcutter will just have to lag behind. If we reach the bridge and get the traitor across, perhaps there'll be time to hold the crossing open for our wounded. It doesn't give them much hope, I know, but I'd say it's the best we can do for them. Captain Chelnikov, follow Lieutenant Tarkarov over to First Platoon and guide them out, please. The others will follow.'

'At once, sir,' said Chelnikov.

As the other officers moved off, the colonel shot out a hand and stopped Sebastev. 'Listen to me, Grigorius,' he said in a low voice. 'Keep it together. Do you understand me? I know you're eager to punish the orks, but the mission comes first. You need to understand that. You'll be in full command soon.'

'I'll do what's needed, colonel,' said Sebastev. 'Let's just get you to Seddisvarr, so the medicae can restore you. If you need me to step in for a while, that's fine, but it'll be temporary, I assure you.'

Kabanov shook his head. 'You never change, do you, Grigorius? I guess that's why Dubrin chose you: stubborn to a bloody fault.'

Before Sebastev could respond, the colonel moved off, calling for his adjutant to get the rebel prisoner up off his knees and marching alongside the others.

CHAPTER FOURTEEN

Day 688
East Grazzen – 15:02hrs, -21°C

THE SURVIVING MEN of Fifth Company crouched in the lee of a crumbling hab-stack, checking their weapons, and fixing bayonets to their lasgun barrels in preparation for the imminent order to push forward. An icy wind whipped along the street, tugging at their tall hats and the tails of their red greatcoats. Captain Sebastev peered out from behind a pile of rubble that had once been the building's south-east corner and scanned the road ahead.

He'd never seen so many orks in his life. The streets were absolutely teeming with them, an impossible press of massive green bodies waving every conceivable type of blade or blunt weapon in the air. Tattered banners bearing the Venomhead clan crest whipped in the icy winds. Many of the largest orks wore trophies from their victory at Barahn: grisly necklaces made of human skulls that seemed impossibly small compared with the heads of the monsters that wore them. Some of the largest orks boasted bulky augmetic limbs that ended in spinning blades or gleaming pincers. The roaring and jabbering of the terrible horde threatened to drown out all but the loudest sounds of Vostroyan artillery and gunfire.

Captain Chelnikov had led Fifth Company up through the streets, heading north-east towards the bridge with all due haste, but the closer they got to their goal, the harder it became to move without drawing unwanted attention. So far, they'd been lucky. Ork aggression was utterly focused on the enemy directly in front of them. The men and machines of the Thirty-Fifth Regiment bore the brunt of the ork attack with bravery and resilience, but they wouldn't last much longer. They were being pressed back further and further with little hope of slowing the orks' forward momentum.

If Fifth Company hoped to gain the bridge before the orks forced its destruction, they'd have to break through the enemy lines from the rear and move ahead of the greenskin advance, and they'd have to do it soon.

As his men crouched in positions of hard cover, Colonel Kabanov moved forward to consult with Sebastev. 'This is it, captain. We have their backs. If we can break through the line up ahead, we've got a solid shot at making the bridge in time to cross.'

'I can't advocate a simple charge, colonel,' said Sebastev. 'The moment they notice us, all the orks in the vicinity will turn to engage. They always fixate on the nearest target.'

'There must be thousands of them,' said Lieutenant Kuritsin. 'If I can raise a nearby Basilisk on the vox, perhaps I can arrange some kind of artillery support. That would go a long way to clearing our path. Captain Chelnikov might be able to help with that.'

'It's worth a try, lieutenant,' said Colonel Kabanov. 'Grab Chelnikov and get to work. He's with Lieutenant Tarkarov's men. As for you, Sebastev, I want you to recommend a man to take responsibility for the prisoner. It may be that none of us get through the ork lines alive, but if even the slightest gap opens up, I want our prisoner rushed through it and carried over that bridge. If you've got a fast man that you trust, make him known to me now. Lieutenant Maro will continue to look after the traitor's case.'

Sebastev didn't have to think on it for long. There, by the far corner of the building, talking quietly with Sergeant Basch, was the man he had in mind.

'That would be Aronov, sir,' Sebastev said with a nod towards the big scout. 'He's particularly capable.'

The colonel voxed a summons over to Aronov, and the scout jogged over to their position. After a smart salute, he crouched beside his superior officers. 'What can I do for you, sirs?'

'The captain here has rather good things to say about you, trooper,' said the colonel. 'He seems to think you might be the man for certain special duties.'

Aronov grinned. 'The captain's a famous liar, sir.'

Colonel Kabanov grinned back. 'Is he, indeed? Well, he'd better not be lying this time, because I'm about to give you a very important job. This is absolutely top priority, trooper. I need you to guard the Danikkin prisoner. If you see an opening in the ork lines during the fighting, I want you to take the prisoner and run for the bridge. This man,' the colonel indicated Gusseff with a thumb, 'must make it to the west side of Grazzen. We're talking about duty and honour here, trooper, not just that of Fifth Company's, but of the entire regiment. Are we clear?'

Aronov nodded. 'Like good rahzvod, sir. How much trouble is he likely to be? Is he suicidal? Will he try to run during the fighting?'

It was Sebastev who answered. 'He's been strangely compliant since leaving Nhalich. I don't think he wants to die. So, no, I don't expect him to give you trouble. You can knock him out and carry him if you think it necessary, but no broken bones and no permanent damage.'

'You take all the fun out of life, sir.'

'I know I do, trooper,' replied Sebastev, 'it's in my job description. Now grab the prisoner and get ready. We'll be push–'

Vox-chatter cut Sebastev off mid-sentence. It was Commissar Karif. 'By the Throne! We've been spotted. Ork warbikes coming in from the east at high speed. Get to cover, damn it. I need heavy weapons over here, now! Colonel Kabanov, Squad Grodolkin is under heavy fire. The orks on the street ahead are turning, sir. They've noticed us.'

The commissar had attached himself to Squad Grodolkin and taken up position guarding the company's east flank. The sound of ork stubbers came from that direction.

'Don't get cut off from the rest of the company, commissar,' voxed Colonel Kabanov urgently. 'Move this way. We have to hold together.'

'It's too late, sir,' voxed Commissar Karif. 'My squad is pinned down. The orks are spilling down the streets on either side. Wait! I think I see a way out, sir. I'm going to try something.'

'What are you going to do?' voxed Sebastev. 'Commissar?'

There was no answer.

'Warp damn and blast,' spat Colonel Kabanov, 'we've lost him.'

'Squad Grodolkin, respond,' voxed Sebastev. 'Anyone from Squad Grodolkin, respond at once.'

Again, there was no answer.

'Khek! It'll be a matter of seconds before those orks come round that corner, colonel. We fight or die.' Sebastev pulled his bolt pistol from its holster and drew his power sabre from its sheath. 'Rits,' he shouted, 'where's the damned artillery barrage?'

Kuritsin looked over. Captain Chelnikov was busy talking into the lieutenant's back-mounted vox-caster. 'All the

Thirty-Fifth's vox-channels are choked with traffic, sir. We're having trouble getting through to anyone. Captain Chelnikov is trying the command channel, but the weather is cutting our range.'

Orks appeared on the road that ran east, just a score of them at first, boots pounding the black rockcrete as they raced towards Fifth Company with their cleavers held high. Then, behind them, hundreds more spilled out onto the road from the adjoining streets.

'Engage the enemy!' bellowed Colonel Kabanov, standing to unsheathe his own power sabre. In his right hand, his hellpistol cracked and an ork at the front of the charge tumbled to the ground, headless. 'Try to press north. Don't be drawn away from our objective. We must gain the bridge at all costs!'

'For the White Boar!' added Sebastev. His men lifted their weapons into the air and roared. Then Fifth Company broke from cover, rushing north up the street to meet the massed orks. The enemy on their east flank came straight on, and soon Fifth Company was surrounded, fighting desperately for their lives in a sea of massive green bodies.

To Sebastev, this looked like it might be the end of them.

But it's not over yet, he told himself. If we fall here, we'll sell our lives dear, by Terra. Maybe, just maybe, we can open a path for Aronov and the bastard rebel.

As THE ORKS charged down the street, Karif looked around desperately for the best position of hard cover he could find. Instead, he spotted a dark crevasse in the road, a tear in the rockcrete surface that had probably been caused by a Vostroyan Earthshaker round during the Thirty-Fifth Regiment's attempted defence of the town. The impact on the street had punched a hole straight through to the sewers beneath. Inky blackness had never looked so appealing to Karif.

'Sergeant Grodolkin,' he shouted. 'We're going down that hole at once. Choose three men to cover the descent of the others.'

So Grodolkin had chosen, quickly and calmly, and three men had stayed above, fighting to their last breaths so that the rest of their squad could escape into the sewers.

The orks hadn't followed. In part, Karif was relieved, but he was also concerned. It suggested to him that they'd spotted Colonel Kabanov and the rest of the company and had opted to engage them instead. He offered a quick prayer for the safety of those men as he led Squad Grodolkin along the tunnel, trusting his instincts, secure in the knowledge that his training on Terrax had prepared him for almost anything.

He tried his vox-bead again, but communication with the other squads had been lost the moment he'd leapt into the hole.

Sergeant Grodolkin walked beside him in silence, radiating intense anger over the deaths of good men. The sergeant was big and broad shouldered, and had lost an eye at some point in his past. It was difficult for Karif to imagine that this dangerous man was as respected for his beautiful paintings of the Emperor's saints as for his combat prowess and solid, squad leadership abilities.

'Those men died bravely,' said Karif. 'We'll honour them at the proper time.'

Grodolkin didn't respond.

The tunnels were dark, and still stank of sewage despite long years of disuse. Trooper Stavin walked on Karif's left, carrying a promethium lamp in one hand and his lasgun in the other. The orange glow of the lamp threw dancing shadows on the curved black walls of the tunnel.

The heavy boots of Grodolkin's squad, just six men left, caused echoes that raced ahead of them into the darkness. Karif cursed the noise, and hissed at them to step lightly. As they pressed forward, however, the sounds of battle overhead became louder and covered the noise of their passage. Tanks and artillery platforms could be heard booming and rumbling through the metres of rockcrete between the tunnel's ceiling and the streets above.

'I hope the others are all right,' whispered a trooper behind Grodolkin.

'I'm more worried about us,' replied another in hushed tones. 'They've got the White Boar with them. He'll get them through. But I've never liked tunnels.'

Sergeant Grodolkin grunted and turned. 'Shut the khek up, you two, or the commissar will execute you on the spot for poor discipline.'

Karif turned and scowled. 'Listen to your sergeant. I'll cut the head off any man that gives us away to the foe. Is that clear?'

'Rahzvod,' said one.

'What?'

'Rahzvod, sir,' he repeated. 'It's clear.'

The sound of metal clanking on stone echoed down the tunnel towards them. By reflex, every man dropped into a crouch with his lasgun raised. Nothing happened. After a moment, Karif ushered them cautiously forward. Soon, they could hear scratching and chittering sounds from up ahead.

'Douse that khekking lamp, trooper,' said Grodolkin.

Stavin hesitated only long enough for Karif to say, 'Do it, Stavin.'

When the lamp was shuttered, it became clear that there was another light source ahead. At a bend in the tunnel just a hundred metres away, the stone walls glowed softly with a pulsing light that suggested a naked flame.

Karif didn't dare speak out loud. Instead, he signalled the others to prepare for an engagement.

Remember your Anzion, Daridh, he told himself. Remember what you read in the man's books. Orks can't see in the dark any more than we can. The noise up ahead doesn't sound like your average orks. They're not sneaky or subtle, but it may be ork stealthers like those we encountered in Korris. What in the warp are they doing up there?

The Vostroyan squad numbered nine men, including Stavin, Sergeant Grodolkin and himself. Karif decided their best chance to minimise casualties lay in a full and sudden frontal assault, catching the enemy right in the middle of whatever business they were about.

Using hand-signed battle language, he communicated to Grodolkin and his men that he believed the sounds to be coming from ork saboteurs. With more gestures, he readied the men to rush forward as one, firing on the foe as soon as they were within sight.

The Vostroyans nodded their understanding and moved into assault formation under the direction of Sergeant Grodolkin. Stavin stayed beside his commissar. He put away his lamp and gripped his lasgun tight in both hands. His bayonet was fixed securely under the weapon's long barrel.

Karif's heart quickened and adrenaline coursed through him, lending extra power and speed to his limbs. His laspistol and chainsword felt reassuringly weighty in his hands.

Who knows how many there are, he thought? Or what we're walking into? The men are ready. There's no point speculating. We attack!

He gave the signal to charge. Squad Grodolkin surged forward along the bend in the tunnel, holding formation as they ran. Before them, a great mob of gretchin, scores of them, spun at the sudden noise, freezing for a moment in absolute surprise.

Squad Grodolkin opened fire immediately. Lasguns cracked with uncommon sharpness in the enclosed confines of the sewers. Beams slashed out, cutting green bodies into smoking pieces. The echoes in the tunnel made it seem as if thousands of Vostroyans were attacking at once.

As the screams of dying xenos filled the air, the gretchin snapped out of their shock and launched into a retaliatory action. But it was too late. Scores of them fell howling as las-bolts carved deep black wounds in their flesh. It was a massacre. The gretchin had been so intent on their task that they were utterly unprepared to defend themselves.

In the light of the gretchin torches, Karif realised with a start just what their task had been.

'Stop firing!' he yelled at the top of his voice. 'Hold your fire, Throne damn it!'

Stavin must have seen it too, because he joined the commissar, his high voice cutting through the noise as he yelled: 'Hold your fire!'

The surviving gretchin, of which there were just over twenty, began firing back. They hefted their heavy pistols with two hands and loosed shots off towards Grodolkin's men. But the Vostroyans saw the reason for the commissar's order. They saw for themselves how close they'd come to disaster. There, fixed to the ceiling overhead, was a mass of ork explosives. Long fuses dangled all the way to the floor, waiting to be fixed to the timing device that lay in the middle of a ring of fresh, green corpses.

A single stray shot, thought Karif, and we'd be dead already.

'Bayonets,' yelled Sergeant Grodolkin. 'Engage at close quarters.'

The gretchin fired again and again as the Vostroyans rushed forward, but the weight of their pistols made it difficult for them to aim properly. Even so, given the volume of fire they loosed at the charging men, it was inevitable that some shots would find their marks. The Vostroyans' cherished carapace armour saved their lives, absorbing most of the impacts from those shots, even at close range.

Only two of Grodolkin's men went down in the hail of bullets. Karif was right behind one of them when it happened. The luckless man was thrown backwards, lifted clear off his feet with his head demolished. Before the responsible gretchin could reload, both Karif and Stavin raced forward, closing the distance at a sprint. Stavin pierced the creature's belly with a thrust of his bayonet, but the gretchin lashed out with its long arms at the same time. Fingernails like talons cut deep red gashes in the adjutant's left cheek.

As Stavin reeled from the blow, Karif swept his chainsword up and lopped off one of the creature's arms. He immediately followed with a savage kick to its bleeding belly. The kick was a blur, launched with a speed and technique developed over long years of daily training on Terrax. The gretchin was blasted backwards, howling pitifully until its skull cracked against the tunnel wall behind it.

As it slumped unconscious to the tunnel floor, Karif turned to his adjutant. The young trooper was shaking with anger and adrenaline. 'Finish it off, Stavin. No mercy for the Emperor's foes. Kill it.'

Stavin stepped forward wordlessly and ran his bayonet through the unconscious creature again and again, driven by rage and shock, fear and pain.

That's the stuff, Stavin, thought Karif. Mercy has no place in a soldier's arsenal. I told you back in Nhalich, remember? The graveyards are full of merciful men.

High-pitched alien screams filled the tunnel as Grodolkin's troopers exterminated the last of the gretchin. The stunted greenskins were no match for Vostroyan Firstborn in hand-to-hand combat.

'Damn, but that was a close thing, commissar,' said Sergeant Grodolkin, stepping up to Karif's side. The big sergeant noticed that Stavin was still ramming his blade into the lifeless xenos corpse. 'That's enough, trooper. It's dead. Save your energy for the next one you meet.'

Stavin stepped back, his chest rising and falling with deep breaths.

'If a single las-bolt had struck the explosives, sergeant,' said Karif with a gesture at the bomb clusters on the ceiling, 'we'd have met a very noisy and, in my opinion, early death.'

'Why here?' wondered Grodolkin.

'I suspect we're very near our destination, sergeant. We must try to find an exit hatch nearby. There must be a ladder leading to a manhole cover. I can hear the rushing waters of the Solenne, so the bridge can't be far. The gretchin were trying to bring down the road.'

Grodolkin nodded. 'Meaning we might just be behind Vostroyan lines?'

'More likely, we're right under them.'

As if to confirm this, the tunnel shook with a mighty boom. Karif said, 'The orks must be closing on the bridge even as we speak, sergeant. We've got to get a move on.'

Another blast shook the tunnel. One of Grodolkin's troopers shouted for his sergeant's attention. Karif and Stavin followed Grodolkin over to the trooper and discovered that the man had found a series of steel rungs set into the stone wall. At the top of the ladder there was a manhole cover, their way out of the sewers.

'Outstanding,' said Karif. 'Sergeant, order your men to carefully dismantle the gretchin explosives. We don't want any accidents after all we've achieved down here.'

'Aye, commissar,' said Grodolkin. He turned and began barking orders to his men.

'As for me,' said Karif, 'I could do with a bit of fresh air.'

CHAPTER FIFTEEN

Day 688
East Grazzen – 15:37hrs, -22°C

THE SKY ABOVE was dark and heavy as Fifth Company charged straight towards the greenskin horde. The churning black clouds matched the moment well. Sebastev bore little real hope that they'd make it through. Mere men, even soldiers as brave and skilful as the men of this company, couldn't hope to survive for long in close combat against enemies as powerful and savage as the Venomhead orks.

Colonel Kabanov had ordered the men into a fighting wedge with heavy weapons spread evenly along the line. Sebastev placed himself near his colonel with Lieutenant Kuritsin at his side. Father Olov was nearby, as was Lieutenant Maro. The other officers placed themselves by the surviving men of their own platoons. Leading the thirty-nine troopers that remained, the officers of Fifth Company charged up the street with weapons blazing, eager to fell as many of the enemy as they could before the two sides crashed together.

The orks ran, too, roaring and laughing as they hefted their blades into the air. They loved nothing more than a bloody battle at close quarters. This was a fight on their terms. For Fifth Company, there were simply no alternatives. If the Emperor was with them, there would be an opening somewhere. Some of them had to make it through. Trooper Aronov ran just a few metres off to Sebastev's right. The rebel prisoner was slung across the big scout's shoulder, hanging limp. Aronov had immediately knocked him unconscious rather than wrestle him forward during the fight. The prisoner was a terrible burden on Aronov. His fighting would be seriously hampered. Still, Sebastev was sure he'd made the right choice. If anyone could get Brammon Gusseff across the ork line, it would be the big scout.

'Vostroya!' shouted Colonel Kabanov as he charged, firing at the closest orks with his powerful antique hellpistol. Adrenaline and desperation had overcome his ill health, at least for the moment. His every blazing shot sent another smoking ork corpse down under the feet of its fellows, but there were just too many. Ten kills, twenty, thirty, it seemed to make little real difference to the wall of green bodies.

'For Vostroya!' yelled the men, pouring fire ahead of them as the distance closed. The buildings on either side of the street lit up with the intensity of the Vostroyan lasfire. The air echoed with cracks, and became thick with the smell of scorched ork flesh. Troopers Mitko and Pankratov, both of whom wielded plasma guns, loosed devastating rounds that were almost too bright to look at. The orks were packed so close that every blast of superheated plasma obliterated dozens of them.

Troopers Kovo, Grishna and Tzunikov sent burning streams of promethium out towards the enemy, scorching scores of them to death and forcing the others back. But the press of bodies was so tight that the greenskins had nowhere to go. In those first few seconds of the battle, the toll taken by the flamers was gratifyingly heavy.

Fifth Company had already lost most of their heavy bolters on the journey. Only a single man armed with such a weapon remained among them. Trooper Kashr strafed the orks with deadly explosive shells, killing scores of them as he ran forward. The weapon's rate of fire was incredible but, all too quickly, his ammunition was spent. He dropped the heavy gun to the ground and pulled his sidearm from its holster, drawing his knife at the same time.

A part of Sebastev's mind processed all of these details, assessing where best to place his own shots, and where the ork line was thinning, if at all. His bolt pistol barked again and again, and thick ork skulls detonated with sprays of blood, brain matter and bone fragments. But it was Sebastev's power sabre, gripped tightly in his right hand, that he knew would do the most damage.

As orks and men crashed together with bone crunching force, Sebastev launched himself into a sweeping series of strokes from the twenty-third form of the *ossbohk-vyar*. The Vostroyan combat art had taught him to target his enemy's extremities first, removing their offensive capabilities at the first opportunity. The orks that came towards him swinging their crude weapons quickly lost their hands. They fought on, attempting to kick out at him, or batter him with the bleeding stumps of their wrists. That was the nature of orks. They seldom fell from anything but a lethal strike to the brain or to certain vital organs, but by stripping them of their weapons, he rendered them far less of an immediate threat. Disarmed in this way, the orks in question could be dispatched far more easily, though they were still frustratingly tough.

As Colonel Kabanov's fighting wedge bit deep into the ork line, the colonel called out for his men to change formation, to form a tight circle with their backs to the centre.

With the orks closing around them, the Vostroyans arranged themselves into a bristling wall of bayonets and power sabres. They fired las-bolt after las-bolt into the faces of the orks that pressed forward, but they were truly surrounded, and in the most desperate fight of their lives.

THE MANHOLE COVER was frozen shut. It may as well have been welded shut given the incredible hold the ice had on it. Even the powerful figure of Sergeant Grodolkin couldn't push it off, though he slammed his armoured shoulder against it again and again. After a moment, Commissar Karif called the man back down to the bottom of the ladder.

'Is there a flamer in your squad, sergeant?'

'There was, commissar,' said Grodolkin with obvious remorse, 'but he stayed behind to cover our escape.'

'Well, I suppose there are a few other options available to us. The one that immediately springs to mind would be lasguns.'

'Lasguns, commissar?'

'They won't damage the manhole cover itself, but if we fire enough las-bolts at its underside, I think they should provide more than enough heat to melt the ice that's fixing it in place, don't you?'

'Easy enough to find out,' said Grodolkin. He called three of his men forward and ordered them to stand at the bottom of the ladder, firing vertically at the disk of black metal above their heads. After a moment, Karif called for them to stop.

'That ought to do it,' he said as he gripped the first of the rungs and hauled himself up towards the exit. At the top of the ladder, he reached out a gloved hand and checked the temperature of the cover's underside. It was still warm, but no longer scalding hot. He braced his shoulder against it and pushed.

As the cover lifted, the pale light of the winter afternoon washed over him. The cold wind rushed past him and down into the tunnel. With his head above ground again, his left ear immediately filled with a stream of vox-chatter. There were reports of Leman Russ tanks being crippled by ork anti-vehicle squads. Platoons across the city were desperately trying to fall back towards the bridge, but the orks had already cut them off in many places. Some of the vox-traffic consisted of little more than screams that cut off sharply.

Karif pushed one more time and heaved the heavy manhole cover from his back. As he pulled himself out of the hole, he listened hard for any mention of Fifth Company. To his incredible relief, he managed to catch the voice of Colonel Kabanov ordering his men to fight hard for the glory of Vostroya and the Imperium.

They're still alive, he thought. There's still time to help them.

'Quickly,' he called down to Grodolkin's squad. 'Follow me up.'

Something very sharp and cold slid into position by his jugular. Karif suppressed his reflex to turn.

'Who the khek are you?' asked a harsh voice from behind him. The owner of the voice kept the edge of his blade pressed tight to Karif's neck.

'I am Commissar Daridh Ahl Karif of the Emperor's own Commissariat. I'm attached to the Vostroyan Sixty-Eighth Infantry Regiment's Fifth Company. And, while I applaud you for both your vigilance and your suspicious nature, if you don't get that bloody bayonet away from my neck, I'll use it in your execution. Is that understood, trooper?'

The blade withdrew from his neck immediately.

'That's better,' said Karif as he stood and turned. 'Now move back while my men exit the tunnel. And get someone in charge over here now. I'll need to speak to him at once.'

GOOD MEN FELL screaming behind Kabanov and the sound filled him with rage, adding speed and power to the strokes of his sword. His hellpistol was empty and there was no time to reload. For every ork that went down, another stepped forward swinging wildly with club or blade. Instead, Kabanov focused on his sword craft, letting his power sabre become an extension of his body and his will. The ground at his feet was slick with freezing blood, slippery with greenskin viscera. The footing was bad, but Kabanov had spent his whole life training for fights such as this. As old as he was, he still retained some of the balance and agility that had made him a regimental combat champion so many years ago. The orks weren't quite as graceful. One slipped on the entrails of its fellows and dropped to one knee. Kabanov lunged forward in a flash and plunged the point of his power sabre into the creature's brain.

'Lieutenant Kuritsin,' he shouted. 'Where in the warp is my damned armour support?'

Kuritsin was close enough to hear. 'Sorry, sir. The vox-channels are absolutely choked. I can't get through.'

Colonel Kabanov knew they were choked. He could hear the panicked transmissions of the Thirty-Fifth Regiment's armour platoons in his own ear. His vox-bead insisted on telling him just how grim things were for Vostroyan soldiers all across this doomed half of the city. As he listened, he recognized the voice of Sergeant Svemir.

'This is Svemir to Fifth Company command,' voxed the medic. 'Can you hear me?'

'I hear you, Svemir,' replied Kabanov. 'What's your status? Where is the Pathcutter now?'

'We've been crippled, sir. We're stuck out on the highway. The orks are cutting their way in. I just wanted to say good luck, sir. I'm giving our wounded something to send them on. I'm sure you understand, sir. I couldn't let the orks kill helpless men. For my part, I intend to go down fighting.'

There was little Kabanov could say to that except, 'You're a brave man, sergeant. The Grey Lady waits to take you to the Emperor's side. Have no doubt about that.'

'Thank you, sir,' voxed the medic. 'They've broken through now.'

At the sergeant's end, the vox went dead. Kabanov felt his stomach twist with anger at the foul xenos. He wouldn't allow this to be the end. 'We have to press north,' he shouted. 'We have to cut through them. Maro, I want you to move into the centre of our circle and start throwing grenades ahead of us. We must thin the ork ranks there if we want to push through.'

Lieutenant Maro did so without question. From the centre of the circle, he began lobbing hand grenades into the packed orks. The resulting explosions showered Fifth Company with hot blood and sent broken green bodies tumbling through the air. The momentary gaps these explosions created lessened the pressure on the circle's north side and allowed Fifth Company to push towards their goal a little at a time. But it was far from enough.

There were fresh screams from the southern and eastern sides of the circle. Fifth Company was losing more men all the time. Pain flared in Kabanov's leg as a cleaver whistled past, tearing a red slash above his knee.

'Fight on, Firstborn!' he roared. 'The sons of Vostroya will never fall!'

But he knew, even as he said it, that he was tiring fast. The fire in his lungs was returning. He started wheezing again. Adrenaline and natural endorphins couldn't hold the pain of his illness at bay any longer.

Just a little more, he thought. Emperor help me. Just give me a little more time.

More screaming sounded behind him and the Vostroyan circle grew smaller and smaller.

'You're in charge?' asked Karif, eyeing the tall, slim officer that stood before him, resplendent in Vostroyan finery that remained unsullied by battle.

'Of this particular platoon, commissar, yes I am. Lieutenant Vemko Orodrov, commanding officer of the

Vostroyan Firstborn 41st Armoured Regiment's Second Tank Platoon, at your service.'

'Excellent, lieutenant,' replied Karif, 'It's your services that I require. You arrived here yesterday from Seddisvarr with very specific orders from General Vlastan, is that not so?'

'It is. We're to hold the bridge open for as long as possible so that your Fifth Company might cross with an important prisoner. I see you and your men, commissar, but I don't see any prisoner. I'm afraid there is little time left before the ork horde forces us to fall back. We'll have to withdraw in the next few minutes if we're to be clear before the bridge is blown. The orks mustn't set one foot on Theqis under any circumstances. The general was very clear about that. You may cross with us, commissar, but you won't find a warm welcome in Seddisvarr with your mission unfulfilled. The general will be displeased.'

'Displeased with you, lieutenant, if you don't do everything in your power to aid me now, particularly with the prisoner in question so close at hand.'

'He's close by?'

'Very,' said the commissar. 'Colonel Kabanov and the rest of the company are attempting to force their way through the ork lines as we speak, but I'm sure you've seen how many orks they're up against.'

'They're trying to cut a path through on foot?' asked the lieutenant incredulously. 'It's impossible, commissar. They're dead men for sure.'

'They will be, unless you assign me three tanks and their crews to help open a corridor for them.'

The lieutenant shook his head emphatically. 'I– I can't, commissar. The ork armour is rolling right towards us. We need every machine we've got just to withdraw safely. No, you… you're asking the impossible.'

Before the lieutenant could blink, Karif whipped his chainsword from its scabbard and up to the officer's neck, thumbing the power rune in mid-motion. The weapon purred threateningly into the young officer's left ear.

Karif smiled. 'Impossible is not a word they teach at the Schola Excubitos, lieutenant.'

SEBASTEV COULDN'T RISK a glance behind him, but he heard Lieutenant Maro cry out and knew that something was wrong. A trooper yelled, 'The White Boar is wounded!'

As those words filled the air, there was a roar of anger from the surviving men. The fighting intensified as if every single ork they faced was personally responsible. More orks fell, and yet more pressed forward. The Vostroyans were few, and each moment was met by the screams of another man as he was cleaved apart by laughing alien brutes.

A monstrous black ork pushed its way through the front ranks and roared at Sebastev, spraying thick mucus into the air. It tossed its head and gnashed its massive yellow tusks together, lifting its axe to launch a horizontal stroke that missed by a hair. The blade of the axe lodged deep in the body of another ork on the right. Before the monster had time to pull his weapon free, Sebastev leapt forward, placed his boot on the bent knee of the ork's lead leg, and stepped up to plunge his blade down through the top of the ork's head.

As the giant body collapsed, Sebastev jumped backwards, returning to his position in the circle. 'Lieutenant Tarkarov is down!' shouted someone.

Hestor's balls, thought Sebastev, not Tarkarov!

'Captain Chelnikov is dead!' shouted another.

'Captain Sebastev,' yelled Lieutenant Maro, 'you have to take command. The White Boar is wounded. The prisoner must get through.'

Khek the prisoner, thought Sebastev, but he knew Maro was right.

'Aronov?' yelled Sebastev. 'Aronov, are you alive?'

A laspistol appeared at Sebastev's shoulder and burned the face from the ork right in front of him. 'I am, sir,' growled the big scout in his ear. 'I won't be for much longer if this keeps up. We can't thin the bastards out, sir. Let me drop the traitor and fight unhindered alongside the rest of you.'

It was a fair request. Aronov wanted to die giving his very best. He clearly believed they couldn't prevail. Sebastev could only agree. Perhaps it had been hopeless from the start. There were just too many orks and every single man who'd fallen so far had sold his life dear. He was proud of them, proud to be their captain.

This is how a Guardsman is meant to die, he thought. There's no dishonour in this, not in fighting with all you've got until your very last breath.

'Fair enough, trooper,' said Sebastev. 'Drop the pris–'

The air was ripped by a mighty explosion. Just a hundred metres or so to Sebastev's left a great cloud of dirt and green bodies erupted into the air. It was deafening. Moments later another cloud burst upwards, throwing hunks of ork meat down onto the Vostroyans. It was much closer this time. The ground shook.

'Armour!' shouted Lieutenant Kuritsin. 'Leman Russ tanks on the north side.'

A cheer went up from the remaining Vostroyans as the sound of heavy bolter fire filled the air. The vicious buzz of lascannons followed before the ground shook again at the impact of another shell from the tank's demolisher cannon.

The orks started to turn their heads.

Sebastev was too short to see over them, but from the frequency of the cannon-fire he counted three separate tanks firing on the ork horde.

'I don't have all day,' voxed a familiar voice.

'Commissar,' voxed Sebastev, 'we thought...'

'I don't care what you thought, captain. We've got the orks blindsided and we're thinning their ranks for you, but if you and your men don't get a bloody move on, it'll be for nothing. The orks have got armour moving in from the east at speed. You've got minutes until the north bridge is sent to the riverbed.'

More explosions rocked the street. 'Maro,' shouted Sebastev, 'get the colonel up and get ready to move. Aronov, don't you dare drop that prisoner. We're getting out of here, now.'

Sebastev stopped shouting long enough to sever the hands of an ork wielding two iron clubs. Then he drove the point of his blade through the beast's throat. A flick of his wrist sent the ork's head rolling to the surface of the street.

'Fifth Company,' he yelled. 'Move, now. For the White Boar and the Sixty-Eighth, go!'

The circle broke and the men surged forward behind Sebastev. He heard Kuritsin urging them on. Father Olov charged ahead, cleaving a broad path through the orks now that there was more room to swing his huge eviscerator.

'Get behind me,' bellowed the old priest. 'I will cut a way through.'

The eviscerator chainsword growled as it chewed through thick ork bodies. Dozens fell in front of the redoubtable priest. Troopers rushed in behind him to protect his back.

Sebastev hacked and slashed as he moved, aware of Aronov beside him, the prisoner still slung over his shoulder. Maro, too, was close by. He carried the White Boar while troopers surrounded him, stabbing out at the greenskins with their bayonets.

Sebastev realised that Maro was struggling to carry both the colonel and the traitor's case. With his free hand, he wrestled the case from the adjutant. 'I'll take care of this thing. You just focus on getting the colonel to safety, Maro.'

The lieutenant nodded.

The ground exploded so close to Sebastev that he was almost knocked from his feet. 'Watch your fire, commissar,' he voxed angrily. 'You'll kill us before the orks do.'

As he uttered these words, more troopers fell howling at the rear of the charge, their bodies smashed apart by savage blows from the greenskins that harried them.

Sebastev kept his sword moving as he pushed through. Everything was a high-speed blur of ugly alien faces and gleaming weapons. More explosions sounded close by and shook the rockcrete underfoot. He could feel the heat from lascannon beams where they strafed the ork line. Heavy bolters chugged as they cut down scores of unprotected greenskins with enfilading fire.

Then, with an explosion that was too close for comfort and a yell of triumph from Father Olov, Fifth Company broke into the open. They'd made it through to the other side of the ork line. Sebastev could see the Leman Russ tanks just ahead. Commissar Karif could be seen at the hatch of the leading tank, manning a pintle-mounted heavy bolter and yelling orders to the crews inside.

'Run to the tanks,' yelled Sebastev. 'Give it all you've got!'

His men raced forward as the Leman Russ continued to pour fire on the orks, dissuading them from pursuit. Orks weren't easily dissuaded, however. They charged forward, unmindful of the horrendous casualties they were taking.

Despite the weight of the prisoner, Sebastev saw Aronov racing ahead. The moment he reached the first Leman Russ, he threw the man up onto the back of the tank, turned, and began firing at the orks with his laspistol. 'Someone, give me a proper bloody weapon,' he shouted.

Other men reached the tanks: Sergeants Basch and Rahkman, Lieutenant Vassilo, Troopers Kovo, Kashr, Akmir: more, but still too few. The moment Sebastev reached the commissar's tank, he threw the traitor's case up beside the man, reloaded his bolt pistol, and turned to stand with Aronov, firing shot after shot back towards

the orks, concentrating on those that threatened Lieutenant Maro as he carried Colonel Kabanov forward.

'Don't be fools,' shouted Commissar Karif. 'Get up onto
the tanks and hold on. We've got to make the bridge
before they blow the damned thing.'

Sebastev stopped firing long enough to help Maro and
Kuritsin lift Colonel Kabanov up onto the vehicle. When
the colonel was safely onboard, everyone else scrambled
up onto the back.

'Go, commissar,' called Sebastev over the drumming of
the heavy bolters. 'We're all on board.'

Each of the huge tanks was covered in Fifth Company
survivors, clinging on for their lives as the tank drivers
kicked their machines into high gear. Colonel Kabanov
lay between Maro and Sebastev on the back of Commissar Karif's machine. As the tank moved off, he gripped
Sebastev's sleeve and said, 'Grenades, captain.'

Blood was leaking from his mouth and nose. His skin
had turned a ghostly white.

'Good idea, sir,' said Sebastev. He pulled two grenades
from his bandolier.

The colonel struggled to sit up. 'No, Sebastev. Give
them to me, both of them.'

Sebastev was confused, but he did as he was ordered.

Colonel Kabanov faced Lieutenant Maro. 'You'll
explain it to him?' he asked.

Maro nodded sincerely, and Sebastev saw tears in the
man's eyes.

'Good,' said Colonel Kabanov. 'Then it's time the White
Boar looked after himself for a change.'

With that, he slid off the back of the Leman Russ.

Sebastev immediately reached out to grab for him, but
Maro restrained him. 'You know it already, captain. This
is what he wants. Would you have him wither and die in
some hospital bed? I don't think so.'

Sebastev wanted to deny it. He wanted to order the
Leman Russ to a stop and go back for the man who'd

been his hero since the day he'd joined the Sixty-Eighth Regiment, but he knew Maro was right. Legends like the White Boar were meant to die in battle. When his own time came, he wished no less for himself.

As he watched Colonel Kabanov walk back to meet the orks, Sebastev saluted.

'To me, you filthy devils!' shouted the old man as he staggered towards the foe. He pulled the pins on his grenades. 'One last gift from the Emperor of Mankind!'

Sebastev forced himself to watch. He owed the colonel that much and more. He couldn't be sure of the exact number, but it looked like the White Boar took a good many of the green khekkers with him as he died.

The tanks rumbled around a corner and the scene shifted from view.

'Almost there,' said Commissar Karif from behind Sebastev. 'The bridge is just up ahead.'

CAPTAIN GRIGORIUS SEBASTEV and the scant remains of his Fifth Company crossed Grazzen's north bridge at 16.02 hours on the 688th day of the Danikkin Campaign. The north bridge was destroyed precisely two minutes later, sending a significant number of pursuing Venomhead orks and their vehicles to the bottom of the Solenne.

Patriot-Captain Brammon Gusseff, known to personnel with the appropriate clearance as *Asset 6*, was delivered to Twelfth Army Command HQ in Seddisvarr in the early hours of the following day.

Captain Grigorius Sebastev was placed under arrest at that time.

A TRIAL ENDS

Thirteen days.

For thirteen days, Sebastev had listened with furrowed brow and gritted teeth as men who'd never set foot on the Eastern Front berated him, belittled the valorous efforts of his men, and placed the responsibility for each and every death firmly at his booted feet.

The trial reached its conclusion. There was General Vogor Vlastan, Old Hungry himself, strapped into his life preserving mechanical chair behind the judges' bench. He would pass sentence personally. Sebastev figured the general must have been anticipating this moment for quite some time. The spectators were anticipating it, too. The grand hall had gone deathly quiet.

The council of judges ended their whispered conversation and turned back to face Sebastev in the dock. Servo-skulls, yellowed with age and bristling with sensors and recording devices, descended from above, drifting through the air on suspensor engines that hummed softly. They registered every word spoken in the hall, by officials and spectators alike. The records would be carefully checked later to help identify dissenting voices and potential troublemakers.

'Stand,' ordered a wizened old major on General Vlastan's immediate left. 'Stand, Captain Sebastev. The general wishes to pronounce.'

Sebastev got heavily to his feet, mentally fatigued by so many days of endless talk, of recounting over and over again the events that had transpired since leaving Korris. He saw, there on the far right, in the shadows below the hanging balcony, the figure of Commissar Karif, dressed, as always, in black. He'd attended the court martial every single day since the beginning, and had given evidence of his own on eight of those days, though Sebastev had been ordered out of the court on those occasions, and knew not what the commissar had reported.

Just as it had on every previous day, the hanging balcony that jutted out over the seats of the spectators contained the same two bizarre, inscrutable occupants.

Sebastev's blood chilled inexplicably every time he looked in their direction. He could feel the eyes of the hunched old woman on him, burning into him as if she sought to scorch away his flesh and view the naked soul beneath. The incredible alabaster giant, whose blood-red eyes missed nothing, sat next to her.

And no one can tell me who the khek they are, he thought.

The general coughed and began burbling through a vox-amp attached to his chair. 'We've heard, honoured attendants, from a broad range of witnesses, analysts and assessors over the course of this trial.' The general's small, black eyes panned across the assembly. 'We've heard how the accused conducted himself throughout the period in question, the ways in which he influenced Vostroyan men of both higher and lower rank. And we've heard in great detail how the events that transpired after the loss of the

Twelfth Army's dominion over Korris have affected the status of this war.'

Sebastev's stomach rumbled quietly, reminding him that he hadn't eaten since daybreak. His appetite was starting to come back, but his complaining stomach would have to wait.

'This honourable council,' continued the general, 'has listened carefully to all that has been put before it. We have consulted with learned bodies and scoured the histories of our proud military past for precedents.'

Sebastev caught Old Hungry casting his glance to the two strange figures on the balcony, just as he had done throughout the trial. It was further confirmation of something Sebastev suspected: General Vlastan was terrified of the strange pair.

Just who are they, he wondered, *and why are they here for this?*

The general continued, but Sebastev was sure he detected a loss of confidence in the man's amplified voice. 'We have reached our conclusions and shall now make our pronouncement. In the name of the Emperor of Mankind, and the honoured tradition of the Vostroyan Firstborn who serve in his name, I now address Captain Grigorius Sebastev of the Sixty-Eighth Infantry Regiment's Fifth Company.'

As was the form, Sebastev saluted the Twelfth Army leader.

'Captain Sebastev,' said the general. 'It has long been held by many worthy officers in the Twelfth Army that your field commission to the rank of captain was a grievous and reproachable error on the part of Major Alexos Dubrin. Indeed, some of your senior officers consider your appointment to the rank of captain little more than a favour from one friend to another. Naturally there is no room for such things in the ranks of the Firstborn, but the late Major Dubrin is beyond our judgement now. You, however, are not.'

Sebastev scowled and gripped the wooden railing of the dock. His knuckles whitened. He'd known all along that the man would make the most of this final, grand opportunity to offend and aggravate him.

'Of course, the matter of your promotion is not on trial. We must turn, instead, to matters of acceptable conduct and proper performance. A man in command has responsibilities to many, both above him in rank and below, but especially to those above. That, I'm afraid, captain, is the root of your worst transgressions.

'Throughout your career, you have consistently been shown to suffer from the regrettable delusion that it is your job to safeguard the lives of each and every one of the men under your command. Let me address that delusion by telling you directly, captain, that it is not so, nor has it ever been. The responsibility of any officer is both clear and singular: it is the execution of those orders given to you by your superior officers no matter the cost in blood, pain, lives or anything else you wouldn't care to spend or endure.

'This regular prioritising of your men's lives above all else constitutes a definitive failure on your part to live up to the duties, honours and expectations placed on you by men of vastly superior lineage, intellect and judgement.'

A sharp sound echoed through the great hall. Sebastev flicked his eyes to the source. The alabaster giant sat glaring at General Vlastan, but it was the old woman next to him who'd interrupted the general's speech. She had struck the floor of the balcony with the metal-shod heel of her walking stick.

A long moment of silence stretched out, during which Sebastev watched the general wither under the old woman's gaze before finally turning back to face Sebastev. The general's usual arrogance and confidence had bled right out of him.

'As I was saying,' he said, shifting uncomfortably, 'it is the opinion of some members of this military council that you, Captain Grigorius Sebastev, have consistently placed the lives of individual Guardsmen above the best interests of the Twelfth Army.'

The general was interrupted again by the sharp rapping of metal on wood. Sebastev followed General Vlastan's eyes as they again darted over to the tiny old woman.

'By the Throne,' snapped Vlastan, immediately regretting it. With obvious effort, he reverted to a more placatory tone. 'Please, honoured madam, I have not forgotten your decree. If you'll just allow me to finish what I was saying without further… interruptions.'

In response, the old woman folded her tiny, childlike hands and nodded from beneath the hood of her cloak. Sebastev couldn't shake the impression that she was laughing, though no sound or motion gave evidence of this.

'Some members of this council believe that, for the role you played in the death of Colonel Maksim Kabanov, a greatly respected man among the ranks of the Firstborn, you should be precluded from any commission for the rest of your life. Others felt that the mere stripping of your rank was overly lenient. Extended incarceration and expulsion from the ranks of the Firstborn were considered as alternative punishments.'

This time, Sebastev had the impression that General Vlastan was deliberately trying to avoid glancing at the figures on the balcony.

'However,' continued the general, 'the reality of our war against secession and treachery on Danik's World has changed dramatically in the short time since Barahn and Ohslir fell. The Twelfth Army finds itself facing unprecedented pressure on two fronts, and this war has attracted the attention of certain Imperial bodies that wield a level of authority even greater than that of Twelfth Army Command. As such, this court is forced to acknowledge your part in the successful delivery of a valuable prisoner, the recovery of a device crucial to the continuation of the war effort, and the survival of a regiment whose long and unbroken history is filled with honour.'

General Vlastan's brows knitted together in frustration as he continued. 'There is also the matter of Commissar Karif's testimony to consider. The statements made by the commissar go a long way to suggesting that your purported bravery, piety and prowess in combat were responsible for the deaths of a great many orks and rebels. With these things in mind, and at the insistence of certain high ranking individuals outside the Vostroyan military structure, this court decrees that you will retain the rank of captain.

'Henceforth you are charged with conducting yourself in a manner more fitting to your responsibilities. And to those responsibilities, this court now adds the command of all remnants of the Sixty-Eighth Infantry Regiment, until such time as an officer of adequate rank and potential can be found to replace you. Once this replacement has been selected, you will immediately revert to your former position as Fifth Company commander.'

Voices filled the air of the court as the spectators reacted to the council's pronouncement. People began chattering, eager to share their opinions with those seated next to them. Sebastev looked for Commissar Karif, stunned that the man had spoken out on his behalf, but the commissar had already left his seat. He was nowhere to be seen.

Sebastev looked up at the balcony, but the strange duo had likewise vanished in the last few seconds.

General Vlastan cleared his throat and raised his voice over the hubbub. 'Captain Sebastev, pay attention.'

Sebastev met the general's glare.

'Your men are billeted in the city's south-east quarter, district eleven. My staff will provide a map and arrange transportation for you. Twenty-eight men are listed as the last survivors of the Sixty-Eighth Infantry Regiment, captain. It's not many, but I'm afraid there won't be time to reinforce you before your next deployment.'

For the first time in over an hour, Sebastev parted his lips to speak. 'Deployment?'

The panel of officers who'd acted as Sebastev's judges rose at a gesture from the general and left the bench. General Vlastan's chair gave a loud, mechanical hiss as its piston legs unfolded. The walking chair shook as it rose to its full height, causing General Vlastan's abundant flesh to wobble.

The general's lips stretched into a lop-sided grin. 'I've always thought you disconcertingly short for an officer, Sebastev. A leader should be tall so that men are forced to look up to him, you know.'

Sebastev didn't bother to respond to that. Instead, he met Vlastan's gaze and held it.

The general's grin dropped. 'Yes, redeployed. The Sixty-Eighth Regiment, such as it is, has been temporarily placed in the service of a higher authority. You'll find out the rest for yourself soon enough. You're no longer of any concern to me, at least for the moment.'

The general grasped the controls of his chair, turned it, and skittered out of the hall, leaving Sebastev speechless. A staff officer led him down from the dock and out through a side door as the rest of the court emptied.

Seconded to a higher authority, he thought? What in the twisted hells of the warp is going on?

SEBASTEV HAD A partial answer soon enough.

Commissar Karif awaited him outside the court, accompanied, as always, by his adjutant. As Sebastev walked towards them, he couldn't fail to notice the wide smile on the young trooper's face.

'It's wonderful to see you, sir,' said Stavin with a salute. 'I'm so glad everything… Congratulations on the verdict.'

Sebastev saluted back and said, 'Thank you, trooper. At ease.' He met Karif's gaze. 'As for you, commissar, I don't know what kind of grox-balls you told them in there…'

Karif stiffened.

Sebastev fought back a grin, and added, 'But thank you. Your presence in that hall over the last thirteen days is appreciated, I assure you.' He reached out and gripped Karif's hand, shaking it firmly.

'I'm sure I'll think of some way you can pay me back, captain,' said Karif with a smile and a nod. 'Let's walk together. There are many things we have to talk about.' Trooper Stavin fell into step a few paces behind them as they began their stroll.

'You're not wrong, commissar,' said Sebastev. 'I can't work it all out. We've been seconded? To whom?'

From behind a thick marble pillar on the left, a voice rumbled. 'Seconded to us, captain, and I promise you, you'll soon wish it weren't so.'

Sebastev gasped as the alabaster giant from the balcony stepped across their path. The huge man wore a simple black tunic, cinched at the waist with golden rope. The contrast between his robe and his deathly white skin was striking. His blood-red eyes, so strange and unnatural, fixed on Sebastev's own, measuring him, freezing him where he stood.

Karif and Stavin halted at Sebastev's side, but their reaction was muted. They hardly seemed surprised at all. Karif looked at Sebastev and shook his head. 'My first reaction was exactly the same, you know, captain.' He raised a hand, palm up, and gestured towards the giant man. 'May I present Brother-Sergeant Ischus Corvinnus, of the Death Spectres Space Marines.'

'By the Throne!' muttered Sebastev.

The brother-sergeant lifted his massive hands to his chest in the sign of the aquila, offered a shallow bow, and boomed, 'Good beginnings, Captain Sebastev. There will be time to become acquainted later perhaps. Your new commander is waiting to brief you on urgent matters even as we speak. Let us not dally here.'

Sebastev was still speechless. An Astartes, he thought. Here!

'Come on, captain,' said Commissar Karif, 'we should get moving.'

Sebastev felt Karif nudge him, and wrestled with his sense of awe.

'Follow me,' said the Space Marine as he turned and led the way. 'Milady's patience is famous only for its tiny measure.'

As Sebastev, Karif and Stavin struggled to keep up with the giant Astartes warrior, Sebastev felt his mind racing, trying to understand just how much the war had changed. The Death Spectres Space Marines were here, and something had forced General Vlastan to release Sebastev into the service of another authority: this 'lady', of whom the Space Marine spoke with obvious respect.

Surely it's the old crone from the balcony, thought Sebastev. If the Astartes are here…

'Well?' asked Karif. 'Aren't you going to answer?'

Sebastev shook himself. 'Sorry, commissar. I didn't catch the question.'

'I asked you how you felt about returning to active duty so soon. That farce of a trial… I'm sure you're eager to get back to what you're good at.'

Sebastev thought of the men he'd lost, the friends he'd watched die. He levelled his gaze at the commissar. 'If you're thinking I want revenge for the men we lost, commissar, you're damned right.'

The Space Marine turned his head just a fraction as he listened to Sebastev's words.

Commissar Karif smiled and nodded sagely. 'That's the spirit, captain. I would expect no less from a fighter like you. After all, what would men like us do without a good old-fashioned war?'

A Transcript

Source: Partial Audio Feed from Pict-Recording 22a/1F31
Originator: Inquisitor Zharadelle Inphius Faulks
(OM/613-7980.1 SC.3)
Date of Recording (Imperial): 5.232.767.M41
Location: Twelfth Army Command HQ, Seddisvarr, Danik's
World, Gamma Kholdas, Kholdas Cluster, Segmentum Ultima

Faulks: 'Try again. What is your name?'

*Asset 6: 'I told you, damn it all. What do you want me to
say? I'm Patriot-Captain Brammon Gusseff of the Special
Patriotic Service, attached to the–'*

<screams>

*Faulks: 'Brammon Gusseff is a construct, nothing more. He's
a role you've played perfectly for the last four years, but it's over
now. Stop resisting. You're just making this more difficult. Oh,
to the warp with this. I want the witch brought in. The drugs
aren't enough.*

*Asset 6: Witch? Please, I- I don't understand. What do
you want? I've given you the codes for the case. You have the
jamming device. I was promised immunity.'*

<door opens, closes>

Jardine: 'You summoned me, milady?'

*Faulks: 'Get to work on him. The last program is rooted too
deep. If you can't draw him out, he'll have to be retired. This
one is a highly prized and decorated asset, so do your best.
Understood?'*

Jardine: 'Yes, milady.'

<door opens, closes>

Asset 6: 'Who in the warp are you? Please, get me out of here. The old crone is insane. I- I don't know what she's talking about.'

<chants>

<screams>

[2 hours 11 minutes of audio censored under security directive 15.331C.]

Faulks: 'Take a drink. You're shaking quite badly.'

Asset 6: 'So would you be, warp damn it. The things I do for the Imperium…'

Faulks: 'Quite. And we're very grateful, lieutenant. It's good to have you back. For a while there it looked like that last graft was going to be permanent.'

Asset 6: 'At which point, you'd have killed me, inquisitor.'

Faulks: 'But I wouldn't have relished the task. Now please, for the records this time, name and rank.'

Asset 6: 'My name is Lieutenant Pyter Gamalov, Vostroyan Firstborn, Office of Special Operations, Twelfth Army Division.'

Faulks: 'Excellent, lieutenant. Now I need to know just how much of Gusseff's memories you have access to. How close were you able to get to Vanandrasse? What's wrong, lieutenant? You're shaking. Why the tears?'

Asset 6: 'You're going to make me remember everything, aren't you? Every act he perpetrated while I was with him.'

Faulks: 'As always, lieutenant. It's how you serve the Emperor.'

Asset 6: 'But this one, milady. Oh, Throne above, no. This Gusseff… I… he did such terrible things!'